BORN
BURNING

Also by Thomas Sullivan

THE PHASES OF HARRY MOON

THOMAS SULLIVAN

BORN BURNING

E. P. DUTTON NEW YORK

Published in the United States by E. P. Dutton,
a division of Penguin Books USA Inc.,
2 Park Avenue, New York, N.Y. 10016.

Published simultaneously in Canada by
Fitzhenry and Whiteside, Limited, Toronto.

Library of Congress Cataloging-in-Publication Data

Sullivan, Thomas
    Born burning / Thomas Sullivan — 1st ed.
        p. cm.
    ISBN 0-525-24782-3
    I. Title.
PS3569.U3579B6   1989
813'.54—dc19   89-1054
                                                CIP

DESIGNED BY EARL TIDWELL

10 9 8 7 6 5 4 3 2 1

First Edition

For Colleen and Sean,
hold fast,
and be not ancient or future children

GENESIS

1

The teak from which the chair was cut was old when China was young. What kept it alive is a mystery of ecology or botany or God. Such trees generally live for two hundred years or so. This one endured for two thousand.

The soil from which it sprang was black and deep with the souls of fierce warriors. They had fought amid the dark forests of what is now Yünnan province and died in sunless depths, their blood black and thick on the forest floor. It may be that the protean caverns of some sanguinary subworld fed the thing or it may be that it had roots in hell, but it sprang lustily from its source at a time when China was six thousand feudal states in two river valleys. Christ was yet to be born—and then so far away. Far, too, to the northeast the Huang Ho and Yangtze life

3

waters spawned dynasty after dynasty. The Shang and the Chou Sons of Heaven came and went, and Shih Huang Ti built the Great Wall while China yet crept west.

Up soared the tree, taller, thicker, radiant with dense flesh, elbowing aside its rivals. Whatever touched it of the surrounding forest withered, even the bamboo, which always accompanies teak. The usual light soil yielded to an ever-widening circle of black loam. In the time of the Sung dynasty to the north, the local tyrant lord, Ati Chan, visited the tree and declared that here was a true Son of Heaven. He made it a symbol of his own feudal tyranny.

But the tree had not come from heaven, and its roots sank ever deeper into the underworld.

A hundred times lightning licked and blasted it, but always it healed. Twice, fire assaulted the forest in which it stood. The barren ring around it held, however, and the flames roared angrily as they starved themselves out. What there was of consciousness in the tree accumulated history and the portents of comets and novas. Revolution, invasion, new orders of ancient travesties teemed all around it, and of all the mighty warlords who ravaged the land, only Genghis Khan dared contemplate the tree's destruction. Six times he swung his sword against its trunk—until the blade shattered—and finding he could not conquer the mighty teak, he urinated on it. "You are mine now!" he cried. But Khan died. The tree lived on.

And on.

After the Sung dynasty came the Yüan and then the Ming, with all its elaboration in stone, ivory, bronze, jade, rock crystal . . . and *wood*. Wood and the idea of wood took on a reverence of its own. The reverence spread with travel, with commerce, even to the dark forests of southwest China where teak and tung grew in abundance. When the last Ming was overthrown in 1644, and the Manchus ruled eastern China, there arose in the forest of the teak a terrible despot named Khi-tan Zor. His dominions were limited, but his fierceness in ruling them was all the more cruel. His tortures were slow and exquisitely subtle. His enemies did not so much die as linger in eternal dying. And it is said that he ate his own male children at birth to forestall plots of succession. But what he is known

4

for, what marked him in the ages of man and beast upon the earth, is that he carved his throne from the colossus in the heart of the forbidden forest.

What's more, it came out of the living tree.

This may be important . . . if understanding is important. For whatever realm the roots of that anomaly were vested in, whatever the concert of its living consciousness with the world around it, the teak was in total contact with both when the chair was torn out of its trunk. Whether it was the incredible strength of the surrounding wood or its sheer girth, the tree remained standing until it dried out and, in the middle of a moonless night some seven years later, came roaring to the ground.

It was another slow and exquisite murder for the Emperor Khi-tan Zor. But by the time it was fulfilled, the chair had long been crafted, polished, and employed in his palace. The original cover was silk embroidered with crescent teeth and a scarlet serpentine tongue entwined among the bloodied shoals of a half-savaged infant.

When the emperor died there was no successor, and a bloody revolt ensued. The palace was looted and burned, and the chair began its odyssey across the mountains from peasant to trader to merchant. Battered and scarred, its cover worn to transparency in spots, it was nevertheless a thing of obvious value. From Mandalay to Katmandu it was traded and bought and sometimes taken with loss of life, until an enterprising merchant fashioned a new silk cover for the damaged one and a new legend more palatable than the old. The chair, it now seemed, was commissioned for an Indian prince on the occasion of his seventh birthday and later became his throne. The legend of Khi-tan Zor and the truth of the chair's origins disappeared forever.

In 1856, the year before the Sepoy Rebellion against the British, a senior official of the British East India Company visited Calcutta. Chester Maynard Whitehall was a proud man, unbending, and with the wealth to make all his whims dictums. At home in England he had a wife and son. The son, Jacob Alexander, would be seven next month—the same age as the Indian prince of the false legend. The senior Whitehall saw the chair and learned the tale from a one-eyed Bihari who led him

5

from his vat of boiling bones, where fat was being removed, to the gloom of some hellhole of contraband for the viewing. It was a magnificent piece of furniture, and Whitehall liked the pedigree of a prince become king in its embrace. There was no reason to doubt the tale; the chair had royalty in its grain. It was a thing of authority, an emblem of succession. Whether mandated by demonic forces and commissioned by an emperor who ate his male children or sanctified by fictitious Indian potentates, the chair was permanence and power. It invited occupation. Whitehall paid extravagantly and took it home to found his own dynasty.

"Jacob Alexander, you are my firstborn male and my heir," he said to his son when the boy turned seven. "Happy birthday."

Jacob sat in the chair and, though it was a bit lumpy, decided he liked it. "May I keep it upstairs?" he asked.

"It will stay in the drawing room. We will call it the patriarch chair. It is only the promise that it will be yours which I give you today. When I die, you may keep it wherever you wish."

Jacob wished his father would die soon. He even thought about murdering him. He would sit in the patriarch chair and formulate ways of accomplishing this. But it wasn't to be. Two weeks after his seventh birthday, the boy disappeared.

The gardener, who had a criminal record and had never gotten on with young Jacob, was suspected from the start. But he fled as soon as he was accused, and the allegations were never proven. Neither ransom demand nor body ever turned up, and when his wife also died, Whitehall went to America, where he had a second son by a second marriage. The chair, of course, went with him, and in due course his last issue was initiated.

"Arthur Clement, you are my only son and heir," Whitehall said on the occasion of the seventh birthday.

Young Clement grew up uneventfully and married in 1890, the year after Chester Maynard died and the family fortune passed to him. Perpetuity was established in the will such that the patriarch chair and the fortune went together, and the creation of the next will had to echo the conditions of the first. It was almost biblical in its chauvinism. There were four daughters and three sons from Clement's marriage. The second male was Robert Chester. Little Bobby Bastard, the neighbors called him.

He strangled a kitten when he was eight and a year later set fire to a playmate's garage. The playmate's father hauled him into court, whereupon little Bobby Bastard looked up at the judge with elfin innocence and declared, "I love Jesus, and Jesus says to do unto others as you would have them do unto you." The judge looked down, saw a nine-year-old boy in velvet Fauntleroy clothes who could not possibly have committed what the accusations said he had committed, and dismissed the charges.

"Did you, Bobby? Did you do it?" his mother pressed him for the half-dozenth time after the trial.

"If you loved me, you'd quit asking," he said, and his amber eyes took on the shade of impenetrable teak.

Lovelessness is the guilt of every disappointed mother, and Bobby understood this. He used it. The role of victim suited him. He stole and lied and cheated, and the less remorse he expressed, the more his mother felt sorry for him. *I am bad, and my mother is to blame because she didn't love me enough.*

But when he was thirteen he did a very bad thing indeed.

He pushed his older brother down the basement stairs. The injury was severe but not immediately fatal. Moreover, his mother saw it happen. He had wanted her to see it. She was standing at the foot of the steps and he simply thrust forward, his face appearing briefly over the shoulder of his big brother. Bobby wasn't exactly smiling, but there was self-righteousness and triumph and challenge and absolute cold clarity in that fleeting look. Here is your choice of sons to love, Mother. Catch him. Save him. But it is I who am falling and whom you cannot catch! *Thrust.*

His mother saw it all, and though she was riveted upon her oldest son, the fleeting expression at the top of the stairs went deep into her soul for storing. Her voice cried out *Bobby's* name. It was that cry, echoing through the house and the chambers of his mind, which Bobby took with him to the study, turning it over and over for scrutiny of its elements: shock, fear, appeal, remorse. He took it apart while the house resonated with the frantic movements of others. Took it apart as he sat in the study.

In the patriarch chair.

7

When the aftermath subsided, they came looking for him, of course. Their footsteps broke the silence of shock, up and down, back and forth. But he was gone by then. He had gone without taking a blessed thing. His parents searched. The police searched. Finally, even the neighborhood searched. A man who sold newpapers thought he had seen him walking along the rail line through the town. But that was where the trail ended. No trace beyond that. A runaway. His distraught mother told the police she thought he might have been afraid he would be blamed for the "accident." It was an accident, she maintained. Bobby had been there when Kenneth tripped. So many times he had been blamed for things, he must have been afraid. Blame. A runaway.

She never told anyone the truth, and in her heart she knew that the rest of the neighborhood was glad Bobby Bastard was gone.

Arthur Clement grieved. One suffering brain damage, another fleeing, all on the same day. It recalled to him the dim tragedy of his own youth and a brother who had been kidnapped. As before, a portion of life suspended itself and the family did not move on. Bobby was not dead; he was *somewhere*. They waited. Grew but waited. Planned but waited. And when the plans and the growing could not be contingent anymore, they let Bobby go as surely as if they had buried him.

Peter Wilson Whitehall was the third son. He was not initiated into the chair until the age of twenty-three, after Kenneth's degenerative death and the family will was changed to reflect a new order of succession. After Arthur Clement died in 1923, Peter took over the declining family fortunes. Theirs was a shipbuilding enterprise on the Great Lakes, but the days of lumber barons and the ships to haul the trade were waning. When the opportunity came to invest in the budding automotive industry, Peter sold the last of the family's holdings in Midland, Michigan, and moved to Detroit. True to the family heritage, the patriarch chair accompanied him. Marriage came late, but not too late for a daughter and a son. By 1955, automotive investments had blossomed into a successful parts supply industry and an impressive house in Franklin Village. In due course, Peter initiated

8

the chair's third generation—and fifth candidate—since Maynard Whitehall's journey to India.

"William Frank, you are my firstborn male and my heir," he said solemnly on the boy's seventh birthday.

Young Frank had already gained a sense of reverence for his ancestors. At this age, he knew nothing of the two previous generations' tragedies, but the family's resolve to survive its traumas intact reached into the past and future and this deeply affected the boy. The patriarch chair seemed to sum everything up, just as Maynard Whitehall had intended. Frank grew to manhood cherishing the heavy chair, so stable and permanent, its deep rich wood so soothing to his own little conflicts. It would be his someday. He would be the keeper of the dynasty. And nothing would flag under his stewardship. He would marry and have a son of his own—many sons and daughters—and present the chair at the proper time, and the family would never again lack for numbers to carry on the surname.

The second son born to Peter was Gerald Lucien. This was when Frank was ten. As a baby, Lucien cried little. As a child he was quiet, patient, clever. He smiled rarely. Everyone remarked on his good behavior. His mother and his brother loved him dearly. But Peter could not. He tried, but something in him always held back. He told himself how lucky he was to have another son, a boy who remembered virtually everything that was played in a card game, who could devise the cleverest ways to coax a cat from hiding, who could sit down and reason out where misplaced items were. The trouble was those rare smiles. It only took one to shatter all the reasoned love Peter felt for him. Because when Lucien smiled his face turned elfin, his eyes became as impenetrable as teak, and the corners of his mouth and the set of his teeth said something silently malevolent. Peter knew it was malevolent because he had lived with that smile and what went with it before. And every time it ate across Lucien's face, he saw again his long-vanished brother—Bobby Bastard.

If Lucien was aware of the uneasiness his father felt, he did not show it. It seemed likely he knew—as Bobby Bastard had instinctively known the emotional subcurrents of others—but,

9

of course, Lucien had nothing to compare it with. There had always been a gulf between him and his father. He never questioned the order of things. That his brother had been initiated into the patriarch chair before he himself was born and would inherit the family business and most of its assets was the way of it. Everything was happy in Franklin Village. They lived in a magnificent house, went to a picturesque church, attended modern schools, took lengthy vacations, and acquired the material goods they wished for. Lucien went on being quiet and patient and clever. And when his father died, he smiled a sad smile. And when he had to move out of the only home he had ever known, which was now his married brother's, he smiled a philosophical smile. He would be comfortable living the quiet life of an artist on his share of the inheritance.

"You're welcome to work for the company," Frank told him. "I need a vice-president I can trust."

"Thank you, brother," Lucien said, "but not just yet." And Bobby Bastard smiled.

So the dynasty was established through its legitimate heirs and the sanction of the patriarch chair.

Maynard begat Clement.

Clement begat Peter.

Peter begat Frank.

Frank begat . . .

THE ACTS

2

N o one.

"What's wrong with us, Frank? Why can't we have babies?"
"We will, you'll—"
"It's been over a year!"
"Lots of people have difficulty at first."
"Something's wrong!"
"We'll fix it. We'll go see a doctor."
"You've said that before."
"This time I promise."
"Frank. What if—"
"We will. You'll see."

———

They went to the doctor. Rose had a full gynecological exam including a Pap smear and personal history. Frank had a physical with a blood workup and a sperm count. The day they went back for the consultation it was raining. Rose got headaches when it rained. The office was gloomy and damp, and she could smell the carpet this time. Rain drummed all around them as if they were inside an egg, Rose had a headache, and the carpet smelled like sodden hemp.

"Nervous?" Frank stroked her neck.

"A little."

"Whatever he says, we're going to have kids, Rose. There are ways and there are ways."

Ways.

Not for Rose. The doctor was going to tell her she had a tipped uterus and damaged tubes or something. They both knew it the moment they saw his face. He was the pure science type for whom smiles and ordinary conversation were radiant deceits, and just now he wore a grin that could have belied terminal illness. They sat in bottomless chairs that seemed to take them out of the doctor's universe altogether while he read them a litany of results from on high. And then he said, without the least adjustment in expression, "So you see, Mr. Whitehall, it is unlikely you will ever father children."

The rain took on a certain clarity above their heads. A terrible fact had crystallized, and it continued to rain as if that was the only thing that mattered on earth. William Frank Whitehall was a dead end. The keeper of the dynasty, who cherished the heritage more than all the others, who had steadied it in all its ancillary aspects, was unable to germinate the next successor.

"And Rose?" he asked slowly.

"Normal."

He nodded.

"Of course, we can try to increase your sperm count and limit intercourse to the most favorable times," the doctor said.

Frank took injections of testosterone and abstained from sexual contact. He exercised moderately, rested well, and followed the doctor's recommendations on diet. When the moments of truth came, he worked feverishly between Rose's

14

thighs, feeling desperation more than anything else—the damp and clammy desperation of one essence pounding itself on another. But the result was not fertility. It was futility. It was bruised souls.

"We can adopt," he said, nearly a year after they had seen the doctor.

"I don't want to adopt," she answered readily.

They quit talking then. She brought clocks into his life—mantel clocks, wall clocks, clocks on desks, and clocks on tables. The house was endowed with them. Some whispered, some spoke crisply, one stroked majestically on the quarter hour and wagged its censoring ticks of the tongue in between. In the silence that settled over their marriage, the clocks prattled garrulously. From room to room you heard them posting each other on the latest gossip—only the gossip was all the same.

The Whitehalls can't have babies!

He thought he understood her disappointment as well as any man could. But he did not understand the anger.

She was a good woman, stockily built, with black sparkling eyes and a clear full face. Red lipstick inevitably glistened on her pretty mouth, and you somehow always thought there was a smile being restrained beneath her perfectly smooth cheeks. He had met her in a shopping mall where he had become hopelessly lost. She had been dressed in a Santa's helper costume as she sat in a sleigh collecting donations for children's Christmas presents. No matter how he had executed the levels and turns, he had wound up back at the sleigh, and there it was, that winsome smile inviting the corners of her mouth to dart in opposite directions. Before they had even spoken, they had laughed together.

It made things easy; they had reached the altar in four months.

Patience was another of her virtues, but she was compelled about some things. Her urges came like seasons and were equally irrepressible. When it was time to do this or that, go here, go there, own one thing or another, it just had to be. Thus she had led him to a variety of experiences—Greenfield Village, cross-country skiing on the eves of first snows, dinners promptly

15

at six, the painting of the house, the planting of a small apple orchard. It was as if she had yet another clock inside her whose hands posted mandates at irrevocable moments.

And now it was time to have children.

She delayed as long as she could, she struggled against the clock inside her, but inevitably the moment came when she had to tell him. The smile that was always just below the surface flickered like a nervous tic.

"I want a divorce," she tremoloed.

They were sitting at the table eating breakfast, and her eyes were so awash he couldn't see the pupils.

"Because we can't have children?" he asked.

She nodded.

"Rose, don't throw us away. I know how you feel, but . . ." He started talking rapidly. "We could adopt a wonderful baby. The world is full of them. Fine, healthy babies that need our love. Would we know the difference when we'd had it, shaped it, loved it? Would we, Rose? A human being is a human being."

"I want my own children." She spoke as though they were already there inside her, and his key would not unlock her womb.

"Think about it awhile. Will you do that, please? Just think about it."

"I've been thinking for a year, Frank. At night it's unbearable, but I waited for a morning to tell you."

"Rose." Leaden, pleading. "Rose, we're happy . . . aren't we?"

The settlement was amicable. She moved out. The lawyers exchanged a few pieces of papers, had lunch together. Frank wanted to go on seeing her, but she said no. All the clichés seemed to apply: It's better this way—a clean break—fresh start—no hard feelings.

Frank was slightly built, thin-voiced, and damn near spermless. Now he had been rejected. It took him a while to get himself together.

He threw himself into the company he had revitalized, had the house repainted the orginal white, and took a good look at the handsome face in the mirror. He had lost a couple of years, but he could still marry, still adopt. Legally creating an heir even offered certain advantages. He could pick and choose that way, practically guaranteeing a strong and able successor. His brother, Lucien, showed no inclination to marriage; surely he would find little resistance there. The candidate must be a bright and inquisitive toddler, even-tempered and healthy. If things didn't work out, he could even adopt a second child, older, displacing the first as successor. But that wasn't going to be necessary. It just showed him how many options he had. There were plenty of those, all right. No reason to get down on himself just because biology had played him a dirty trick. No reason at all.

So he began to seach for a second spouse. Search. The word itself belied romance. You would have thought society had the system down pat by this time. Millions of people were out there hunting for the right mate. How unreasonable that there wasn't a single graceful way. The bars, parks, libraries, malls, clubs, and social events of a city seemed wholly inadequate for meaningful relationships. The atmospheres were contrived or comical or sordid. Frightened and angry divorcées hunted for self-esteem under cheap neon lights, and the daylight variety moved mistrustfully in public places. He didn't really have any success until he quit looking.

That was when he noticed Carolyn. He had known her even longer than he had known Rose. In some ways he knew her better. She was his private secretary. And he could already tell what kind of mother she was, because she had a child. A boy. A wonderful boy.

The picture on her desk said his name was Chip. He was just two. Sandy-haired, a tentative smile, but already his mother's self-assured eyes. Clutching *Dr. Seuss* in both hands. It would be Einstein's *Relativity* someday, his mother said. Frank bought the boy a Christmas present—one of those preschool math fact electronic games—and began to take Carolyn out.

The courtship went even faster than Rose's had. Of course, the practical side of it had been marinating for years. They worked well together in the company because she was exacting and rational with paperwork, freeing him up for decision-making. But still their relationship had remained like a brother and sister's in church. Each had known when the other's divorce took place. She had seen the beneficiary changes on his W-4's;

he had given her time off for court appearances. Ironically, her husband had died after the divorce, and that made Chip very special to Frank; the boy could be adopted. Carolyn, extraordinarily efficient Carolyn. She had even filed a son for him as if by dictation. And now he noticed the pert nose and full lips that softened the imperiousness of steel-blue eyes, and her long legs and full shoulders began to haunt him. She, in turn, let down her defenses, her fears, her doubts, all in a rush. This was not the way she had expected love to return—not through a man she had known. She gave him a little speech at lunch one day.

"The part of me you don't know is the worst part," she said. "I've never been very secure emotionally, and now that I'm a marriage casualty, it's worse. I can't stand criticism, and I can't take failure. I really don't reach out very well and probably never will."

"If we stay close enough together, you won't have to reach out at all," he said.

The wedding was like a tardy gesture.

Where Rose had brought clocks into his life, Carolyn brought pictures. Pictures and plants. She did their taxes and kept the household budget and very slowly waded into a social life she had never known. When it came to human dilemmas, she tended to freeze in place. It had been one of the problems of her first marriage. A misplaced sense of guilt was part of it, and the inability to make a decision about relationships. Asking for a divorce in itself had been very difficult for her. Chip was both the problem and the impetus that had finally gotten her to make the break. She needed someone to understand that. Frank did.

They had been married three months when he told her about the chair. In that time he had spent as many moments with Chip as he possibly could, and he felt more certain than ever about his choice. The boy was intelligent, even-tempered, quick, and strong. Chip was going to be the Whitehall heir, he said, when he had finished recounting the chair's history to her.

"Of course he's going to be your heir," Carolyn responded with a nervous laugh. "You're legally adopting him. Succession is statutory."

18

"Only in the absence of a will. And there *is* a will. Inheritance is contingent on what I'm telling you about the chair. I intend to initiate him, Carolyn. At the proper time, I'm going to place the dynasty right in the middle of his lap as he sits in that chair."

She didn't see that it would make any difference as far as the inheritance was concerned. Who else would be in line for it? But she understood the significance of the patriarch heirloom. The strength of this family, its sense of permanence and stability, had given her a personal security her own roots lacked. She wasn't about to question it.

But Lucien was.

He sat across the table in the little café where Frank had invited him to tell him what he was going to do, and he was livid.

"I may not be firstborn, Frank, but I'm your brother and a Whitehall by blood. How could you even consider initiating an outsider without at least asking my opinion?"

"You're here now, and your opinion is quite plain."

"This is the end of the family, you know."

"The end of the family is inevitable without it."

"What about me?"

Stunned silence.

"What about me, Frank?"

"Are you suggesting that I turn everything over to you—that I waive my birthright? I never knew you resented the way things were."

The carved corners of Lucien's mouth were straight for once, as if crushed flat. "Not for me. For the family, of course."

"Well, that's a short-term solution, isn't it?"

"Who's to say I won't marry yet? Who's to say I wouldn't have children, if there was a reason?"

It weighed on Frank.

His younger brother had never shown any serious intentions toward women. There were whores, he was aware, perhaps a model or two who had lived at his studio, but so far as he knew Lucien never spent a dime or a minute beyond that to cultivate a romance. A sense of family heritage had been just as

19

lacking. On the other hand, Lucien had never been mercenary. Quiet, clever Lucien.

It weighed on Frank very much.

And it might have changed everything, if everything hadn't changed.

The long legs he had delighted in were wrapped around him nearly every night now while he poured his essence into her—that feeble essence which had been unable to stir Rose's womb—and perhaps it was the sheer volume of it, or some germinating force of carnality, but there came a night when he lay deeply invaginated between her thighs in the aftermath, and her hands stroked silkily along his spine, when she whispered with irrepressible joy that she thought she was pregnant.

The doctor said they had beaten some pretty high odds. Nature wrote the footnotes, he said, and seemed quite unaware that Frank had changed mates. He didn't venture any odds about whether the baby would be a girl or a boy. But Frank had no doubt whatever.

"Joseph Scott Whitehall," he announced at the dinner table, and he nodded to the empty fourth chair.

"Rebecca Anne," Carolyn contradicted in fun.

"One of each?" he offered.

"Dreamer."

But she dreamed too. She would stand at the kitchen sink, her hands limp in dishwater, momentarily lost in a future where two children played outside the window. Or she would sit in the patriarch chair, conjuring up childhood idylls for a duet. In fact, it was during just such a dream—in the fifth month—that the nightmare happened. She was sitting in the chair and wondering how they would work out the inheritance now that there were going to be two children. It was the kind of thing she hated to deal with. Thank God she had Frank. He would work out something fair. And that was when she felt the stab.

It was sharp and sudden, and it came low in her womb. The wave of nausea that followed was probably fear. Something had twisted or ripped; the baby was strangling! Imagination. Only the hemorrhaging—that was real.

They rushed her to the hospital, gave her a shot of estrogen and phenobarbital. She had almost lost the baby. The doctor said no more tennis, and she had to stay in bed a good deal of the time. But the rest of the pregnancy was uneventful. By the ninth month the baby was kicking lustily, and she was sure everything was all right.

"I think I'm carrying a mule," she told Frank.

"I'll settle for a field goal kicker."

All was well. Her second marriage was working out, Chip had a father, and the baby—the baby was just fine despite the near miscarriage. Whenever she needed reassurance of this, she sat in the patriarch chair. It was then that the sense of life in her belly grew keenest. She would sit in the patriarch chair, and the baby would kick and kick and kick and kick and kick and kick and kick and kick and kick and kick. . . .

3

Joseph Scott Whitehall.

Firstborn.

Second in line for the patriarch chair.

Born with a silver spoon in his mouth and a Chip on his shoulder. But the portents of his future were lost in the forever of his infancy.

For all the kicking, he was a tiny baby, slow to cry, with big nocturnal eyes. Noises set him off, bright lights, frantic movement. But for the most part he was quiet. Like his Uncle Lucien. It was not the quiet of the hunter, though. It was the quiet of the prey.

"We have a very serious scholar here," Frank declared.

"He's more the wise elder-statesman type," said Carolyn.

"Or maybe he's just trying to hide the fact that he's got a dirty diaper."

"Babies don't hide that." She handed him a box of Pampers. "Fathers do."

She was grateful for Joey's temperament, and she prayed fervently that it wouldn't change. Disciplining children was not her strong point. That was another thing fathers should do. But she needn't have worried. Frank *was* there. Would be there. She saw how lovingly but firmly he dealt with Chip. There was never any self-doubt with Frank. He knew what was proper and right for people, any people—corporate moguls, garrulous spinsters, little boys. They sensed this sureness in him and accepted the handling. How lucky she had been to marry this man, she thought.

Chip's infancy had been a trial of colic, sleepless nights, and persistent rashes of one type or another. He had endured a kidney infection and biweekly visits to a pediatrician before he was a year old. She had felt guilty for this: guilty for the ailments, guilty over giving her baby medications, guilty when he wouldn't eat, guilty when he wouldn't sleep. Consequently, she had been secretly glad when Frank told her he couldn't father a child. But by the time she became pregnant again she had grown to trust him and, more importantly, to trust in herself again. And now she had Joey, a perfect baby, quiet and regular in every way.

Everyone said so. Everyone loved Joey. Everyone came to see him.

Even Uncle Lucien—eventually.

He came on a windswept day six months after Joey was born. There was no call or warning, simply the old black Fury creeping to a halt in the driveway, as if the momentum of its journey had barely been sufficient. Out he stepped, white and raptorial looking. His jet eyes burned on the house; his black hair lay back like quills.

Carolyn was watering her houseplants when she saw him coming up the steps. Frank was at work. She had only seen Lucien twice, but she rather liked him. Once, before her second marriage, he had come to the office to pick up a check. The other

23

time had been at the wedding. On both occasions he had put her at ease with his quiet, patient manner. Here was a relationship that asked for nothing, posed no problems. But then, he was a Whitehall.

"Frank won't be home for two hours," she told him when he was seated in the living room. "Would you like a cup of coffee?"

"No, thank you." He had a resonant voice that somehow surprised you—all mellow murmur or abruptness from one sentence to the next. Almost theatrical. "I've come to see my nephew."

She cocked her head, smiling. "Really? I'm delighted. I'd written you off as a W. C. Fields type when it comes to children."

He looked amused.

"Well, the little prince is due to surface from his nap," she said. "He's been waiting all his life to see you."

"That long?" Dipping into his inner coat pocket he extracted a necklace strung with wooden cartoon faces. The tiny effigies were hand carved and painted with obvious skill. "Maybe I can bribe his forgiveness."

Carolyn oohed and held it up to the light. "This is beautiful. Where did you get it?"

"I carved it."

She looked at him with real awe now. "Lucien, this is really beautiful. I had no idea you—"

"Dwarfs are easy. Snow White was a bit of a challenge. I nicked her cheek. Do you think he'll notice?"

"He won't notice anything for a year or two. But if I give this to him now, he'll try to eat it."

Lucien smiled, shrugged benignly.

"So I'll put it away until he's old enough to appreciate what his uncle has done for him."

He dropped his hand on her wrist then. "Give it to him now. I can always carve another."

"But he might strangle himself with it."

"Oh."

He looked so disappointed that she almost laughed. "You don't need a gift. He doesn't even know he's got an uncle. Come on up and introduce yourself."

They glided upstairs, a duet of shapeliness and lank leanness. He walked the same way his voice carried, seeming to loom up and unravel all over the house. At the door to the nursery, she peeked in and waved him through. He flowed past, slowing in three deliberate steps and stopping a little short of the crib.

Joey lay on his back, arms and legs pulsing, seemingly unaware that he had company. Suddenly he turned his head and beheld his uncle. A grin of sorts distorted his lips and he gave a little cry of joy; but almost immediately the tiny brow puckered and the dark eyes grew intent with searching, as if he had just realized that this was not a familiar face.

"You've got a visitor, Joey," Carolyn said, breezing to the crib. She picked him up, held him in her arms, swaying slightly. "Would you like Uncle Luce to hold you, baby? Would you?"

Lucien looked startled.

"Would you like to hold your nephew?"

"No, thank you."

"Anyone who can carve faces on beads can handle a baby."

"Wood doesn't squirm."

She laughed, and then the phone was ringing like the concerted cry of infants everywhere, coming from extensions all over the house.

"Excuse me, Lucien," she said. Laying Joey back in his crib, she darted down the hall to the master bedroom.

It was her father calling long distance. It had always been long distance between them, even when they were in the same room. But the phone calls were worse. No windows to stare out, no plants to pretend to fuss with, just ungodly silences while each clung self-consciously to a telephone receiver, like a handshake suspended, like an idiot grin through soundproof glass. He kept saying he should have called months ago. "I should've called months ago to say I should've called months ago to say . . ." She asked him about his stiff back, his headaches, his diabetes. He was beyond wanting to talk about them. He was "fine," he kept repeating. Finally he asked her about the baby, and all she could do was echo that Joey was "fine."

When she got back to the nursery, the door was closed. She was sure she had left it open, but now it was closed. A twinge of apprehension slid like ice from her heart to the pit of her

25

stomach. What did she really know about Lucien? She had left her baby alone in a room with a man she had met only twice. And then she had the door open and Joey was there in the crib exactly as she had left him. The momentary nonsense of a mother's fears evaporated. Lucien was family. Lucien was Joey's uncle. Lucien was . . .

Gone.

She glanced back into the hall. He certainly was a shy man. Perhaps she had embarrassed him—asking him to hold the baby and all. He didn't know how to behave. Men could be like that. And then she saw that Joey wasn't exactly as she had left him after all. He had something in his hands. She crossed to the crib. Took the object. It was another carved head.

Men.

They didn't want anything to do with babies. Leave them alone with one and they started giving them presents like they were warding off an evil spirit. She had warned Lucien that Joey might strangle himself with the necklace, but he could as easily swallow this and choke. She held it up to the light. The wicked witch, yet!

So Lucien came and went, like a courtier paying homage to an heir apparent, and Joey would not see him again for seven years.

It was hard to say just when Joey's fear of the chair began. Frank came home one night and lofted him from his crib in a high arc that had never failed to produce glee: Joey grinned. A second arc: Four tiny fingers disappeared in a tiny mouth. Third arc: Drool on Daddy.

"That's my little man, catch as catch can—"

"Frank?" Carolyn calling upstairs. "Bring him down, will you? It's time for his bath."

"Okay, Joseph. You heard your mother. March." He held Joey above his head, wiggled him. "What'samatter, don't you know how to march? It's easy. Watch."

And he trudged downstairs in thumping steps, hugging Joey against his shoulder.

"Water's running," Carolyn called from the downstairs bathroom. "Entertain him for a few minutes, will you?"

"Yes, ma'am. That's what I are here for. Funny Frank's Baby Buffoonery." He held Joey out horizontally, like a model airplane. "How about the old loop-the-loop once around the house?"

"How about not getting him too excited?" Carolyn shouted, swirling water around the tub. "*You* loop-the-loop, around the den or someplace. Let him *watch*."

"A spectator," he said to Joey. "Boy, what a party pooper. Okay. Tell you what"—they were moving into the den now—"I'll introduce you to the amazing Rub-a-Dub, man of a million faces. You sit back and politely applaud while I dazzle you with expressions. I'll even let you sit in the patriarch chair, okay? Here. Ker-plunk. Now you are royalty, and that makes this a command performance—"

Almost instantly the horizontal creases of Joey's grinning face went all to little O's of breathless surprise.

"Hey, quit hamming up my act!"

Whimpers now. Frank took Joey's foot and wiggled it. That always worked. The baby loved to be touched and teased. But not this time. The crying was paroxysmal, rapid surges of breath as if he couldn't get enough of screaming. Carolyn was already in the doorway.

"For heaven's sake, Frank!"

"I didn't do a thing." He snatched Joey up. "I haven't even started to make faces."

And by the time he got the words out, Joey stopped.

"You must have frightened him."

"Carolyn, I didn't do a thing. I just sat him down like this—"

Crying. Great voluble bursts.

"Frank!"

He snatched the baby back and in the sudden silence said, "That's amazing."

"What's amazing? He wants to be held."

"It's the chair. Listen to him." He returned Joey to the chair before she could protest and snatched him up at the first outbreak.

"Would you please stop that?"

"All right." They both stared. "It's the chair."

And it was.

Now and then, despite Carolyn's prohibition against it, Frank would put him in the chair just to make sure. The result never varied. At first Joey seemed not to make the association. The sight of the chair as he was carried closer made no impression. He sat in lots of them, after all. But as he went from infancy to being a toddler, he sorted it out. The chair. *That* chair. Soon thereafter he would not even touch it. Not even to keep himself from falling.

"That's amazing," Frank said.

Not so amazing, thought Carolyn. Babies had their whims and phobias just like adults. What they didn't have were explanations for things. Joey must have remembered being upset as he sat in the chair. It seemed like an unhappy place to him. It had *become* an unhappy place to him. That was all.

But such a phobia.

Now when she held him in her arms and approached the patriarch chair, he trembled. You couldn't get him to go near it to retrieve a toy or a present. Frank even tried it with a piece of chocolate. Joey loved chocolate. At first discovery of the marvelous stuff he had sent them all into hysterics by trying to lick the brown rubber doorstop they kept in the hall closet. One evening Frank unwrapped a Hershey bar and placed it in the center of the chair. Joey stood a few feet away, for all the world like a child staring through the plate glass window of a confectionery shop. Not an inch closer. Not a hint of indecision. As if the barrier was something other than in his mind.

"That's amazing," Frank said.

When had the fear begun? Not on the night of the bath, Carolyn believed. The crying had already been too hysterical. It could not have been because he wanted to be held. Frank was right about that. Something else had happened to Joey.

And then it came back to her: the only other occasion. He had been in the chair for a feeding. Strained peas for the first time, and it would have been funny . . . except he had nearly strangled! She had been holding him on her lap. He was already an old hand at strained pears, peaches, apricots, veal, chicken, lamb. But not peas. He had been fussing even before, and then the spoon came in with the green mash, and the stuff never got

28

all the way down, because he gagged, or maybe it met something on the way up. She had inverted him, patted him, finally slapped him hard on the back. But the choking had gone on and on, his little brow turning violet, and if he hadn't started to throw up, if she hadn't jumped up with him—

I don't want to remember this!

That must have been it, though. The bad association with the chair. It couldn't have been anything else. She didn't think there had been another time he had sat in the chair. It wasn't something they did every day. Chip wasn't even supposed to sit in it. In fact, the last time she remembered being in the chair with Joey before that, he was only a would-be human being in her womb kicking and kicking and kicking. . . .

She told Frank about the feeding and Joey's choking, but he didn't seem impressed with her theory that this was the cause of the fear. All he said was, "So why does he still like peas?"

Which was true. Joey loved peas.

Frank had no theories, but he spent hours watching and contemplating the baby. He had become fascinated with Joey's night silences. They were like truces with the powers of darkness. "The dark ickies," Frank called them. Joey was afraid of them, he said. The dark ickies came at you when the lights went out, as every child knew. During the day they hid in sealed closets and behind picture frames and under beds and up the holes in perforated ceiling tiles. But let the lights even blink and they rushed out to get you.

Dark ickies. Joey was afraid of them. Frank would stand at the door to the nursery whenever Joey fussed before bedtime and flick the light switch up and down. The crying and the light seemed to be synchronized. Light on: whimper, fuss. Light off: silence. On: fuss. . . . Off: silence. On . . . off. Fuss . . . silence. As if he had an electric baby. As if light and darkness were incompatible ethers.

And Frank would say, "That's amazing."

4

Joey at four.

The mouse, they called him. Not with malice. Everyone liked Joey. But a mouse was quiet, shy, apt to go unnoticed. That was Joey.

He liked being a mouse. He would snuggle up against his mother's side in a room full of adults and nibble the atmosphere, or savor the aromas of leather and wood and baking dough on a foray through the house, or stand quietly at the window on the border of a storm. He knew the safe havens and the things to avoid. Few things to avoid. Chip when he was feeling malicious. The chair.

At four, he *knew* there was something wrong with the chair.

It wasn't just a feeling now. It was a thought. And he knew no one else knew. The way he found out for sure that something was wrong with it was to sit in it. Again. He hadn't actually sat in it since that evening as a baby. But he had touched it. Run against it and planted both hands on the silken seat. Something restless went through him each time, like low voltage. But he didn't actually sit in it again until the summer of his fourth birthday.

It was one of those electric days when the air lay motionless and damp on everything and the sky was a ghastly green. The tornado season was supposed to be over, but there was a watch in effect until dusk, and he and Chip had been told to stay in the house.

"Let's play search-and-destroy," Chip proposed.

Hide-and-seek with a boy's dynamics was what it was. Not Joey's favorite game. Chip liked to jump out and scare him. But he liked to do that anyway, and playing it in a game gave Joey the advantage of knowing when it was coming. Even then Joey was learning to negotiate with terror.

"Okay," he said, "but it has to be in the basement."

"No way."

"I don't want to play, then."

"Okay. Give me my Thundercat back."

Joey looked fretful.

"Give me my Thundercat back or else play the whole house. It isn't any fun just in the basement." Chip's face relaxed into something ugly with victory.

His brother was going to jump out at him the first chance he got, Joey knew.

"You hide first," Chip said.

Joey went straight to the basement. The smell of paint thinner and detergent was strong in the humid air and seemed vaguely assertive. He wandered out of the laundry and his father's workshop, but the rest of the basement was just as territorial this day. Spiders held the wall by the windows, and the half-sorted largess of abandoned goods dared him to defile his mother's recent efforts at spring cleaning. From high up in the house he heard Chip's cry, reverberating tinnily in the heating duct that went to their room. Stairs next. Snapping and rumbling directly toward him, as if he had left a trail. He got behind the furnace and played mouse.

Chip descended to the foot of the stairs and said, "I see you behind the furnace!"

His shadow. That was it. The light from the windows threw his shadow across the damp floor.

"My turn," Chip said.

Joey trudged upstairs.

He counted a long time. To ninety-nine, he thought. Maybe it was only twenty or thirty, though. He had trouble after thirteen. Chip had been able to count to a hundred when he was three, they said. Chip was smart.

When he was done counting he hollered, "Ready or not!" and plodded back down to the basement. There wouldn't be any shadow from behind the furnace this time. Not with Chip. Joey edged around the water heater and whispered, "I see you." But nothing stirred, and he thought he knew already by the stillness and the smells that no one was there. He went into the workshop and then the laundry room. Chip had once hidden in the dryer, and the door flying open had sent a surge through Joey like a bolt of lightning. "I know you're there, Chip," he said. But he didn't, because Chip wasn't.

He tried upstairs then. The library, the living room, the hall closet, the dining room, the downstairs bath, the pantry, the foyer, the kitchen. His mother was in the kitchen.

"Looking for your brother?" she said without glancing up from the letter she was writing.

"Yes."

"He's a good hider, isn't he?"

Joey raised his elbows to the table, barely clearing the edge. "I hate this game."

She wrote, frowned, scratched something out.

He added, "I don't think I'll look anymore."

"You had your first turn, didn't you?" she murmured.

"Yeah." Reluctantly.

"Chip will be disappointed."

"Oka-a-y."

"Why don't you try the den?"

The den.

No. He wouldn't try the den. Even though he knew . . . now. Even though she had practically told him. Upstairs, first. Maybe, just maybe, Chip had gone there. Because that was the last place you would think of.

Upstairs he went. The bedrooms and the baths, the sewing room, the closets and the sun porch, the upstairs study, the playroom, even the attic—an awful place. But no Chip.

So it *had* to be the den.

He came back down, letting his feet catch up on each step, even though he could descend stairs like an adult. Just inside the door he stopped.

"I know you're in there, Chip," he said.

Joey felt the room coiling like a jack-in-the-box. Chip might be behind the curtains. They were a deep apple red, like the rug, and no light got through. He tiptoed to the side of the room, peeked along one wall. Not behind the curtains. There was a brown leather couch and speaker cabinets. Cautiously Joey checked them. Not there. That left the *chair*. It was in the corner, and you couldn't get behind it without squeezing by the arm and the wall. Chip would get him then. And it would scare the heck out of him. It didn't matter that he expected it.

"Chip," he said sharply. "I see you behind the chair."

Long silence.

"Chip?"

There were only two sides to choose from. Chip couldn't be ready to spring from both. Two sides—unless he climbed over it . . .

Everyone else sat in the chair, and they all said nothing was wrong with it.

Straight over the top . . .

He wouldn't really be sitting: kneeling, maybe.

Then he could look down on Chip . . .

He could do it really fast and be off in no time.

And then the game would be over.

"I didn't mean to! Honest, Mom! Joey just started crawling over the chair, and I jumped up and—*I didn't think he'd start screaming*

33

like that! He didn't even look at me. He was just rolling around screaming. I didn't mean to. I didn't mean to, Mom!"

Adults hide their secrets behind big words, but a mouse uses silence. Joey never said what he saw in the chair. He did not even know what it was, except that it shrieked like a million cats and twisted like a million snakes. And he was no longer sure that it only happened when he sat there. Maybe everyone felt it. Maybe it was a family secret. Why did his parents talk about the chair as if it was so special? Why did they use those big words and lower their voices when it came up and he or Chip was near? Occasionally he caught snatches:

". . . made our decision, let's stick to it—that was before . . . I don't care . . . what's more important . . . over a century of tradition . . . vested authority . . . legally recognized . . . instrument of succession. . . ."

And on one particular night, tossing between the sanctuary of sleep and the compelling discord of parents in conflict, Joey crept to the head of the stairs and caught it all.

"But Chip *already* knows," his mother was arguing heatedly. "What do you think that will say to him if you change your mind now?"

"You shouldn't have told him." His father's voice, delivered in stone.

"There was no reason not to. I took you at your word—"

"Before Joey was born. And he wouldn't have remembered, if you hadn't kept reminding him."

"You didn't say that anything had changed after I got pregnant, and you didn't say anything when you saw we had a boy."

"It was self-evident. You shouldn't have told Chip anything."

"Frank. We've been over this and over this. The point is Chip *does* know, and he'll be terribly, terribly hurt if you don't initiate him into the chair on his birthday. That would be like disowning him."

"Carolyn, I love the boy. You know that. He knows that. But this is a matter of blood. I have an obligation to the past—"

"The past is dead."

"Dead? Is the family dead? It would be the first time the chair and the family inheritance have passed out of the bloodline."

"You were willing enough to see that happen when you couldn't produce an heir."

"Well, now I have. And Joey has the right by birth and blood to be initiated into the chair on his seventh birthday."

"So . . . you just used Chip." She started to cry. "And now that you don't need him anymore, he's not really your son—"

"Carolyn."

"I thought you adopted him with no strings attached. I thought—"

"Carolyn!" Silence. "All right. I won't change it."

There were dim edges all around the meaning, but Joey understood that the chair was central to it. He wondered what "initiation" meant, and if Chip was his real brother, and what could happen on your seventh birthday. It sounded like it was going to happen to Chip instead of him. And that made him glad.

He didn't have to wait long for some of the answers, and they were reassuringly undramatic. On Chip's seventh birthday his father merely took his brother into the den and sat him in the chair. It was the first and last time Joey heard Chip's christened name.

"Clark David Whitehall, you are my oldest son and heir," their father said solemnly.

"I'm Daddy's *air*!" Chip boasted at Joey's bedside that night. "I'm seven and I'm the air in this family. That's one of my birthday presents."

He still had chocolate cake in the corner of his mouth, and his eyes held the mad gleam of an overindulged child. Joey saw the gleam and wondered if it had been put there by the chair.

"I don't want to be the air when I'm seven," he said.

"*I'm* the air," Chip repeated. "You can't ever be."

"How do you know?"

35

"Because there's only one."

One. And Chip was it.

"I'll still be the air when you're seven, Joey."

"Good."

Chip stared at him hard now. "You can't sit in the chair if you aren't the air, ya know."

"That's okay."

"I'm the only one. I can sit in the chair anytime I want. Maybe I'll do it tomorrow. Maybe I'll get up in the middle of the night and do it."

Joey would have said "Good," but Chip had flicked the switch by the door and only the night-light remained on.

"Maybe I'll sleep in the chair," Chip said. "Maybe I'll sit in it all day tomorrow."

It was what Joey thought of first when his mother asked him where Chip was the next afternoon. They had gone shopping for shoes in the morning and eaten lunch in the backyard, and after lunch Joey was supposed to take a nap so he could stay up and watch *Superman III* on channel four. But when his mother peeked in he sat up and grinned.

"What have you been up to?" she asked, grinning back.

"I've been asleep."

"Mmm-hmm. You wouldn't happen to have your brother in the covers with all those toys, would you?"

"Nope." He pulled up the blanket. A book fell out; something jingled.

"I've looked all over the house for him."

"He said he was gonna sit in the chair."

"In the den?"

"Yup."

"Well, he's not in the house. You can get up now and run down to the Witherses to see if he's there."

Still barefoot, Joey plodded downstairs and out the door. The Witherses were two houses down, which in Franklin Village meant an acre or so of the finest Bermuda blend, well-watered and cropped close. He looked for Chip along the culvert and among the several dozen birch and pine in a stand behind the

36

Atkinsons' tudor. But he saw no activity, and the Witherses weren't home.

"Did you ring the bell?" his mother asked when he returned with the news.

"Yup. Rocky barked the whole time."

The Witherses' Llewellyn setter. He always barked when they weren't home.

"Damn that boy!" Carolyn said and went out to look herself.

When she returned, her anger had become anxiety. A pair of phone calls followed and another sortie through the neighborhood, this time by car. She took Joey, and they both hollered through the open windows as they crept along winding roads.

She phoned Frank at three-thirty.

"His bike is here and I've been looking for over two hours and I'm really getting worried, " she said.

"You called the neighbors?"

"I called just about everyone. The Witherses weren't home."

"Maybe he went with them."

"He wouldn't do that without asking."

"Maybe he thought it was okay, or maybe you got your signals crossed somehow. Happens."

Maybe.

But the Witherses returned from a shopping trip to Fairlane Mall at a quarter after five, and Chip wasn't with them.

Carolyn phoned the police at five-twenty.

Frank got home at five-forty.

By six-thirty a small search party of police and neighbors were tramping the fields and back lots around the Village.

By ten o'clock, it was a big search party.

There was a pond in the woods behind the church property off Greenwood. They dragged it at dawn the next day. They found a stolen bicycle, a stroller, a kitchen sink. House-to-house interviews were next. The last time anyone had seen Chip he was with Joey. Scent dogs were borrowed from the county sheriff, but they furrowed through nearby fields in opposite directions and finally tracked back to the house. A TV crew showed up at noon, shoved a camera into Carolyn's face, elicited a tearful plea for aid and information, and left.

The faces that came next were disturbing. Strangers' faces full of some terrible eagerness, as if in vicarious pursuit of disaster. They gave the afternoon a leering complexion more awful than the gnawing fear itself. By sundown the family's hopes seemed to have been dragged down from the sky and eaten by an eternal night.

Morning dawned gray as cardboard. A deadness in time hung over the house. The search had passed beyond their grasp now to a network of police interactions and useless tips. The phone seemed never to have stopped ringing as it resumed again, and Frank answered all calls with a terse "No statements. We're in seclusion."

Joey understood the sense of what was happening, but not the reaction. The reaction was a rending, murky thing that shook his world, and the more tightly his mother held him, the more terrifying it became. Chip was missing. That was bad. It meant he didn't have a brother to play with. It meant he had to sleep alone. And he had enough compassion in his four-year-old soul to feel sorry for Chip. But what he sensed stealing up from the foundations of the house seemed out of proportion with even that. What was it? What was he missing?

"Is Chip ever coming back, Mommy?" he murmured in her arms on the second night.

For a full minute all she could do was breathe heavily. "We don't know, baby," shuddered out of her then.

But that wasn't the extent of the horror Joey felt drifting through the house.

"If he doesn't, where will he be?" he asked next.

She took a deep, regular breath and tried to smile. "We've got to keep our faith up. Chip is all right. Wherever he is, he's all right."

She was lying, of course.

She was afraid.

There was danger all around. Joey was especially sensitive to that. But it wasn't until he came back down to the doorway of the den just after bedtime that he thought he understood.

It was the chair.

38

"I'm the only air," Chip had said.

Air.

Chip was the air now. And the chair was empty. Waiting for the next air. The next little boy to turn seven. And Joey knew who that was. Stunned, he crept back up to bed and lay very, very still.

5

I'll tell you my secrets, if you'll tell me yours. Then we'll be friends. I'd like us to be friends, okay? . . . Okay? You don't have to talk if you don't want to. Just give me nice pictures, okay? Give me nice pictures of your secrets, and then I'll know we're friends."

Joey gave her a picture the next day. She had been a school counselor for three years, and an art teacher before that, and she knew that here was a first-grader whose fine motor skills made most fifth-graders look as if they lacked opposable thumbs. The greens and the reds were meant to be dissonant against the arrangement of pastels; there was balance and a real sense of composition. Not so easy for a six-year-old to control, considering that the figure had the cosmic anatomy of a Dali. There were deliberate gaps in the arms and legs as if it were dematerializing. On the whole it was a remarkable picture. But that wasn't why she called Mrs. Whitehall and asked her to come in. The reason she called was because the face in the picture had snakes coming out of its mouth and stark horror in its eyes and because it was called MY BROTHER.

"Mrs. Gaylord?" Carolyn stood just outside the counseling office door, a softly arrived breath of fresh air in raincoat, scarf, and see-through umbrella.

"Ah, it's still raining out there," the counselor observed, pushing back from her desk in a chair that spoke with thrums and clicks. "Hello, Mrs. Whitehall."

They shook hands and small-talked their way down to seat level, a desk in between, white hands seeming to negotiate the amenities. The gestures stopped when Mrs. Gaylord said busily, "Joey, Joey . . . yes, Joey."

"I hope he hasn't done anything too terribly wrong," Carolyn said lightheartedly, though the ease in her voice never reached her eyes.

"Oh, no. Joey is perfectly well-behaved. Almost too well, actually. Sometimes we all wish he'd throw a tantrum or something, just to loosen up."

Carolyn nodded, though her eyes remained intent.

"He's very quiet, I'd even say withdrawn," Mrs. Gaylord resumed. "His teacher, Ms. Farthing, asked me to try and coax him out. He's so serious, so on his guard all the time. She feels something is troubling him. Mrs. Whitehall, does Joey have a brother?"

Carolyn sagged reflexively, one knuckle moving toward her lip and arrested by an act of will. There it was. The question again. She felt her eyes going raw and beginning to mist. "I don't know," she managed aloud, and while she daubed her eyes with a Kleenex she laughed briefly at the nonsense of that. She liked this woman. They shared a certain directness that businesswomen acquired. But the counselor's business was "people," and Carolyn tied up on "people."

Does Joey have a brother? She had never been able to say he did not. Chip's body had never been found. His clothes were still in the closet, the bureau drawers; his toys appeared here and there, untouched by Joey. Does Joey have a brother? Do you have two sons, Mrs. Whitehall? It's eleven o'clock, do you know where your child is? It's January . . . it's June . . . it's Christmas . . . it's his birthday. In what tense do you speak of your son, Mrs. Whitehall? Where *is* he?

The counselor kept her composure and waited.

"He disappeared," Carolyn said with a sniff. "Two years ago. He was seven . . . well-adjusted . . . happy. He disappeared right out of the house. There never was any ransom demand, no hint of an accident or a crime . . . nothing. Just gone. I don't know where he is. Or even *if* . . . you know?" She tried to smile, a plea really. "I suppose you could say he and Joey were close, as close as Joey gets to anyone. I know Joey is withdrawn, but he's always been withdrawn. We started him in a different school, so there wouldn't be any reminders, and . . . and that's why you never had Chip."

Mrs. Gaylord leaned forward on her desk and had the good sense to say only a quiet "Thank you."

Carolyn nodded, gestured futilely.

"So you don't think being withdrawn has anything to do with Chip?"

"No."

"I don't mean to pry—and I won't be offended if you tell me it's none of my business—but I know you're here because you don't want to overlook anything that might benefit Joey. Could there be anything else troubling him?"

Carolyn shrugged. "Nothing. His father and I get along perfectly well. It's a second marriage for both of us. But Joey is ours. Chip is his half-brother."

Mrs. Gaylord looked away. "It's really difficult to tell what's going through a first-grader's mind. Sometimes the super-bright types are off in entirely different universes—"

"I don't think Joey is exceptionally bright. He's just normal. Just right."

The counselor's eyes went back on her now. "Well. They're very hard to measure at his age. Surely you know he's quite gifted as an artist, though?"

"He likes to draw. He always has. I buy pictures like other mothers buy magazines, and Joey has come to feel they're a natural expression."

There was nothing natural in Joey's portrait, Mrs. Gaylord knew. "Is there any particular type of picture that Joey likes best?" she probed.

"No. I don't think so. He likes landscapes. Clowns. Why?"

"Well. It's nothing to get upset about, and I hope you won't, but . . . apparently Joey does think about his brother more than you realize."

And then she showed her.

It was raining harder when Carolyn left, and the chocolate-revel sky writhed like serpents coming out of the mouth of God. She walked to the car, scarfless, umbrella folded and dangling from her wrist. The rain on her face was necessary to obscure the tears, to cool the hysteria simmering just below the surface. How could Joey have drawn that? He loved Chip, didn't he? Why would he imagine such a blasphemy? The theme was so alien to anything she had seen him do before. He always drew laughing eyes with blue in them. Blue was his favorite color. Where was the blue? Where were the clouds, the birds, the grass? He did not know how to draw eyes like that!

But he did.

He had seen them somewhere. It was the most *real* thing he had ever done. And there was no question it was his. She knew his every crayon stroke—the tight smooth circles, the length of the sketch lines, the angle of the shading, the amount of pressure, differing only in the uncharacteristic firmness of those god-awful green snakes.

She did not go home. She drove in the rain. Drove and drove and drove. If she went home she would have to see colors, the serpent green of her plants, the blood red of her baked enamel potware. Here on the road in the rain the sky was the whole canvas, and it was the color of her insides: a black-and-white wound.

It ended about two-thirty. The rain had subsided to a tympanic drizzle by then, and she was stopped at the intersection

43

of a two-lane highway and a wide country road. There was a traffic light and she sat through several cycles, *red . . . green . . . red . . . green*, before she remembered. Joey! The bus! He was on his way home from school!

She had been thinking of nothing but Joey, and yet she hadn't been thinking about him at all.

He was waiting near the garage, his yellow slicker as cherishable as a rainbow, when she drove up. It brought back the color and the reality of her world. For two hours she had been adrift in a neurotic fugue of the type that had poisoned her first marriage. She had been convinced she was an inadequate mother then, and the child she could not rescue was still lost and unaccounted for. And now she had damn near done the same thing to Joey. At least she had left him vulnerable. She had sworn never to let the bus arrive without being there, but she had. Thank God he was waiting for her! She didn't care how overprotective she was being or how much she was overreacting to Joey's picture—

"Mommy, where have you been?"

She gathered him up, hugged him. "I'm sorry, precious . . . I'm so sorry."

"I thought you weren't coming, Mommy."

"Oh, of course I was. I got lost for a while, baby. That's all. I just got lost. I promise never to do it again."

Beneath the smell of his rubber raincoat she thought she could smell his heat, his anxiety. And it was so much a part of their relationship that she felt she knew every atom of him. Was there a meaningful experience he had had that she hadn't shared, a single book, a TV show, a trip from home? Not in this life. But God only knew what messages traveled unread from long-ago ancestors. Genes and chromosomes. That was where the model for the drawing had come from. Some cosmic fluke. A momentary intrusion in the soft wax of a child's mind she knew as well as her own.

But later, watching him fret at the dinner table, she wondered what he was thinking, if it had anything to do with Chip, and when she tucked him in for the night she had the feeling that this was the border of the world she didn't know about, this was when Joey went searching for his brother. "The dark ickies," Frank called them. And wherever Joey went after she turned out the lights, he would go in silence.

"Do you think he has nightmares?" she asked, lying in the dark next to her husband.

"Who?" Frank rolled over to face her.

"Joey."

"Why don't you ask him?"

"I'm not sure he knows what a nightmare is."

Frank laughed slowly. "Well, if he doesn't, he'll certainly appreciate having it suggested to him."

"Don't make fun of me."

He heard the tremor then. "Sorry. You're a good mother, but it's after hours now. We should be talking about the moon."

"There isn't any tonight."

"We'll gossip behind its back, then."

She let the playfulness die. "I went to the school today."

"And . . . ?"

"I saw the counselor. She's a nice person, and we had a long talk about Joey. She showed me a picture he'd drawn—" Here her voice tightened up.

"What's wrong?" he soothed.

She sighed with exasperation. "It's just . . . me. I swore I wouldn't do this again. I waited till now to talk to you because I thought I could keep control in the dark—"

"Carolyn." He took her in his arms. "You don't have to talk at all."

"I want to tell you. Just hold me, okay?" She took a deeper, freer breath now. "The picture was of Chip. And it was terrible. It had snakes coming out of his mouth"—she swallowed—"blood coming out of his ears—and his body was dissolving and his eyes were . . . were—"

"Why did she show you this?" he demanded indignantly.

"That's not the point. The point is he drew it. It was a sick, sick drawing, Frank, and our son drew it!"

"The counselor said it was sick?"

"That's what she thought. That's why she called me in there."

"She said that?"

45

"She said his teacher, Ms. Farthing, thought he was troubled and withdrawn. She said the picture might mean he had a lot of conflicts about his brother. I told her about Chip."

"What did she say to that?"

"She said we ought to encourage him to express himself. She meant his feelings for Chip."

"Oh. That's not quite the same as saying he drew a sick, sick picture, is it?"

"Lord, am I the only one who can see it?" She lay like spring steel in his arms for a few seconds, then gradually relaxed. "Okay, I'm a guilt-ridden mother of one-and-a-half sons, but they didn't call me in there to tell me how well-adjusted Joey is. And she did suggest professional counseling."

"They called you in like they probably call half the mothers there at one time or another," he said, clearly annoyed. "They called you in because the teacher has twenty-five little kids who don't all conform to the role model and because the counselor is, after all, a counselor, and she gets paid to look for the kinds of problems counselors look for and to make referrals. They got a sample of a very imaginative little boy's darker visions—which they probably asked for—and so they rattled your cage; all in a day's work. You can overdo this interpretation stuff, Carolyn."

"It wasn't like that at all," she said wearily.

He took a few seconds to come down off his high horse. Then he said, "All right. I didn't mean to get defensive. We're both being extreme. You're seeing Joey as an apprentice sicko, and I'm making him out to be a Cub Scout. Husbands and wives at chess. Let me confess that I'm apprehensive for Joey too. He has lots of fears, I think. I don't know when they started or why. But I also don't think they're hideously abnormal. And I do think you can make problems where there are none, just by surrounding a kid with a lot of career professionals frantically signaling him that something is seriously wrong. Everyone is different, and everyone has to develop their own mechanisms to cope. If he's allowed to face that without interference, Joey will presumably do it in the way only he can, and I'd very much like to see him do it without psychological surgery and the scarring thereof."

46

"But what if he can't?"

"Life isn't cut and dried, Carolyn. There are degrees of success and a great deal left to chance. I'm not taking a macho attitude toward this, I'm not saying we don't all need help; I'm just saying let's be sensitive to Joey without making him a basket case of introspection and without a crowd to stand in his head with him."

So self-assured, she was thinking. Frank, her knight in shining armor. The color was coming back into balance now. Not just reds and greens.

"We give him love and understanding," Frank was saying. "We listen to him, but we don't panic, we don't go off the deep end when he draws a picture—which, by the way, got something troublesome out of his head. We don't put him through the dubious benefits of analysis with a paid stranger, who will— if he's lousy—suggest a lot of things to him, and—if he's competent—merely listen. We *do* encourage him to find listeners among those he chooses: us, his friends, the minister, the teacher, and, yes, the school counselor, if he feels like it. I think he's got an invisible companion already, and that's good."

"What?"

"An invisible companion. Someone to talk to. It's not unusual for children to imagine a friend."

"What are you saying?"

"I'm saying I've heard him talking to himself."

"Where? When?"

"I don't know. Sometimes. In the den maybe."

"What does he say?"

"I've never gotten close enough to hear."

"Maybe he's talking to Chip."

"Maybe."

He had his hand on her breast then, playing the nipple as if it were a turntable, stroking warm music with the stylus of his finger. And the glow of that merged with the exhilaration his certainty brought her. An invisible companion . . . Chip, maybe. It made Joey's journey seem less lonely. And then Frank had his hand beneath her nightgown, tracing out the melody of her body. She pulled the gown off her shoulders and up over her hips and hungrily offered him harmony.

47

So why haven't I heard Joey talking to himself?

It was the first thing she thought of when she awoke the next morning. Frank was hardly ever with him. How had she missed the signals? And that marked the beginning of a new watchfulness on her part.

But in two months' time she never once saw or heard a clue that Joey was fantasizing a relationship with Chip. He would sit alone, read alone, play alone, and his games seemed to be solitary in nature. Once, she tried to sound him out. She was sitting on the edge of his bed at night just before Christmas, and the house and the room seemed particularly right, with the winter locked outside and soft light and warm air wafting up the stairs like a caress. Everything was right except for that one dull pang.

"I think I miss Chip most at times like this," she said. "Do you ever think about him, Joey?"

He looked at her with great sad eyes from the bed and made a slow shrug.

"It's all right to think about him," she said. "I wouldn't want you to forget him. Not at Christmas. Not any time."

"I remember. . . ."

"Do you? What do you remember best?"

"Mmm . . . His birthday."

"That's a nice thing to remember."

"He sat in the chair."

"Yup. He did. Your father was very proud."

"Am I gonna sit in the chair on my next birthday?"

"Yes. Your father especially wants you to be initiated."

"What if Chip comes back?"

Ah. Here it was. The conflict. "Honey . . . if Chip comes back we'll pick up just like before. Your father and I talked about this, and we agreed"—after long soul-searching arguments!—"that we need to go on as a family. We can't stop living. Chip wouldn't want that. So now it's even more important for you to fill your role and be our little man. It doesn't mean we don't love Chip or that we've given up hope or . . . or that he won't come back. But we can't just *wait*. Do you understand that?"

He understood.

"I don't like to sit in the chair, Mommy."

"I know. But you will, won't you? For Chip. For Daddy. For me."

She took him shopping that weekend. The malls were thronged with spirited people searching industriously for the right gifts or waiting not too impatiently in long lines, seemingly mesmerized by the color and sound of Christmas-apparent. Joey waited his turn to sit on Santa's lap and when it came had his picture taken. Carolyn stood a few feet away, trying to overhear the privileged wishes of her six-year-old. But Santa himself—perhaps deafened by his own incessant bells—could not hear. She saw him crane his hoary head closer to Joey's mouth, and when Joey's lips moved again, Santa's eyes shot up at Carolyn's. Then Joey was off his lap and a nubile elf was giving him candy. Carolyn's gaze never left the puzzled emptiness of old St. Nick's face as she stepped closer, already feeling a premonition, to receive the child's most secret desire.

"He says he wants Chip back," Santa said.

The face receded then, leaving the faint impression of an indictment, which Carolyn absorbed leadenly. The mall itself seemed to be receding, as if the whole imbroglio of song and shoppers and Santa were sleighing away to the remote acoustics of the past. Gone was the glee. "Joy to the World" . . . but the world was apart from her.

Her eyes stinging, her hand like ice around her son's, she walked numbly through the concourse, and when he was drawn suddenly to the gaily lit façade of Circus World, she let him go. But it was not the fuzzy nap of some stuffed love bear that had caught his eye, it was something quite the opposite. And suddenly she realized that the predominant colors of Christmas were red and green, just like the hard scaly serpent with the scarlet tongue forking out of its mouth, Joey was now entranced with.

She knew then what he wanted. How could there be any doubt? she thought. Frank was right. Chip had never left him. And somehow snakes were a part of it. A vision of death? of decay? It was ghastly, but she knew she absolutely must repress

49

her revulsion and outrage. This was Joey's haunting, Joey's specter. *He* must exorcize it, as Frank had said. Let it run its course or it would never leave him.

"I want that," he said with uncharacteristic firmness when she came up behind him.

"Do you?" she asked, trembling. "Why, Joey?"

"I want to give it as a present."

For Chip, of course. And she bought it for him, and they walked back through the mall, the mall that was receding, only now Joey was receding with it . . . joy to the world, Joey to the world . . . *Joey to the world.*

But it wasn't for Chip.

And it wasn't a Christmas present.

Joey waited until his father was at work and his mother was outside, and then he went into the den and laid the rubber snake in the middle of the patriarch chair and said, "I'll tell you my secrets, if you'll tell me yours. Then we'll be friends. I'd like us to be friends, okay? . . . okay? You don't have to talk if you don't want to. Just give me nice pictures, okay? Give me nice pictures of your secrets, and then I'll know we're friends."

6

"Happy birr-thday, dear Joe-ey . . . happy birthday to you!"

Applause.

Sixteen friends and relatives beamed their glowing faces at him as he hyperventilated to blow out the candles. It was a monstrous cake, four tiers high, but he craned all the way over it to get the seventh flame, shimmering there on a cleft of butter frosting.

"What did you wish for, Joey?" shouted little Johnny Withers.

There was only one wish to make. The same wish he had made for three years. But it wasn't going to come true. He knew that now, and so he was already steeling himself. They played the games and tried out his presents and one by one the cars came to take them away, until there were just the three of them left and it was time.

"Well, son, are you ready?" his father rumbled.

Joey met his look and tried to smile. It came out tremulous and intent, but his father must have thought it was suitable because he smiled back with stoic pride. His mother followed them into the den, her reservations all smothered in a kind of blind faith.

Joey had been preparing three years for this moment. He had studied every detail of the chair's heavy teak turnings, its red and green silk cover; he had sat with it, talked to it; he had tried to make friends, had even made an offering of a rubber snake, in fact—a bribe against the future and the terrible pictures it caused in his mind. Now the moment had come.

Pale and light-headed, his blind faith was no less than his mother's, no less than the world's elite group of sacrificial virgins who have walked into the mouths of volcanoes or the human offerings who have laid themselves on altars, as he shambled slowly to the chair, slowly turned, slowly dropped down, down, forever down, on a piece of furniture whose seat was as deep and enveloping as its past. But volcanoes and the blood basins of altars are insatiable and relentless. No less the throne of Khitan Zor.

The first thing was the howling.

It erupted exactly like a cat—a million cats—who have been stepped on all at once. And the sound filled his head like a fluid, imbibed by every nerve until it seemed to resonate along his spine. Immediately afterward, he saw the snakes. They were sluicing out of some obscure darkness, great green waves, faster and faster. His thoughts flowed faster too, compacted like time itself. It was, in fact, just a second or two, but the only measure he knew was the impulse to catapult himself out of the chair, and this he fought down again and again.

The howling ate the flesh off his bones and set them rattling. Then it reamed out his skull until his nightmares whirled without anchors, and images popped out of nowhere with bits of landscape. There was a ceramic tile tunnel and the sensation of flight. There were other people . . . running . . . a migration of panic, dotted here and there with camp fires, with torn clothing, with demonic carnage. There was snow and sliding, sliding. The tunnel had pitfalls and great heavy doors and sudden vistas. He had no words for some of what he saw, but the visual links came out of his subconscious, from comics, cartoons, and Goya-like paintings—a surrealistic Chutes and Ladders journey. Somewhere there was a beast for which he had no name. The satyrlike creature erupted from this passage or that. It moved and sated itself with a terrible urgency that was fascinating for its singleness. Joey could hear it snorting and wheezing. It seemed to come from behind, then in front, then below, and he would flee with the other screaming humans just before its hairy, horned head shot up from a sewer opening in the floor of the tunnel. He became aware of a door, heavier and more massive than the others, and it was behind this that they all cowered. The thing was slammed shut, the bolts shot home, and in the breathless silence of waiting they heard the satyr coming, rooting happily, slathering over the hapless few on the wrong side of the door. Closer and closer it came, until they heard the terrible roar of surprise. The bolts rattled, the frame shook under a fierce fusillade. Tiles fell, splashing in the fulvous scum on the floor. But more terrifying was the sudden silence. Then, in the nether light, Joey saw the rusty drain cap at his feet do what it could not do. It began to swell. Like a bubble. Like a balloon. From below his feet arose the sound a little boy makes inhaling and blowing out candles, an awful huffing sound. And the drain got bigger and bigger. Except for the cavernous respiring, it grew in utter silence to the size of a head and burst with a wet, mucous sound. And by then it was a head. Chip's head. Grinning malevolently and saying in his father's voice, *"Joseph Scott Whitehall, you are my firstborn and my heir."*

And after the words came the snakes again, spilling out of Chip's mouth as volubly as uncontrolled laughter.

7

$$W$$inter.

The earth simplified by snow. White on white. Like layers of gauze. And beneath it the world slowly healed. But not Frank and Joey Whitehall.

Frank hadn't been able to hide his disappointment at the initiation. Barely were the words of the ceremony out of his mouth when Joey was screaming like a baby, and though he recognized that his son needed to be given time and understanding, he felt very much that Joey's phobic attitude was stubborn and unnecessary.

The central artifact of his life had been that chair and what it stood for. His boyhood insecurities in a family struggling for survival and the chair's role in keeping them together had been the main influence on him then. The fact that as a seven-year-old he had already vowed to make the dynasty what it had once been was another. And then to have done it and secured a natural son after the shambles of his first marriage . . . how could his heir presumptive have picked the very symbol of what was important to the future to be hung up on?

That it *had* been picked by Joey in some fickle way was not open to question. Something arbitrary and cruelly ironic had been set in motion in Joey's infancy. It really wasn't the boy's fault, but it was an obstinacy he must conquer. Not just for the family's sake, but for his own. A child was afraid of moths, of loud noises, or the dark ickies. He had to get over these things. Frank had discussed this with Carolyn and she had finally understood: the key to Joey's coming out in all phases of his life was victory over the patriarch chair.

"But before you come down too hard on him, remember you can't order a fear to go away," she had admonished. "You might make him sit in the chair, but you can't make him like it. And I hope you realize what a tremendous amount of courage it took for him to sit in it at all on his birthday. He didn't want to be afraid. He really tried, Frank."

Nevertheless, the estrangement had grown. The chair was the seat of Frank's emotions. You couldn't force love, either.

But it was time to reach out, and Frank had visions of a new rite of passage. He would take Joey camping. No highway cabin just off I-75; they would tent. In the wilderness. Tent and ski and go ice fishing. And one more thing. They would take someone else, someone whose boyhood Frank knew well. Someone who had liked just this sort of isolation and rigor back then.

Lucien.

"Uncle Luce?"

"What?"

"Did you really ski up Mount Everest?"

Lucien exchanged an amused glance with Frank across the van. "Twice. But I only skied down once."

Joey's head swiveled toward his father at the wheel. "You said he took the lift down, Dad."

"Right. The second time. That's why he only skied down once."

Joey grinned. He liked being teased, though Uncle Luce's capacity for this was as yet unknown. "Lifts don't take you *down*," he said after a minute.

He had his new cross-country boots on and his dark blue Salomon gloves, though the heater was blowing full blast. They hadn't even cleared the driveway, and he had a half hour of skiing in. His father had loaded the gear while he tried the elevations above the frozen culvert and worked on his diagonal strides through the Atkinsons' birches. He had been out four times already this year, and he was going to get wax skis if he stayed with it; his parents had promised. They had picked up Uncle Luce at seven-thirty, and now they were in transit to the Upper Peninsula.

Joey did not remember his uncle, though the white face and raptorial eyes seemed to stir something in his memory. The voice so mellow one moment and inert the next, and always deep, also found a twin in his mind. He wasn't sure whether the faint echo was good or bad, and it took the present-tense Lucien to redefine it for him.

"Now *that's* a ski jump," his uncle said when they passed an ill-fated construction project near Saginaw; the Zilwaukee Bridge hung unfinished and partially collapsed against the sky. And again, near Standish, "Look, a herd of deer," when they saw a half dozen cows at the edge of a copse.

Joey decided his uncle was funny.

At Grayling they really did see a deer, and then they crossed the Mackinac Bridge and took Highway 2 west along Lake Michigan. At Engadine they got groceries and turned north.

"Where are we going?" Joey wanted to know.

"I own nine hundred square miles of virgin paradise," Lucien said, and when they actually passed into Luce County, Joey thought there was something magical and wonderfully surprising about his uncle.

They pitched camp near two frozen sheets of water called, indiscriminately, Little Two Hearted Lakes. The woods were dense and sheltering. The sky was incredibly clear, a vaporous blue trailing off into the sure thick girth of a snowstorm.

"All able-bodied men grab a shovel," his father directed, and Joey took the short implement with the detachable handle and began to help clear a site.

The tent went up next, a North Face geodesic dome, and then their sleeping bags, which his father called "gophers"—though the label said Marmot—went in. They made a fire ring and stuck their skis and poles in the snow. By that time the first flakes were falling.

"Going to catch a corner of it," Frank said, appraising the sky.

"No sense breaking a trail till morning," said Lucien.

It snowed off and on throughout the afternoon, and they fried hamburgers with the flakes sizzling off the pan. Joey thought the smell was richer, the taste heartier than any McDonald's he had ever visited. The woods darkened and closed rank shortly after five, but the ground snow and the sky stayed lit. There was stark beauty in the coming of night: slivers of brilliant cream with bruised edges, pockets of iridescence, great gaping eyes filled with sunset motes. The air was so crisp and potent it seemed to flow into you without the need of breathing. And then, with a suddenness that could only have been orchestrated, the black wing fell and it was night, and they knew they were intruders.

Fire was their host. It gave warmth and prepared food. It made pictures, stirred thoughts. It whistled, snapped, and sighed. It flavored the air. The one thing it didn't do was invite touch. For that they retreated to the embrace of sleeping bags. The last thing Joey remembered as he sank into sleep was the meaningless benediction of voices, arguing the merits of a pole sleeve tent over something called an oval-in-tension. And then he belonged to the night.

He awoke with a precipitancy and a joy that only the very young know, made keener still by the bite of the air. The hush outside the tent was magical, as if energy waited there and his emergence into the morning would trigger a boisterous welcome. Inside the tent was the faintest syllable of light sleep. His father lay in front of him, a green reef of insulation. Behind him was his uncle. The bulk nestled between them consisted of water bottles, stored upside down so that any ice would form at the bottom, and the tent stuff sack turned inside out and filled with their wet boots. This was to keep those items from freezing, he had been told. He could not hear his uncle breathing at all.

And all at once he knew—

Uncle Luce wasn't there. Joey twisted suddenly and beheld the rolled sleeping bag.

"Daddy," he whispered, still intimidated by the stillness.

"Hmm? Good morning, Joey."

"Uncle Luce is gone."

His father hesitated, then turned slowly like a sea lion to survey what Joey had already seen. "Yeah," he said, moving his lips to stir moisture in his mouth. "Doesn't look like he just went out to use the facilities, does it?"

"Maybe he's making breakfast."

His father rolled to a sitting position and unzipped the window. "Nope. His skis are gone, though."

They found the note written on a grocery bag and pinned in the woodpile after they were up and about: GONE TO BREAK TRAIL—WAIT FOR ME. Lucien's tracks led northeast away from camp.

"Well, that leaves breakfast to you and me, Joey." Frank snapped a birch stick in two. "What'll it be, eggs and bacon or bacon and eggs?"

It was a good two hours before Lucien came knifing out of the forest, his breath trailing like a streamer, frost clinging to his sideburns and bib.

"Excelsior!" he shouted. "God lives!"

"You must have crossed through Sault Sainte Marie and made Hudson Bay," Frank jibed. "Joey and I were worried you might not beat the spring thaw."

"Never fear. There's ice and snow for a millennium out there. I have seen it! Tasted it! And the trail is exquisite. All the way to the river and back in a breathtaking loop."

"You must have left in the middle of the night to set it."

"It's slow going, breaking trail, brother."

Frank looked at his son.

"I can make it, Dad," Joey said.

Frank smiled. This was the kind of test they had come out here for.

They left a half hour later, Joey in between his father and uncle, feeling their way into the trail. The two men exchanged views on the wax color they had chosen relative to the temperature, but other than that the only sounds were the hissing of the skis and an occasional branch cracking somewhere close at hand. The beauty was awesome. Four inches of powder made a confection of a million branches and tendrils bowing over the trail, and the effect of all that silence was to stifle inner voices and smooth minds into "now" things that remembered or planned nothing. And when the sun hit, the explosion of light nearly stopped them in their tracks. The urge to strike a rhythm, to match one's pulse to the flow of grandeur was overpowering. But Joey's slower strides set the pace, and soon his father was alternately gliding ahead and waiting for them to catch up.

"Take off, Frank," Lucien suggested. "Joey and I will bide our time. We don't need you."

Frank paused indecisively. "That's okay. We've got all day." But it was clear he wanted to set a rhythm for himself, shooting the sweeps and climbing hills on momentum.

"Go ahead, Frank," his brother urged.

"I'm all right."

Then, finally: "Somewhere in here there's at least a half mile of drops you've got to try, Frank. Hit 'em hard, and when you bottom out keep kicking. There's another half dozen miles of forgiving roller coaster after that. Joey and I will make an afternoon of it while you wait in camp."

The prospect was too tempting, and the last Joey saw of his father was the blue-and-red fanny pack bouncing with his kicks as he poled around a stand of pines.

"Let the rabbit run," Lucien said behind him, and Joey thought he heard amusement in the amber voice.

After that it got very silent.

The fish-scale texture of Joey's skis whining on the snow seemed to be the only sound. His uncle's waxed bottoms ran so easily they were inaudible, and Joey kept twisting around to make sure he had not been abandoned in the great forest. Each time he did this he saw the same hawklike smile, with hoarfrost dripped onto his uncle's bib like crystal saliva. The jet eyes never varied. And since he had removed his cap, Lucien's black hair flared back like the horns of an ebony ram.

"If you *did* get lost, you could follow the tracks, nephew," he said at last. "Would you like me to ski in front of you?"

"No, it's okay," Joey said.

But a few minutes later his uncle suddenly flitted past through the powder and cut back in.

"The more traveled the tracks in front of you, the easier they'll ski," he said. "See if this doesn't help."

Lucien kicked and double-poled, and again with the other foot, again, again, and having gained speed fell back into alternate striding for several seconds. The gap between them stretched to some thirty yards before he dug in and waited.

"A fast set makes a fast track," he said when Joey had closed to ten feet. "Don't worry if I get out of sight, just stay in the tracks."

But Joey did worry. His uncle went farther and farther, and he didn't like being alone, even for a few seconds. It was beginning to snow now. Time and again the figure in the midnight-blue bib pants blended with the trunks of the deep woods and then vanished altogether in a curtain of falling snow. Joey would come upon him again then, standing next to a sentinel pine or around a sharp turn. But the intervals got longer. The tracks won't go away, though, he told himself. Unless it snows really, really hard, the tracks won't go away.

And that was when it began to snow really, really hard.

He tried to ski faster. He tried to kick harder and lengthen his stride the way his father had. But that made him fall. The first time he fell he got snow in his gloves, and the second time he got a whole mouthful. He wanted to cry. He wanted to call out for his father. All around him was a vast white room and the snow was blinding and he was lost. But his father would be ashamed of him if he cried out. He knew that. He had been brought up here to be a man, and men didn't cry out. He got up. Got up and skied the white room. His uncle was in it. His father was in it. Their tracks were still here, though he had to squint to see them. He would find them, the way they wanted him to. Because maybe they had planned this, he thought. Maybe his uncle had gone out in the middle of the night and set the track just so they could—

"Joey."

His uncle's voice. Close.

"Over here, Joey."

Joey stopped, looked left. There was a silhouette against the curtain, a half-formed shape against the scrim of the storm. It looked like the satyr thing from his nightmare in the chair, the thing he didn't have a name for. And he realized that the ram's horns and the dripping saliva and the hawkish eyes were all like the thing. And the white room was like the ceramic tile tunnel of that trauma. And he could feel the chair, here, among the trees, as if wood itself were its agent, its familiar in a subterranean world where roots groped and conspired and sent messages through the earth. Joey's mind saw these things without terms or explanations. Like the pictures from the chair.

"Joey . . . follow me."

But the tracks went the other way. His uncle was turned around.

"We'll never make it, Joey. The storm will cover the tracks. We've got to go back the shortest way."

How had his uncle gotten over there without leaving a trail?

"Just ski toward me, Joey."

Joey skied toward him: awkward, stumbling strides that caught in vines under the snow. And then he saw that there really were tracks. Another set.

Another set?

They led in both directions, parallel with the first track. When had they been made? But the snow was swirling and he heard a distant click, as if a ski pole had struck a branch, and he looked up to see the phantom figure of his uncle already fading in retreat.

Joey followed.

The wind was part of the chase now, pushing and nudging in no particular manner except gracelessly. How it entered the high forest of white pines was a mystery. But veils of snow dropping from the tops of the trees suggested that it blew straight down from the universe at large. Joey knew only that it milled along the forest floor, now rushing, now turning, in disarray like the migration of panic in his nightmare. It seemed to bounce and well up off the snow, kicking out special effects like the frictionless orb in a pinball machine slingshotting out of baffles and traps. It could do this with a vengeance. Because something else was happening. The terrain was changing.

Gone were the long inclines and gently banked slopes of the first tracks his uncle had set. These new ones fell away abruptly, or climbed like rickety ladders over ganglia and roots. The earth seemed to have healed badly from some sort of bone-breaking cataclysm. He would watch the sticklike figure disappear around a switchback, reappear seconds later, disappear, reappear . . . and now and again a cry of exultation or feral glee or something else would come back circuitously through the trees. Joey's skis were slower, but the steepening descents were too fast for him. He wanted to sit down, to slide on the seat of his pants, but even this would have exposed him to a battering as the trail narrowed and dipped ever more sharply. And besides, his uncle—if that really was his uncle and not the resurgence of a nightmare—was leaving him farther and farther behind. The occasional distant cry was no longer ecstasy but mournful, limberlost. Joey had to keep his feet.

And that was when the fog started.

It lay in the deepest pockets, a bottom-of-the-world fog, and Joey feared it immediately. He saw it from the corner of a sharp descent, snaking lazily over a vast basin. Somehow he kept his balance and came up the other side, climbing, climbing, as if vicious dogs raged at his heels. But it was everywhere now—lakes of the stuff—and he couldn't see his uncle at all. He couldn't see his skis at times either, though the track seemed to grip them relentlessly, rocketing him down, around, up. The whine on the drops rose higher and higher, giving him another symptom of speed.

He was sweating

He was thirsty.

He was aching.

With ice forming on his lashes and a sting on his cheeks, Joey was in the early stages of heat exhaustion. He could not climb as his uncle did, attacking the rises with herringbone strides. He had to hang on his poles for every foot he bought. And there came a hill, a very long hill, that seemed to go up forever, and when he got to the summit he was so faint, so knotted with anxiety and fatigue, that he did not immediately recognize the sound he heard. He did not recognize it until he slid off the tiny sanctuary of level ground at the top. But then he did.

It was the insidious rushing of a river.

And *he* was rushing now, faster than ever before, the whine of his skis becoming a thin shriek. The drop twisted sharply and suddenly he was in a snow tunnel, running a gamut of benedictions from snow-laden branches, and then he shot free and the trail narrowed to nothing and there, straight down and half a galaxy away on his right, was the river.

He couldn't actually see it. It was bedded in fog and mist. But he could hear it. He could *feel* it. A tumult. A torrent. Raging in a nether chasm he did not dare look into. But there wasn't time to dwell on that, because the trail was all twists and ruts now, and the scream of his skis was like a never-ending zipper yanked hard. And the hill was never-ending, too. There was no bottom! At least, he never got to it.

He never got to it because he fell.

It was a forward fall, his shoulder hitting first, one of his legs—or maybe just a ski—snapping clean off. Thereafter he rolled and half somersaulted toward the next turn, which is to say the next edge. It lay perhaps forty feet below him, and he took all of that at a ferocious rate, and if he hit the knoll that was rising there first, and if it had something in it besides snow, he was going to be all right. Beaten and bruised, maybe, but all right. Only it didn't. It burst like a Christmas ornament. And Joey went over the edge. . . .

8

$\mathbf{M}$y God, Lucien, how could you let him take that hill by himself? If I hadn't come back and seen your tracks, he would've hung there on that underbrush till he dropped."

"I thought he was right behind me, Frank. As it was, you were closer to him than I was."

"Which couldn't have been any too close. He was damn near frozen!"

"With the wind hitting him exposed like that, it wouldn't take long to get cold. It was probably only a minute or two."

"Well, we won't know from him, he was too disoriented. You must have been going pretty damn hard for quite a while."

"Hills, Frank."

"Hills, hell."

"You don't control the speed of the downhills, Frank. And you don't stop on a climb."

"You should've waited for him at the tops, don't you think?"

"I *did* wait for him."

"How come he didn't see you?"

"Damned if I know. He had his head down. It was foggy. I thought he was fine. He looked okay. When he got close, I went ahead."

"Geez . . . hanging over a cliff. If I hadn't come back and seen your tracks—"

"I'm sorry, Frank."

"Yeah."

"I should've gone behind him, I guess."

"Yeah. I shouldn't have gone ahead either. We both fucked up."

"No, no, I told you to go ahead. It was my fault."

"Well, he's okay. I just want to get him home now. As soon as he's awake, we'll break camp. Oh, shit."

"What?"

"Carolyn. She'll never let him out of her sight when she hears about this."

"No. Probably not."

"I mean, you can't blame her, after all we've been through with Chip and all, but . . . *damn*. Why did this have to happen?"

"It's done."

"Try to bring him out of his shell, give him some self-confidence, and look what happens. She'll have a nervous breakdown and he'll be a terminal momma's boy."

"Does she have to know?"

Frank looked at his brother, pursed his lips.

"Why tell her?" Lucien posed. "For her own good you could just not mention it."

"Joey will tell her anyway."

"You could talk to him. Would he keep a secret if you talked to him?"

65

"As a matter of fact, he would. Volunteering information isn't exactly his strong suit. Chip even trusted him to keep mum. It's one of the things that makes him such a loner."

"Well . . . ?"

"I suppose I can talk to him. Tell him not to make his mother worry. Too bad I can't make him forget, too. He'll be a long time getting over this."

9

But he wasn't.

Joey went skiing the next weekend. He went with just his father to a local place called Snow Gulch, and he took its most ragged descent—a twisting, beknotted incline ending in an obligatory wipeout—with two falls and no complaints. The next weekend was Maybury State Park, icy and hard-packed, and the weekend after that Independence Oaks. He skied the high trail at Independence Oaks with its convolutions and pay-in-advance sweeps that you had to climb to earn. The last one—a quarter-mile drop—he made without falling. Afterward they sat in the warming house, where idle conversations were struck with strangers, and his father told a man from Boyne City that

Joey had made the advanced trail. Paternal pride. Joey lapped it up like a thirsty kitten.

The truth was he had been ashamed after the camping trip. He had gone to the U. P. in shame and failed to exonerate himself. The drive home had been one long silence, except when they stopped in Gaylord for lunch. They had sat in a Burger King, and when his uncle went to the bathroom, his father spoke to him about keeping everything a secret. He said it was to prevent Mother from being upset, but Joey understood.

A secret.

Shame.

"Do you think you can just forget to mention this, son?"

He thought of his counselor then, because the name of the town was Gaylord and because of what she had said that day: I'll tell you my secrets . . . then we'll be friends. Secrets were supposed to make friends, and now his father was asking him to keep one between them. It hadn't worked with Mrs. Gaylord, because she had shown his mother the picture anyway, and it hadn't worked with the chair because the chair hated little boys. But it was going to work with his father. It *had* to work with his father. He could at least do that.

Don't worry, Dad. I won't tell anyone why you're ashamed of me.

And then Snow Gulch came. And Maybury and Independence Oaks. Joey would have hotdogged off the Zilwaukee Bridge on one ski by that time. He would have skied up *and* down Mount Everest with his uncle, if his father had asked.

Second chance.

Joey took it and ran with it.

Skied with it.

"My boy took the advanced trail this morning," Frank said unabashedly, sitting in the warming house at Independence Oaks. "He's just seven."

Frank whistled as they drove home. Joey's cheeks burned with the heat from the blower and with pride. "Independence Oaks," his father mused, as if the name were hallowed. "You've certainly become independent, all right. My little man." And then he said something that made Joey's blood run cold. "To think just a few weeks ago you were afraid to sit in a chair!"

Joey sat very still. The mouse was back.

The ax didn't fall until the following Friday.

By that time his father had told and retold the exploit of the advanced trail, and each time it came out a little hollower in Joey's ears. "I never learned to ski until I was fifteen," Frank would say. "And I don't think I tackled anything like that until I was in college." But nothing more was said about the thing Joey still feared with all his soul until Friday.

That was when his father got out the maps to plan the weekend and suggested they go into the den and then, as casually yet cautiously as a man turning on the lights in a long-disused room, said, "Sit in the patriarch chair, Joey. You've earned it now."

Déjà vu.

Joey was stuck at a point in time and in a relationship that would not go away. There would be no appeasement until he had laid himself on the silk and teak altar to be consumed by whatever it was that boiled within. And though the terror of that melted his bowels and all resolve, he would try one more time. *He must* or forever lose his father.

And he did.

Both.

Because the moment he grasped the cold, blackened wood and slid against the silk, he was falling, falling in a long white tunnel that smelled of wildness and hunger, falling and scream-ing—

"Joey!" His father holding him in the chair. "Stop it, Joey!"

"No, Daddy! Daddy, Daddy, please! Please . . . no, no . . . *plea-se!*"

The plea in *plea-se* echoed through the night.

They did not go skiing that weekend. Or ever again. There was open warfare between them now. The kind of love-hate thing that exhausts a relationship.

Frank left no doubt that he considered Joey's attitude to be baseless hysteria. "Protracted by parental indulgence," he added for Carolyn's sake. "What's needed is a systematic plan to over-come this nonsense. He's going to sit in that chair once a week. Once a week, Carolyn!"

"Oh, Frank—"

" 'Oh, Frank,' nothing. We can't let this go on."

"Why can't we? What's it harming?" Her blue eyes were tragic, her voice stricken.

"What's it harming?" He blinked at her, as if the answer were so obvious that it defied articulation. "Don't you see what this is doing to Joey?"

"No."

"It's his attitude toward me, toward the family. Why do you think he won't sit in the chair?"

"I don't know."

"Because he's defying us, Carolyn. He doesn't want to grow up and take his part in the world. And he won't ever grow up and be well-adjusted and do well in school or get along with his peers or any of the other things you want him to do if he doesn't lick this thing *now*!"

She looked at him with deep doubts but also with fear for what he said. This was Frank, the man who had put her life together again, the consummate businessman she had aided for years, the consummate lover who occupied her body, father to her orphan, father to their son. *His* family was a dynasty. So, he must know.

"The key to this whole logjam is that chair, and Joey knows it," Frank said. "It's the tangible symbol of what we are and will be, and don't you think for a moment that he doesn't un-derstand that—has understood it. He knows it from our atti-tudes. And he's afraid of the responsibility. He's a child who has always had fears, and he's got to conquer them before it's too late. Now it's all boiled down to the chair for him and what it stands for. He doesn't want to take responsibility for growing up, for stepping into the role he has to follow as head of the family. Surely *you* can understand that, Carolyn."

Because you couldn't handle the stress of running your own family, Carolyn.

That was what he meant, she thought. Bad genes. It was her legacy that had pissed in the soup. Hers that froze up over

70

relationships, like Joey did. Stasis. Stasis and worry. That was how she had handled relationships. And a family was lots of relationships.

"Once a week," he affirmed.

"What if he won't?"

"Then he'll lose privileges."

Joey lost privileges, of course.

He lost TV, lost movies and outings, lost events and friends. He lost people. He lost his father.

It wasn't so bad. He liked to read, read and think. He thought about a lot of things, and he talked to his mother about some of them. Did she know that sharks could drown if they didn't keep moving, or that a battleship made of ice and wood pulp had been planned for a war once? He thought it was a very long-ago war, back in the 1940s. Diamonds were really just coal, and mistletoe was poison. Someone had once buried a horse in a soldier cemetery, and the soldier was still on it. There were lots of things he thought about that he didn't tell his mother, though. Like the trip up north and how Uncle Luce skiing in the ground fog had looked like the horned thing he saw whenever he sat in the chair. Or how sometimes he was so afraid Daddy was going to make him sit in the chair that he wished he didn't have a father at all.

And that thought led to a lot of guilt feelings. Because one Saturday late in the merry, merry month of May his father left the house early in the morning to fish on Echo Lake and didn't come back.

Carolyn called the state police at eleven-thirty that night.

A sergeant listened politely and checked his traffic reports. No disasters involving a red van with a green canoe on top. Red and green, she was thinking now. The sergeant took the license number over the phone and suggested that a lot of fishing trips ended this way.

"This wasn't a trip!" Carolyn insisted with just that note of oscillation which police everywhere recognize as barely controlled hysteria. "He was going to be back by *dinnertime*."

"Yeah, well, he's probably on his way or maybe his vehicle

broke down or maybe the fish were biting so well he stayed over another night—"

"You're not listening to me, officer, this was Echo Lake! It's just a few miles down the road. He would've called if he had trouble." She knew she was being hysterical and hated herself for it.

He started repeating her name, then. "Mrs. . . ."—checking the note in front of him—"Whitehall, I *am* listening to you. Your husband had a day off and he went fishing. He's a few hours later than he thought he would be, which isn't too remarkable, is it, Mrs. Whitehall? Now, I don't know your husband, but most men like to unwind after a little recreation. You know, a-few-beers-with-the-boys sort of thing. He may be telling some friends about the big one that got away right—"

"He doesn't go drinking with friends! And you can't fish at night! The van is new, and so is the canoe! Tomorrow morning at nine o'clock he's supposed to usher at *church*—"

She broke down in frustration at that point, and the sergeant let her shudder and gasp a little over the phone.

Then he said, "I want you to know, we take every report seriously, Mrs. Whitehall. But if we put up a search every time a fisherman was a few hours overdue, we'd have no one left to handle crime. Why don't you wait until morning. Then, if he isn't back by, say, noon, give us another call."

So that was it.

She wanted to scream at him, to tell him she had been through this before, that it wasn't fair—that if this whole cruddy thing was going to happen to her again, she wanted a body—mangled or crushed or shot neatly between the eyes—because she couldn't live in limbo anymore!

She called Beaumont Hospital.

She called Pontiac General.

She tried Providence and Sinai Day.

Then she put her light blue jacket on and woke Joey up and took the big six-battery torchlight from the cupboard and got all these things into the Escort in the garage. She didn't tell Joey what the matter was, and he didn't ask. For once she was grateful for the fears that kept him wide-eyed and silent, wrapped in a blanket beside her. She felt less hysterical now. She was doing something. She was going to find Frank.

The lights and the night seemed peripheral as she sped through the vaguely commercial sections of West Bloomfield, her mind fixed on the lake. The smooth whisper of asphalt changed to a gritty roar when she hit the dirt roads. Plumes of dust reflected her brake lights going into the curves, and more often than not she startled a possum or a rabbit coming out of them. She could taste the dust, she imagined, and through the dash vents came the slightly clammy, effluvial smell of a lake at night.

She drove to the brink, the Escort's high beams appealing to a black, barely agitated expanse for clues. She thought it might be as quiet as it looked, but when she rolled down the window the water seemed to be giggling and murmuring. She rolled the window up again, opened the door, clicked the lock, got out.

"Stay here," she said to Joey and slammed the door.

His blank face sought hers through the glass, but she looked away. The sound of the door had initiated a partial stillness. Frog songs and night whirs were arrested nearby, and now there was just that giggling and murmuring. Oily little secrets. Some ill-defined turmoil in the belly of the lake.

The torch shot across the swath of headlights, poking here and there in the corners that it could reach. She realized suddenly that she was looking for a body. What else? She had come here because she couldn't wait, couldn't hope anymore. She was still waiting for Chip after nearly four years, and there just wasn't any more she could offer the dead and missing. So where was he? Where was Frank? She wanted an answer. Now.

Now!

Giggles and murmurs.

She took a step in the obscene jelly that was the doorstep of this gloating lake. Then another. And another. Her light shot accusatively this way and that. It was not a big lake. Just enough for the echo that had given it its name. It seemed to be mimicking her journey around its weepy edge in a distorted way. *Squish . . . squish/giggle . . . murmur.* And all at once a

73

laugh. Harsh and furious as her foot broke through reeds into water.

But there was nothing out there.

Nothing.

Until . . .

It was just a hump gently rocking in the reeds. She caught it in the sweep of the torch, left it, caught it again. Her throat went dry and seemed to be passing knots down into her chest. Her stomach was awash with some chill fluid not unlike the dank lake. She had her body now. Here it was. The punctuation she needed. Dangling participle gone. Frank, Frank, Frank! Oh, God, what was she doing out here? Their son was in the car and she had brought him out mindlessly in the mdidle of the night to witness . . . what?

Because it wasn't Frank.

It was the canoe. Green. Smooth. The canoe. Not Frank. It's all right, Joey, this isn't your father lying here face down in the reeds, after all. Sorry for the scare. Sorry for the horror your little soul went twisting through. But it might as well have been.

Because if this was the canoe, then Frank must be . . .

And now she couldn't wait. Blasphemy be damned. Let the night's entertainment begin! Up with the canoe! There's the paddle over there. Never mind the bloodsuckers leeching at your ankles. Never mind the slime. Over she goes! Now, sit in it. Never mind the water still in the bottom, the six-battery torch shining a little while longer beneath it. Paddle. Paddle. Around and around. Through the night, through the headlights, until the car battery goes dead sometime in the dawn. And now and then calling out from the thickening viscosity of your mind, "Frank . . . Frank!" As if he could free himself from the slathered chains of organic matter on the bottom. As if he could rise, rise, rise before his time, before the gases could swell his body obscenely and tear him free, bursting through the surface of Echo Lake, as smooth and featureless as an inner tube: *Frank*-n-stein!

They found them that way.

The County Sheriff's patrol saw the van on the other side

74

of the lake, and then the woman paddling around in the sun-light, and the boy huddled in the Escort across the way. They finally dragged the lake. Carolyn would not have to wait for this one, would not have to identify a cadaver bloated beyond rec-ognition. Here was the body she needed. In the merry, merry month of May.

10

At the funeral, Carolyn laughed and laughed.

She sat stone still in the front row of the little chapel, swathed in black, and the laughter roared around inside her head like wind in a bottle. Laughter was necessary. It meant she wasn't screaming.

There were lots of funny things to make her laugh. There was the closed casket and the dismal tintinnabulation of rain on stained glass. There were incipient children who never really *were* and inchoate lovers with one foot in eternity. Life was a series of abandoned foundations. She laughed at a winter that had bent the days with the weight of gloom and ice, only to

76

melt into the blood of spring. Horror was funny. So godlessly funny.

The blood of spring.

Again.

Chip's and Frank's flowing together now. The stuff of grass. Only, she thought for a moment that they were both there in the gunmetal coffin, and her hand actually went out to the lid, fumbling at the seam, as if to insert a thumbnail under the seal of a monstrous envelope and burst it open. The funeral director, posing with airbrushed perfection next to a plastic frond, flashed apprehension from his opal eyes. Lucien, suddenly on her left, dropped a hand as pale as a lily over her own, quieting her fingers.

The touch brought her around. Linkage to here and now.

"Let him go, Carolyn," he whispered in a voice that creaked like a rope coming taut. "The good part of him is his memory."

She laughed out loud now. Just a throaty little sound, but it gave Lucien worlds of insight into her state of mind.

"Would you like to leave this?" he asked softly. "Nothing says you have to stay."

"No." She grinned harshly, and her eyes were brimming with tears.

He led her to a chair, sat next to her. Joey sat on the other side, mute as a mannequin. The minister spoke knowingly of death, but the room was leaden with the silent forensics of terminal mystery. When it was over, the cortege crept through the dreary rain to the cemetery and an awning that rattled and hissed while the final consecration was made. And after that there was the great awkwardness of continuing to live, of coming home to an ostentatious house, of brewing coffee and slicing cheese. The last of the business associates and neighbors departed just before six, leaving Carolyn with a sudden feeling of panic. In a few minutes she and Joey were going to be alone.

"If you want, I'll stay the night," Lucien said then.

"I'd be bloody damn glad," she said tightly. God bless Lucien. Whatever else he was, he had an uncanny sensitivity.

"Joey went outside. I think he's checking puddles with a stick."

77

She took a deep, resurrecting breath. "Let him play. Sweet Jesus, let him play."

Lucien dropped into the chair as silently as a bat on velvet and dared to laugh softly. "You're going to make it, Carolyn. Frank told me you didn't know how strong you were."

She shook her head, clasped and unclasped her hands. "Everything I've tried to hang onto has gotten away from me. It's driven me back into a shell I don't want to live in anymore. Joey's the same way. I've already warped him with my fears. Frank knew it. He tried to do something about it. God. He picked a fine time to die, didn't he?"

"A boy finds his way."

"You mean he may grow up despite me."

Lucien's smile faded to faint. "Role models be damned. A clever boy like Joey rights himself whatever the storms. If you go around blaming yourself, he'll have to fulfill your expectations."

"Frank said I treated him like cotton candy."

"Cotton candy has a way of evaporating."

They sat in the gathering gloom for a while and the peace accumulated in redemptive rhythms—tires swishing on the road, the ticking of the mantel clock, the rushing of air. Carolyn felt she had never thought more clearly. The twilight and Lucien's calm were steadying her.

"I've never been any good with people, and it's best to recognize that," she said. "My first marriage failed, and I haven't a clue as to how to handle Joey. No sense at all when it comes to being a mother. But I'm a practical person when it comes to *things*. I can handle a budget for a household or a corporation and read a tax code for entertainment. As long as there aren't any people decisions, I'm a whiz with flow charts and demographics. That's why I'm going back to work."

"Good for you."

"It will be. If I can find somebody to do what Frank did." She tried to discern his eyes, but the light had fallen too far. "I'm offering you his job."

Lucien tucked his chin, grasped his knees. He could have been Abraham Lincoln contemplating the fate of a nation. "Carolyn, Carolyn," he said, "I've never pretended to be anything but a frustrated artist. Where you tie up emotionally with people, I'm as indifferent as ice water. I'd do almost anything for you or the family, but what possible qualification do I have for that?"

"You're Frank's brother. That counts for something. You're Joey's uncle."

"Ah, Joey's uncle. If I could help that way, I would. Not that I could ever replace a father, but I'd be glad to spend some time with him."

Her head dropped back against the chair. "I was hoping you'd offer. I'm desperate. Joey's desperate."

"I'll see him whenever you want. An artist is always looking for an excuse not to work."

"Lucien?"

"What?"

"Would you consider moving into the house for a while? You'd have the place to yourself until Joey got home from school. You could choose practically any room for a studio. God knows we have enough space."

The front door opened and closed softly then. Joey moused across the archway, freezing when he saw them sitting quietly in the dark.

"It's okay," Carolyn said. "Come in and sit with us. We need to be together now." She held out her hand, took him in as he shuffled forward. "Joey, Uncle Luce is going to stay overnight, and then . . ."

"—then Joey and I will start to transfer my studio to the room next to his."

God bless Lucien, Carolyn thought. She could see his eyes now, moist crescents in a palpable gloom. He might be exactly what he said he was—as indifferent as ice water—but she knew there was passion deep inside him, the kind she had that she couldn't express. They would be comfortable together in the house. A pair of social lepers. One who couldn't deal with people, one who wouldn't. No demands on each other. God bless Lucien!

Joey had wished his father wouldn't come back and he hadn't. He had cried at the funeral home, but this was because his mother was crying. He had been frightened. Frightened because

79

the sound of her sobs was so deep and uncontrollable, frightened because his father was there in the room, in a box, and he felt somehow that he was angry—*So, you didn't want me to come back, did you? Just wait till I get this coffin lid off!*

The one thing Joey didn't feel was sad.

Not yet.

The emptiness that would pang him in unfathomable ways at every rite of passage seemed almost like relief now. A boy without a father walks in the wind and is a stranger to himself, but for now he could think of only one thing: he would never have to sit in the patriarch chair again.

His father had been buried for five days when he and his uncle moved the studio. It was not something he was anxious to do. He hadn't forgotten Uncle Luce's wildness on the ski trip, and his uncle's theatrical voice—full of magic one moment, flatness the next—made him uneasy.

"Why can't we live alone?" he had asked his mother.

"Joey! Lucien is your uncle. He's part of the family."

She sounded disappointed in him, but he didn't think it was the way she felt deep down. "We don't know him," he had said, and she had immediately answered in a different, calmer voice.

"No. But if it doesn't work out, we can always go back the way we were before."

"Then we could live alone?"

"Would you want that, Joey? Would you want to come home from school to an empty house?"

He thought he might but didn't say so. And when she drove him to the studio to help with the moving, he only said he wished she would come in too.

"I've got to go to the plant, honey. Mommy goes every day now. It's not easy to run a business, and I have to be there a lot."

But that wasn't the real reason either. The real reason was because she wanted him to be alone with his uncle. To like him. He knew that. Knew already that all of this sudden contact was because Uncle Luce was supposed to be his new father. His mother had taken great pains to deny it and to tell him that no one would ever take his father's place. "Uncle Luce is an artist, honey. Uncle Luce is going to work at our house now because we all need each other."

Uncle Luce is going to be your father, Joey!

He touched the buzzer outside the glass doors and they unlocked and he pushed one open and—and then he heard the shrill whir of a drill and looked quickly to the single door on the lower level. The smell of a dentist's office closed around him as the glass knifed home with a click. When he turned back, she was gone. It was just the kind of thing he hated: losing track. Now you see it, now you don't. That's what Uncle Luce was like. He had come here to Uncle Luce's place and it had distracted him for a second, and now his mother was gone. He leaned hard on the glass, his feelings smarting, hot tears making him blink. The cadence of his breathing pulsed in steamy circles on the surface, and somehow this cooled him. When the drill whined again he started up the heavily carpeted stairs to the second floor and the only other door. All of this had been described to him carefully, as if he would pass a test if he could just walk up these stairs and find his uncle.

There were pieces of packing material on the upper level— the kind that look like wrinkled paper noodles—and ground-in mud led all the way to the door. He stood there at last, wheezing a little from his allergies and rocking from foot to foot as if the next move was up to whoever was in the studio. He had once overheard his father tell his mother about a naked woman he had come upon when he opened this door. His father had laughed at this, but Joey felt a premonition of shame. He wiggled his hands, pulling the cuffs of his shirt over them, reaching into a pocket, withdrawing. When he finally ventured a knock, it was a single tap, barely audible. But the response was immediate and energetic, as if he had tripped a beam of light or added the grain of sand that tumbled the castle: "Come in, come in, come in! I've been waiting an eternity for you!"

Joey went in.

If he had expected anything, he supposed he had expected a naked lady. What he saw was just strange enough to keep him on his guard and just wonderful enough to bring him five slow steps into the room. It was a lavender room. Floor, walls,

81

ceiling—lavender. Light poured in from a window that ran the width of the far wall at the top, and Joey could see every detail of a perfectly square studio. There was no furniture, no easel, no brushes or paints or canvas. What there was . . . was *hands*.

Hundreds of them! Hands of glass, hands of metal, hands in white gloves. There were ancient hands and young ones, tiny hands and a single huge wooden one, cocked, with fingers spread like the gnarled and grasping roots of a tree. Hands prayed, hands clenched, hands gestured lightly or made taut fists. They came out of the floor and the walls or dangled from the ceiling. Fingers pointed at fingers, palms were raised in supplication. Some sat on pedestals; a chain of them climbed one wall. For a moment Joey forgot that he had been invited in by a voice. And that was a good thing. Because there couldn't have been a voice. Because there wasn't a soul in the room. Just hands.

Until one of them . . . snapped its fingers!

Joey's eye wasn't quick enough to catch which one. He only heard it. Was it the one with all the rings? The one with the crimson nails? Or was it on the big glass thing—a very large transparent prism that scattered rainbow effects among the shadows and alabaster shapes?

The surface of this was bored, and out of these holes at all angles rose more fingers and hands. As Joey watched, there was a sudden flick, no more than a blur, followed by a gleam at the top of the prism. A silver thing had appeared there. It was wafer-thin and curved. And it was notched between the thumb and forefinger of a very white hand. His attention was riveted there when the second snap came. This one was on the other side of the prism. He should have known better than to look away. He should have expected it to be a distraction. *Now you see it, now you don't.* And in the brief flick of his eyes away and back again, the first hand was empty and the silver curved thing was hurtling at him, at his feet, where it fell with a ringing sound and rolled to the base of a pedestal.

It was a half-dollar.

He barely had time to see that when the second hand let fly, and that was a silver thing too. This one stopped on his foot—another half-dollar. He would have picked it up, only now the first hand had flicked again and there was *another* silver disk there. This time it was thrown across the room to his right . . . followed by the second hand—*flick*. To the left. And again. Again. Silver blurs . . . ringing, rolling coins . . . *snap* . . . *snap*. And now he was laughing and scrambling after them. The room tinkled and flashed. Half-dollars everywhere. John F. Kennedy's silver profile—like the Tin Man of Oz—rolling all over the floor. Joey was all over the floor too, dancing circles around the hands. Picking up treasure. Forgetting the craziness. *Snap* . . . *flick* . . . *blur*. Fun. Only, when he got to the coin by the praying hands and glanced up, the fun was over.

From this angle the facets of the prism aligned in a kind of window. And Joey saw through it. Saw eyes. Huge and terrible. Dark as teak. Eyes that swallowed him whole.

He literally jumped back. Immediately the eyes vanished. But then the hands that had made the coins fly were waving at him, fingers gently wagging up and down. "Surprise!" said his uncle in an energetic voice that somehow remained a whisper. He stepped out, his face very white in that lavender room, nearly as white as the greasepaint on his hands. He was wearing a dark baggy suit and a dark turtleneck. "You found me," he said. "You came to help me move. Another pair of hands is just what I need."

Joey smiled tentatively.

"Paid in advance," his uncle said. "You can keep the half-dollars." He gestured around the room. "What do you think of it?"

Joey's eyes roamed obediently. "Did you make all of these?"

"Yes . . . yes, I made them. All of them. One good hand deserves another, don't you think?"

Joey took a few exploratory steps.

"Look around, nephew. The boxes we have to pack are in the other room. Ah. You don't see the other room. Right there. Shake Abdul's hand."

He indicated a brown jeweled hand reaching out from the wall.

"Don't be afraid. Shake it."

Joey grasped the cold ceramic and tried to shake it, but on the first pump it latched downward with a *click*. Which made

83

the door open, the door that hadn't been there a few moments before. Its seam appeared in the smooth lavender as if a giant cleaver had sliced through from the other side. But the magic didn't stop there. It went on into the next room.

This was a workroom, a place to store mistakes and half-formed things. There were skeletal hands and hands in liquid-filled glass jars, hands encased in amber and one monstrously large set of fingers poised over a tiny ebony piano in the center of the room. The tables and materials of an artist were here, along with dozens of boxes overflowing with packing.

"All the boxes are empty," said his uncle, but the voice didn't come from behind Joey.

Which was funny, because Joey was still standing in the doorway and nothing had gotten by him. Except that his uncle was stepping out from alongside a packing case at the other end of the room. And suddenly Joey felt weak as putty. Because the wonderfulness of all that was strange was very, very close to something terrible, something that was rearranging too much of what he took for granted. But his uncle seemed to be ahead of him there, too.

"Has it stopped being fun, Joey? It's really quite disappointing when you look closer."

He went behind the boxes again and Joey heard his voice as he walked along one wall toward his end, the end that separated the rooms.

"As you may have noticed, the partition is very thin. That's because it's portable"—here he pushed a box aside, revealing a missing section of the wall—"and collapsible"—he began to fold other sections of the wall like a pullout greeting card . . . *slam . . . slam . . . slam*—"with painted hinges on just one side"—he passed Joey at the door, folding the section above his head toward the remaining segments, one after another—"so that the whole thing winds up looking like a deck of cards and you end up in the middle with just"—*slam . . . slam . . . slam*—"a door!"

Joey stood in a doorway from nowhere to nowhere.

"Not so frightening, is it?"

"Are you a magician?"

His uncle seemed to consider, tapping his lip, eyes flitting.

"Am I a magician, am I a magician . . . no! I don't do tricks. I . . . expose things. I expose what's there—what's been there all the time that no one ever saw. I like to find things. I'm a . . . *finder*."

A finder.

And he was.

But it would be months before Joey really understood what that meant. The hands were an example: a single theme played to exhaustion. Whatever Lucien examined, he turned inside out, distorted, stretched into grotesque shapes that exposed every element. What Joey did understand in those first few weeks was that his uncle knew where things were when no one else knew— a lost key, pennies in the grass, a misplaced pen, even where a flower was waiting to push through the soil. It was the ultimate misdirection: Joey was so caught up in the mystery of what his uncle *did*, he never saw the mystery of what he *was*.

The day they moved the studio he had thought of a question. It was an obvious question. But uncertainty had kept him from asking it, and the minor miracles of succeeding days had kept him in awe at the same time that they made the question throb.

His uncle knew something was on his mind, of course.

"Is it the new studio? Do you want to see it?" They were at the foot of the stairs, and his uncle led the way up. "Here be dragons!" he exclaimed and threw open the door.

But it was just a white room. Perfectly white. White-white. As if it had been painted over and over. And there were no hands. No tools or furniture. Joey had smelled the paint for weeks, but he had not seen where the boxes they had moved in went.

"No?" His uncle was staring at him. "Well, if it isn't the studio . . ." He leaned down, eyebrows lofting, and whispered explosively, "What then?"

"I want you to find Chip," Joey said.

11

"Mirror, mirror, on the wall . . ."

She took a long gander at herself on a Monday morning and saw Carolyn Whitehall alias Carolyn Booth née Carolyn Smith (Smith, for pity's sake!), survivor. Time for a new identity. The face in the mirror was starting to look like potato salad. Too much lying awake in the night wondering why the hell this was happening to her. Too much crying crocodile tears. If she cried any more her face was going to need rain gutters and downspouts. How long since she had laughed? You couldn't count the funeral, that was hysteria. No more hysteria. Tell yourself a joke, Carolyn.

I'm going to work today and I'm going to kick ass!
Ha-ha.

Let's not get cynical. First things first. The subject is facial renewal. You put enough cream on potato salad and the lumps go away. She had been ignoring her makeup, her Oil of Olay. Such a shame, because she still had the beautiful steel-blue eyes, the pert nose, the puffy lips that softened the imperiousness of the rest and made her look vulnerable to men. No lip gloss today. She didn't want to look vulnerable. Thin red lipstick—Toro by Revlon—fudging the lip line on the narrow side. Then, after she was done being a corporate entity, she could come home, take a hot bath, put on lip gloss, perfume, mascara, and . . . and . . . go out to Kentucky Fried Chicken or something.

Chicken.

You are what you eat. And she was too chicken to think about circulating again. (Had she ever circulated?) Under that tweed business suit she still had a knockout body—long legs, full shoulders. But she didn't want to circulate. She just wanted to feel like a woman—after she was done feeling like a man (being *made* to feel like a man) at Whitehall Automotive Parts Manufacturing, Inc.

Kick ass! Ha-ha.

Downstairs. Breakfast. Joey had his cereal out. She finished the toast. Lucien brewed coffee like an alchemist. Communal living. It was working.

Joey seemed to be doing very well, considering what he'd been through. She'd checked with his counselor. He wasn't what you'd call a hail-fellow-well-met kid, but he didn't get in fights. And no more nasty pictures. Mrs. Gaylord said he was resolving his conflicts. Carolyn had watched him with Lucien, too. No problems there. Lucien was clever. You were always finding out something new about him, and Joey seemed fascinated by that. She wouldn't exactly call it closeness, but Joey had not repeated his question to her about why couldn't they live alone, and Carolyn supposed a bond of some kind was forming there.

"How's the science project going?" she asked him, rumpling his hair.

"Good."

"Did you find something for Mars?"

"I'm going to use the Ping-Pong ball."

"Mars is red, kiddo; use a Magic Marker on it."

87

"Uncle Luce painted it red for me."

Carolyn smiled at Lucien. "Well, crew, we'll circle the universe twice and meet back here at oh-one-zillion hours, okay?"

And then she got in the Escort and tooled off for the expressway.

"Why don't we search for Chip today?" Joey asked his uncle.

"I told you, it has to be a day when your mother won't know. We don't want to upset her, do we? If you don't go to school, she'll want to know why. The first day you're off and she goes to work, that's when we'll search for Chip."

She took Northwestern to the Lodge Expressway and the Lodge to the Grand River exit. Traffic was dodge-'em cars where it could move and a noxious crawl of fumes where it couldn't. Overhead, a local radio station copter beat past while its station broadcast tardy tidings of a "clean and green" status on the metro freeways. The complexities of people were already pressing in on her. Here were tens of thousands of her kind, elbowing into the city, the vortex of hustle, of dog-eat-dog and bureaucracy. In a few minutes she would drive through the plant gate and they would all start to manipulate her. Snide looks. A flurry of pretended activity. False graces. Once, she had been a secretary here, and what had gone on was all quite naked to her. Then she had married Frank and the façades had gone up like so many movie sets. It was one of the reasons she had decided to stay at home. But now she was back, without Frank, without anyone she could trust—except maybe for old Walter Barths, a gentle man, soul of integrity, who kept to his molding machine and smiled unconcernedly at the malcontents as he had ever since the company opened its doors.

She shimmied over a lane on Grand River, hit the flasher, took the turn-in like she was Pac-Man on the scent. Here I come, teeth bared. Better give me some respect, 'cause I'm the boss. I are the boss, hear? *The boss!*

But there was Sinswicki, the gate guard, grinning that stupid little grin. Had he grinned like that when she had come to work as a secretary? Well, well, here comes the little lady in her husband's shoes again. Hello, Mrs. President (heh-heh). Nice day (heh-heh). Going to play boss again today, are we?

Wipe that grin off your face, Sinswicki. Pick your nose, like you usually do.

Snide looks. All the way to her office. She deliberately walked through the main assembly room, just to let them know she wasn't going to hide out in the ivory tower. But, oh, shit, she hated that. Activity pushed ahead of her like a wave, leaving in its wake a curious silence that pricked at the back of her neck. If she turned around they would all be grinning like Sinswicki. Frank had brisked through damn near hourly, checking tolerances, examining finishes, finishing inventories, asking questions, questioning quotas. She wouldn't have known the difference if they took to turning out condoms. She wouldn't have known the difference if they started making dash moldings out of papier-mâché. Frank had built the damn place machine by machine. Did they think she was aspiring to his management style? Who the hell did they think had taken care of the paper half of the company? She might not understand the thermodynamics of the paint-drying operation, but she knew to the penny what each of the stations cost and what the maintenance and depreciation factors were. Snide looks. Silence at her back. She ought to turn and give them all the finger one of these days. One of these days she would.

But that was paranoid.

And she knew she could be paranoid.

Maybe they weren't grinning at all. Maybe they were milling and dipping and grinding and boring and assembling things just like they were supposed to. The plant hadn't missed a beat, had it?

She hadn't been in her office ten minutes before Daryl Millman, the union rep, knocked and came in. Grinning.

"Morning, Mrs. Whitehall, thought I'd best advise you officially of how things stand before you get it secondhand." He was standing there with a gearshift knob in his right hand, as if borne in by some invisible transmission, and she should have offered him a chair but deliberately did not. He parked himself on one anyway, still grinning faintly. "We're all shocked about

89

Frank, and I want to make that clear—the members said to make that clear about being shocked and all."

Members. They weren't auto part workers who practiced a skill but members of a union.

"Frank was a damn good man," he said, dropping the grin. "But this whole business has got the members upset in other ways, too. And I guess I'd be derelict in my duty if I didn't let you know how things stand."

He waited for her to say something, and she should have but didn't trust her lips not to tremble, because she knew what was coming, of course—some monstrous demand she couldn't handle and they knew she couldn't handle—and he was grinning again, politely, but grinning all the same, and gesturing with the shift knob, putting it in second gear now. . . .

"So I've got to tell you that the union and Frank had some understandings, some very important understandings, that will mean changes around here."

Pause, gesture, shift: third gear.

"Like in the work rules about breaks and seniority. Frank even said we needed more regular breaks. Especially on overtime. You can't expect a worker to be sharp and avoid accidents when he's already put in a full . . ."

Blah, blah, blah. Carolyn drifted in and out of the sense of it—the nonsense of it. Millman had become a liability and a union activist in that order. First it had been the closed shop, and when his work began to fall off he got himself elected steward. Now he exuded a casual arrogance she disdained. It came out of his lazy blue eyes and that maddening grin. It embered when he took a drag on a cigarette and seemed to take forever to exhale the smoke while you were talking to him. He was gesturing with the shift knob again: high gear now.

". . . job classification . . . machine operators hadn't ought to be doing the supply clerks' . . . going back in the storeroom any time they feel . . . now, that ain't right."

Gesture, shift: overdrive!

". . . Frank promised . . . thirty-two cents an hour the first . . . retroactive . . . pension."

She couldn't remember if she answered him or not. Just

90

that he finished what he had to say by paraphrasing, softening everything with a picture of labor peace and prosperity, assuring her of how badly they wanted to avoid a costly strike. And then he had left. Grinning.

The next thing that happened was the panic attack.

She had had several of them after Frank's death, but—oh, shit!—this one was a doozy. Room spinning, head rolling around like it was on ball bearings, sweat popping out all over. Edison was inventing electricity in her intestines, and she could taste orange juice and coffee grounds. She went for the blue pill in the center drawer. There were blue ones and yellow ones. The doctor said blue, if she needed it. She needed it. Give me a V . . . give me an A . . . give me an L, I, U, M! After that she breathed funny for a while and then she got kind of limp and then maybe a long, long time passed, like a couple of hours, because her neck was stiff when she got up and started to walk around the office, talking to Frank, asking him what to do, and then . . . then she called Daryl Millman into the office.

She didn't remember exactly what she said, either, just that she could take it or leave it as far as running a company was concerned, and that she had heard from some Japanese corporation, Sony (good grief, *Sony!*), and if you'd asked her tomorrow she wouldn't have been able to remember the fucking name, but they were interested in a buy-out, and the offer was very attractive, though of course it would mean realignment and maybe layoffs or terminations (you know how the Japanese do business, don't you, Daryl, jumping jacks every morning, fortune cookies on payday) but it wasn't that hard a decision if there were going to be so many changes around the plant anyway, and she would be derelict in her duty if she didn't tell the members officially just how things stand before they got it secondhand: that she would run things the old way or not at all!

Daryl wouldn't buy it, of course. It was a transparent ploy, and he would just sit there grinning. *Japanese* fortune cookies? Even Daryl would laugh at that.

But he didn't. Maybe it was the Valium and the lazy way she slurred the whole thing at him, maybe he considered her too witless and frightened to try it, but he wasn't grinning. He was white. The blue of his eyes was almost white. Like something flash frozen. She told him to let the members know for her and left for the day.

Kick ass. Ha-ha.

It was going to work. All of it. It was going to work. She bought some flowers and a painting of a sunrise and went home. Lucien was busy in his "studio" and Joey was doing his math (with the TV on, of course).

"Everything okay today, hon?" she asked, hugging him from behind.

"Okay," he said.

Okay. It was going to work.

She hung the sunrise in the upstairs study and took a long hot shower. The Valium was just a buzz now, like a before-dinner cocktail. Valium and a shower. Tingle on the outside, tingle on the inside. She felt good about herself for the first time in a long time. She had handled people, and it felt good. "Thanks, Frank," she said. For what? For dying? No. He wasn't dead. She mustn't let him be dead. "Thanks for showing me how, Frank. Thanks for listening. You always listened well. It's going to work."

She ought to hang the sunrise in the bedroom, she thought, wrapping a towel around herself. Right in front of the bed. Wake up rain or shine and there's your sunrise. The big promise for the day. Yes, yes. On impulse she went to the study still wrapped in the towel—Joey was downstairs, and you couldn't blast Lucien out of his studio before supper—and reached for the picture. As she raised her arms the towel fell. Standing naked in the sunrise, she thought. It felt good. She would get the towel later; right now she was wearing sunshine in her own private world. But as she turned with the painting, there was Lucien sitting on the wing chair by the bookcase. She had wafted right past him without even looking.

He was as startled as she. Each of them remained frozen for a moment. Then she made the sun set over her private parts, laughed awkwardly, and skipped from the room. Lucien! What a pose he made: too embarrassed to speak, to apologize—you didn't catch him off guard often. And what a pose she must have made. He got a good look at all of her, she supposed. Was that awe or maybe good old-fashioned desire she had observed greening his gills? Poor man. He didn't come down for dinner, and when she brought him up a plate, he took it without a word. He certainly was a shy sort. They would survive under one roof. No worry there.

It was going to work!

$$\boxed{12}$$

It's Memorial Day."

"I know."

"I don't go to school today, and Mommy went to the office to catch up on her paperwork."

"I know."

"Is . . . can . . . ?"

"I've put what we need in the car. Are you ready?"

There was nothing in the black Fury except a pair of wide-soled hunting boots. But then, they *were* going hunting.

Chip was out there and they were going to find him. And when they did, the dreams would stop. The bad pictures would go away.

94

They drove and drove. Drove with purpose. Down the expressway. Sixty-five . . . seventy miles an hour. The old Fury rattled and roared.

"How do you know where to start?" Joey shouted above the din.

"I've always known," his uncle rumbled.

Always? Then why—

"Almost always," he amended. It was part of the magic sometimes. Hearing Joey's thoughts.

They were leaving downriver now. South on I-75. Monroe and Toledo exits next, the green sign said. But they didn't get that far. They turned off left suddenly, then right onto dirt. Dust plumed behind them, and the Fury seemed to live up to its name as it tore at the roadbed. Joey fidgeted, glancing from the cattails and drainage ditches to his uncle and back again.

"How did Chip get way out here?" he shouted again.

Lucien looked across, slowed a bit. "I don't even know for sure that he did. I don't know how I find things. Echoes, maybe. At any rate, we're not likely to find him."

Echoes?

There were gulls in the air, flapping leadenly into the wind, then sweeping down into an area behind the cattails. The only thing Joey could see on the horizon was a huge smokestack pumping out black billows like muddy water. The smoke climbed briefly and lay on the wind as the gulls had but remained aloft, thinning from a smear to a trace half a sky away—a sky that in its haste looked cold.

"We've got to get over water," his uncle said. The car was just crawling now.

"Is Chip in the water?"

"I don't know, but the road is just going around it."

It?

They stopped. His uncle rolled down a window and Joey followed suit. The smell of sediment and decay wafted in, perfumed but not covered by a more redolent suffusion. He could hear water lapping, and the black liquid of the drainage canal on the left curdled in the wind as far as he could see into the cattails. With an oscillating whine they backed up, stopped, and

95

turned left into the reeds on twin tire tracks. A sign bleeding rust said JASON'S LAKE ERIE MARINA 200 YARDS.

"We'll rent a boat," his uncle said.

Joey had never seen Lake Erie. He stood on the rocky shore, gazing out at an enormous expanse of slate-gray water, wondering how they could possibly find Chip out there. A pair of ducks rifled across his field of vision. He watched them low over the water until they were out of sight, and then his uncle emerged from the weathered storefront that was actually a house, carrying two orange life jackets.

"Number seven," he said, indicating one of several flecked and sodden hulls tethered to a narrow dock.

Joey edged uncertainly over the jumble of dried boards until all of a sudden he felt himself lofted off the edge and lowered into the boat numbered 7. He turned and squatted involuntarily as it rocked, his eyes level with his uncle's boots.

Boots?

When had he put them on? When Joey was standing on the shore, apparently.

A fulvous scum swished along the battered sheet-metal bottom and fish scales winked from the gunwales. Bits of amber worm clung flattened but still ridged like so many fingerprints here and there, and the oarlocks rattled like the distended sockets they were when his uncle fitted them.

"No need for the jackets," Lucien said. "We'll be close to shore."

"Did Chip drown?"

"Yes. I think so."

Little waves clubbed them as they came around, and then they were swiftly dipping and knifing along, his uncle's wiry arms knotting with blue veins on each lunge and pull. Joey could see where the smokestack was anchored now, right on the shore in the roof of a large red building. He thought it must be made of brick, but it was too far away to tell. White pinpoints of light flashed up and down the stack, despite the daylight.

"Are we going there?" he wanted to know.

His uncle was facing him, and his eyes closed with each stroke of the oars. "Where?"

"That building."

96

"No. Closer than that."

The shoreline was uneven, broken into little islands.

"Here," his uncle said a few minutes later.

Here was a series of natural channels dotted with flooded scrub trees and bushes. They were perhaps a half mile from the incinerator plant, but it loomed huge to Joey, windowless and stark against the flatness. Reedbeds huddled close as they rowed inland, the mud bottom rising up like lumpy bedding out of shallow pools. There were no rocks here, just the smooth, drab mud, and the oars caught bottom or scalloped spray into Joey's face or whickered against the trees. And then the boat itself began to nudge bottom. Smooth caresses. And still they wriggled inland. Wriggled. Over this bridge and that. Slipping pools, begging entrance to a labyrinth of mud and reeds. Until Uncle Luce said, "I think this is it."

It. At last. What the road ran around. The land of *It*. Except there wasn't any land. Just water. And mud. And reeds. And the wind passing through like a thing you could see now— meandering in the cattails, wrinkling pools.

"He's over there," Lucien said.

There. The capital of *It*. *There* was more reeds and mud and wind.

"I don't see him," said Joey.

"We have to look. But he's there, all right."

Here. It. There. They had taken roads of concrete and dust and water, and now there was one of mud. His uncle already had one foot over the side, going down—yuck—in the muck.

"Give me your hand, nephew."

Joey looked uncertainly over the side, but his uncle had him by the wrist and the boat was tipping, tipping, then wedging as if on a reef. What happened next was a single fluid movement, though to Joey it seemed like a grotesque ballet. The hand on his wrist tightened and led while another grasped and lifted him at the hip, his body soaring suddenly as his uncle's big hunting boot lunged out of the boat and dropped a giant step away, his arms stretching farther still, planting Joey—*planting* him—seven or eight feet from where he had been sitting. Joey's shoes drove down with alarming ease, and the ooze came up his pantlegs like cold splints halfway to his knees.

"Don't stop moving," his uncle grated.

But Joey never started.

"That way, nephew. Straight ahead. Just keep lifting your feet."

Joey lifted and discovered Newton's third law of motion: For every action there is an equal and opposite reaction. His right foot was coming up, but his left was going down.

"Big steps," Uncle Luce advised. "Slowly."

"I lost my shoe!"

"Leave it."

Boots. When you had high-laced, wide-soled boots, you didn't lose them. When you had high-laced, wide-soled boots you didn't sink as fast or as far as you would without them. Joey lifted against the sucking mud and made progress: three steps, four. Already he was exhausted. Why were they doing this? How could they find Chip this way? His child's legs were rubbery, and the chill slime seemed to be squeezing him with real meanness.

"Where are we going?" he kept asking.

And his uncle kept answering that it was just a few more steps, that he was closer to the reeds than to the boat.

This was true. Ten or fifteen feet. The muck got very light-colored in front of him, too. It must be shallower. Like a shore. Like a beach.

But it wasn't shallower. It was deeper.

Joey brought his left foot down as far forward as he could and it kept on going. Past his calf. His knee. No chance of rearing back. His right foot was hopelessly twisted, his weight drawn forward, driving the left foot down.

"Help me!" he cried, unable to turn and see where his uncle was.

The stuff was inhaling him. Where was bottom? The slime tightened and climbed, immobilizing his knee, creeping onto his thigh. His right foot had been coming up in a slow-motion step, and suddenly it popped free, allowing him to roll his leg forward but not straighten it. The knee entered first, momentarily righting his body. Bottom! He'd hit bottom, he thought. But then he felt the chill rising again—more slowly, but rising. He was still sinking, and it wasn't going to stop!

98

"I'm stuck!" he hollered.

Silence.

"*Help* me!"

His uncle's voice, when it came, was calm and flat. And behind him. Where the boat was.

"I'm afraid you really are stuck, Joey," it said. "You've gotten into what they call the ash, down here. It's pretty treacherous stuff. If I go into that lighter area, I'll be caught too. So I'd better go for help."

"Give me an oar!" Joey demanded petulantly. "You can pull me out with an oar just like they did on *Hawaii Five-O.*"

"That's in water, Joey. It won't work in ash. We need a rope."

"Let me have an oar to lean on. Maybe it will reach bottom."

"Ah. Clever boy. That's a very good idea, except . . . how can I go get a rope if I don't have oars?"

Joey started to cry a little then. "I'm sinking," he whimpered.

"I'm going to get a rope. I'll row as fast as I can."

The oarlocks chattered and moaned, measuring out the rate of recession. It didn't sound like he was rowing fast, but he must have been, because it faded quickly. That left the wind. The wind and the reeds and the mud and Joey.

And Chip.

Chip was out there maybe. He must be a skeleton now. Joey had seen a real skeleton when the first grade visited Cranbrook Institute the year before. Chip had probably turned into one by now. A small one, probably. But it didn't seem like he was dead. Joey had never seen him dead, and he could still picture him with his burnt-orange jacket and his Detroit Tiger baseball cap and his Pumas trudging down the street. It would be just like him to be hiding in the reeds, as if they were playing search-and-destroy again. Waiting to jump out and scare him. And if Joey was any more scared, he'd die, he thought. He'd die and then they'd both be skeletons. The wind plied slowly through the reeds with a rustle and a hiss, and Joey couldn't help himself.

"Chip?" he called tentatively. "Chip?"

The wind. But he was hiding out there, all right. Joey was

99

the one doing the searching, and Joey was the one who was going to be destroyed. It wasn't fair.

"Chip!"

Chip never played fair.

"I know you're there. I see you."

And then he thought, What if he isn't there? What if he's hiding . . . in the . . . mud?

Oh-oh. The mud. Chip had crawled out of the reeds, under the mud, and he was coming for him and it didn't help to know that he was doing it, because he was going to jump up, screaming suddenly, like a fencepost thrusting into the sky, bulging out all covered with yuck and slime and whatever else was down there, and then his eyes were going to open and his mouth would be a red hole in the mud and . . . and . . .

No.

He wasn't going to come up at all.

Joey was going to go down.

Joey *was* going down. Slowly, slowly, slowly. He had sunk almost to his hips, and it was funny, but way down there at his feet the muck felt different—colder. Colder and tighter. Like hands. Around his ankles. Chip's hands, of course. His half-brother was pulling him under the mud to share whatever kind of night was down there, and Joey wanted to scream—maybe was screaming—he couldn't tell, because just then he saw that the reeds in front of him were moving kind of strangely again, only this time it wasn't the wind, it was Chip. Wearing his burnt-orange jacket and his Detroit Tiger baseball cap (he couldn't see the Pumas). And between the cap and the burnt-orange was just a skull, all hollows and flaming hair and grinning teeth—fangs, in fact—baring back and suddenly snapping, and Chip said, *Woof!*

Again and again.

Then Joey calmed enough to understand that it was a dog, an Irish setter with burnt-orange fur, barking at him from the edge of the reeds, and that someone was calling, "Rusty? Rusty!" Joey remembered seeing signs along the road that read NO HUNTING, but the man who appeared in a few moments had a shotgun and heavy boots like Uncle Luce's. He wore a crimson windbreaker with a hood tied off at the chin, and his face hung out like a big baby's bottom, soft and shapeless, finding focus around a pair of blister-pack eyes.

"Good God!" he kept saying with the heavy languor of a sea lion. "How'd you get in there, boy? Hang on, hang on. Good God." He squatted, reached pointlessly for Joey—they were a dozen feet apart—stood, tramped back and forth. "Hang on, hang on. I got a rope in the car. Can you hang on? Take me five minutes. Don't struggle, boy. Good God!"

And he was gone, leaving Rusty behind to bark effusively and keep Joey company. Joey was glad for that. The barking would keep Chip away, he thought. But the poacher had scarcely disappeared when the setter grew more excited, and Joey could tell by the angle of its muzzle that it had seen something *behind* him. His mouse instincts told him to freeze, to hunker down, to *not* look around. Chip or some phantom of his half-brother was rising out of the mud there, angry at the interference, come to claim him in a cold, slimy embrace before a human witness could return. And then he heard a familiar sound. Chattering and moaning. Oarlocks. Uncle Luce was back. Already.

He certainly had rowed fast.

"Joey . . ." he called. Almost a whisper. "I couldn't find a rope. We'll have to try the oar after all."

It worked, of course. It had worked on *Hawaii Five-O* and in a Tarzan movie and an Abbott and Costello movie. He knew it would work. His uncle slogged out to him over the darker stuff and reached out with the oar and then caught him by the hand, the arm, the shirt, and in no time at all he had him out and in the boat and they were rowing, rowing, out of sight before the poacher could even return, and it was just Rusty, barking away in a language no one would understand, who witnessed the timely rescue.

Later, his uncle cleaned the car and washed Joey's clothes and threw the one tennis shoe away. It wouldn't do for his mother to know they had been looking for Chip or that she had nearly lost another son. Joey remembered her deep, dark depression at the time of the disappearance all too vividly. She had been unreachable for months. It had frightened him enormously. And she still went into cold funks, especially around holidays or Chip's birthday. He had thought—hoped—that if they found Chip, she wouldn't wonder so much. But they hadn't found him. And Joey doubted that he was even there. Which didn't mean he wasn't going to see him again. Because the other reason Joey had gone searching was to stop the nightmares. And tonight he wasn't going to have any trouble finding Chip at all.

13

"Why can't we live alone, Mommy?"

He hadn't asked her that since the day of the funeral. And he asked her now as she was about to pull out of the driveway for work, his hands over the sill of the Escort window after she had kissed him good-bye. She studied his mouseness for a moment—the deep brown eyes that had glimmers of adulthood in them already and the slight puffiness above the corners of his mouth so hauntingly reminiscent of Frank—but it was the color of his voice, a white voice, the French called it, stretched thin with fright and urgency, that stirred her mother's heart.

"Joey, how can you feel that way about your uncle?" she said with dismay. Which was stupid. Because now she had

103

rebuked him, and if there was one thing about Joey it was that he was getting harder and harder to draw out.

"I just wanta live alone," he said.

She stared, blinked. "Well," she said. Chucked his cheek, stroked his shoulder. "Well, we can talk about it. But my feeling right now is that we all need each other. We're good for each other."

And she thought about it driving down the Lodge Expressway. They *were* good for each other. She could not have dealt with an empty house, an adultless home after the accident. She would never have been able to hang tough at the plant without a sense of balance in her private life. She would have shrunk. She would have warped Joey and shrunk him with her. *Poof!* One day they would have evaporated into thin air, a couple of microbes frightened out of existence. Lucien had given her perspective. Just by being there, he had done that. He was a reason for her to maintain the motions of an ordered life. You had to get dressed when there was a stranger around. You had to wash the dishes and vacuum and brush your teeth. And even after he had stopped being a stranger, there was a sense of routine, of duty owed to civilization, and a world of reading newspapers and taking out the trash on Thursdays.

But he had been more than just there. He had been a listener. An *uncritical* listener. Even when she was babbling nonsense or upset or just acting out the paranoia of her life, he listened amiably. Amiably but not patronizingly, not with secret scorn. And he helped. He cooked, cleaned, washed. No one kept a tally sheet, but he bought his share of the groceries. He bought a new bath mat, replaced the garage door opener; he had planted morning glory along the fence, and a box of oregano was starting to perfume the kitchen. He helped with Joey too. That was the best thing he had done. Because in her heart she knew that there were too many things she couldn't do for Joey and that she was failing him. His weaknesses were hers. He needed an Uncle Luce.

That was probably the problem this morning. Joey was resisting the hard path. And not very hard at that. A little discipline, a little courage, those rites of passage only men know and need. Luce had taken him to a baseball game and several shows.

104

They had built and flown a kite together. They had gone bowling and Joey had returned incandescent because he had gotten two strikes in a row. But now he was withdrawing.

Funny kid.

You never knew why. He could be balking at anything. A fear, most likely. That was the part of him she knew better than anyone else. Knew, but didn't know. He could build a universe out of an anxiety, complete with the nuances of events and relationships. It would be elaborate and detailed and real—very real. And false. All of it. She understood the crystal structure, the totally engulfing nature of the architecture, but she couldn't read the blueprint.

She talked to Frank about it.

She talked to him in the office with the door closed, the way she often did. They talked for hours sometimes. She could do this now because she had done a very smart thing after the confrontation with Daryl Millman. She had made Walter Barths vice-president in charge of operations. Good old Walter, soul of integrity. He knew every routine, sequence, and flake of rust. He knew the pace of assembly, the shortcuts each shift took, and the compromises on quality. He knew every trick of the Daryl Millmans. He knew where Daryl Millman spit and in which pocket he had the most lint. And he didn't owe the union—the "members"—a thing.

So Walter Barths kept things running in the plant and spoke jargonese to the clientele when that was necessary, and Carolyn hung out in the paper palace doing the fine print and talking—*talking*—to Frank.

But Frank didn't have anything to say about Joey.

Which was probably why (thank you, Freud) she got into it so easily (she didn't want to think about it as some bullshit transference thing, but that was what it was) with Luce later on that night. They were puttering with the garbage disposal, which had gone on the fritz while she was doing the dishes, and while Luce was stripping a new wire she said, "I don't know what I'm going to do about Joey."

Lucien cocked an eye at her, half smiling.

"He's gone solo again, Luce," she said. "Have you noticed? I mean, no calls after school, no 'Mommy, can Johnny come over and play,' no nothing. He's a hell of an extrovert. Just like his mother."

"Everybody doesn't have to be an extrovert." Lucien said it almost to himself.

"You don't think that's abnormal? Seven years old and no friends?"

He twisted the stripped end of the copper wire."Maybe it's abnormal. Depends on the kid. But it doesn't have to be bad."

"Of course it's bad. He doesn't relate to people. I've done a crap-o job of teaching him." He went on arranging the wire end in a hook, and she added, "Haven't I?"

"No."

He said it very quietly. Like he meant it. Like it didn't need hyping.

"Well, gosh-o Pete, how's that? I mean I taught him everything I know about hysteria and clutching up and twenty-five ways to say the wrong thing—"

"He'll make friends."

"What?"

"He'll make friends when he finds someone he wants to make friends with."

"How will he find someone? He's not looking."

"He sees dozens of children every day."

"That's the point, he doesn't seem to like any of them. Pretty damn select. Or is it the other way round? He'll be great in a leper colony."

Lucien screwed down the connection and stood up. "He'll be whatever he is. The important thing is that he likes himself."

"Oh. Like I should like myself." He didn't answer, and she knew she was doing it again: blaming herself, internalizing everything, milking a relationship to assuage her own insecurities. Self-effacement is the vanity of the insecure. "I'm sorry," she said and dropped her head on his shoulder.

There was a moment like the brilliant silence between the welling of a droplet on the tip of an icicle and its fall, and then she felt his hands circumnavigate her back, and it wasn't just a brother-in-law's consoling but a man's age-old protectorship, with all that it implied.

"What Joey needs is to feel strength coming out of himself,"

106

he said. "And what you need is to trust strength coming out of others."

So she threw a party. On Joey's eighth birthday. The summer was well along, then, and people would be away on vacation, she reasoned, so she invited every last soul she could think of, beginning with the entire second grade. And they all said they would come, naturally. All except the Hildemanns, the Millers, and the Daggs. But so what? This was a coming-out party. This was a Joey-you-are-important gala affair. Häagen-Dazs and Sanders ice cream. Balloons by Bozo of Bloomfield. The more the merrier. Joey was already starting to feel important.

"Everybody?" he asked. "And they're all bringing presents?"

"That is the custom, I believe."

"Wow."

"May I quote you for the program?"

His eyes went to umber under glass and his seed pearl teeth flashed as they rarely did. Oh, my, yes. This was no mean event. She moved the thing to the lawn with a tricolored canopy tent that the American Legion Post used for their Fourth of July hoot. She hired Bozo to bring the balloons himself and rented a seven-foot TV screen with the necessary video hookup for nonstop *Laurel and Hardy*. There were party favors by the gross and crepe by the mile and tables end to end as long as bowling lanes. She decided against a skywriter to put *Joey Is 8* on the heavens but did have a banner made up—gold with blue lettering. Bozo swore he could play "Happy Birthday" on the bass drum, so she rented one from Hewitt's, and after that there wasn't much else except an ocean of pop and enough food to feed the Boston Marathon on carbo-load night. Then she dared God to make it rain, and fortunately He was in a good mood the morning it rolled around.

But it was a bit much to expect perfection. Either Joey had been drinking the same potion as Mr. Hyde or she hadn't noticed how shaggy his hair had gotten.

"I'll cut it," Lucien offered, when she began lamenting the oversight at the breakfast table.

"I don't want it cut," Joey said.

"Cut it," Carolyn decreed. "It's a local ordinance for birthday parties."

He looked thoroughly miserable, perched stiffly on the kitchen stool with an orange bath towel draped around his shoulders. The scissors were snipping in Lucien's hand, alternating with the deft click of a comb, and already Joey was looking as curried as a coronation prince.

"I wish your father could see you today," she said and immediately wanted to swallow her tongue. It was a cliché she had promised herself never to utter.

"Frank knew he'd turn out to be a dashing little man," Lucien supplied.

Yes. He had. She'd tell him about it anyway when she went in to work. Tell him about it? It struck her then that her dead husband had become her invisible companion just as Joey's dead half-brother had become his. There were too many ghosts among the living, altogether too many. Today they would have a chance to exorcise some. Today there would be a bridge from the dead to the living, from weakness to strength. She'd called the world in to help them today, called in all the elements of their conflict for an Armageddon. Maybe she *wouldn't* talk to Frank when she went in to work. Maybe she wouldn't talk to him ever again.

It was two-seventeen when the first of the children arrived.

The Aragons came first, then the Bakers, and she wondered if the rest of the guests were going to show up alphabetically. But after that she lost track and Bozo chugged up with his bass drum wanting to know what key she preferred him to play "Happy Birthday" in. She looked at him uncomprehendingly, and he had to explain that it was just his little joke. Having devitalized a clown, she went on to parade the caterers through four different locations before entrenching them at the back of the canopy tent. She did it with firmness and tact, however, and they remained good-natured. (Today we will conquer, today we shall overcome.) The grass had never been greener, the sun and the sky never more pleasant. (Thank you, God, for being in such a good mood.) An ice-cream truck crept by, looking like a hearse by comparison with the festivities on the Whitehalls' lawn, its diminutive bell almost mournful, tolling.

The kids hollered and screamed at *Laurel and Hardy* and ran around with chocolate mustaches, blowing horns and party favors into each other's faces. They stumbled through a sack race, pinned donkey tails on Bozo's bustle, revealed social alliances and the beginnings of romance in their preferences at Sly Wink 'Em. And what really got them, what really knocked their socks off, was what happened at exactly a quarter to four.

Because that was when the Legendary Light-fingered Lucien showed up completely unheralded. He wore a topper and a black vest over a silk shirt, and he found cards and coins everywhere. But mostly he read minds. "Look at the card, little boy. . . . Don't tell me which boy you'd like to sit next to, little girl. . . . Is someone here going to have a birthday next week? Let me see, why, it's *you!*"

And after that—at about twenty after four—the whole thing seemed to come together as they sang "Happy Birthday" while Bozo paced out the accents on the drum. Then Carolyn sprang the first of her two surprises, eight separate birthday cakes, each with a solitary candle. Joey had to run the length of them while he blew a single breath to put them out. And that was good, because now the spotlight was all on him. Everybody watched, everybody clapped. Joey is important, they seemed to say. Then came the second surprise: the presents! And the way it had been set up was really a dramatic coup. Because they were heaped in two huge mountains at the end of the canopy where the caterers had been. And above them was the blue-gold banner that said *Joey Is 8.* Only you couldn't see the banner yet because while they had been cutting the cake, the people who had made the banner put up a drape and hung the sign behind it and arranged the two mountains of gifts on either side of . . .

The chair!

The chair they had brought from the house. The one that looked most like a throne, because it was. Had been. The throne of Khi-tan Zor.

And there was Joey. Halfway up the carpet runner when the drape dropped. And there was his mother, her heart in her throat as she saw what had been done, quailing to herself, Today we will conquer, today we shall overcome.

But not Joey.

Not for the world on a string.

109

No, no, no, no, no—

The chair contained his death, his haunting, his stereophonic three-dimensional wide-screen nightmares.

No. The end.

It was thirteen minutes to five when Bozo started to beat the drum. The children began calling for Joey to sit in the chair then and open his presents. His mother went quickly to his shoulder and tried to move him along, whispering urgently, "Come on, Joey. It's your birthday. Everyone is watching."

But he wouldn't.

The shouting was getting impatient now, a little derisive, and his mother tried to stay calm, but he heard the rubberiness in her throat. "What's the matter, Joey? Is it because it was Chip's chair? Do you see Chip sitting there?"

The drum kept pounding and the sounds grew ugly—really ugly, like they did on the playground when he wouldn't play soccer—and that was when he began to shake and cry. Mercifully, he would remember nothing of the rest of it—his falling down, his screams, clawing at the grass—nothing except that his uncle was walking quietly around the side of the tent for a better vantage and that, when he got it, the perplexity on his hawkish face melted insidiously into a terrible look of deadness and joy.

By five-thirty everybody was gone and it was raining violently on the tent, and the lawn, strewn with bits of sodden crimson crepe, looked like the aftermath of a Roman circus.

God wasn't in a good mood anymore.

14

I've done a crap-o job of raising him."

"You haven't finished, is all."

The kitchen again. They sat across from each other in the breakfast nook, and the explosive rain had gone to sheets in the wind, lit by more or less constant fulminations, which was why they left the lights out. That and because the intermittent darkness was balm.

"*Eight* years old and no friends."

"There's still time."

"He isn't going to find friends."

"Not until he finds himself."

She waited for the next flash, a sickly, sulfurous one that bathed Lucien in hell green. He had the calm conviction of his

111

brother: she could see this despite the taint of the light. Arrowed lips, immutable brow, eyes like banked black flames. Harsher than Frank, but strong—so strong.

"How could I have been so stupid as to not tell them," she droned. The banner people, she meant. "You knew about the chair?"

"No."

"Oh, yes, he's been terrified by it since . . . I don't know, maybe before he was born." She laughed in a kind of single-syllable hiss but didn't try to explain. "It was the big event in his life, the thing between him and his father. Frank wanted it to be the symbol of the family's unity like it's always been, but to Joey it was the source of his separation."

"I knew about the chair," he said. "I didn't know about Joey's fear of it."

"Frank used to try and make him sit in it. It was terrible. Like what you saw today."

"Frank knew, then."

"Knew what?"

"That Joey had to have his victory there."

The darkness settled in momentarily against the growling in the sky. *God help her, it was exactly what Frank believed.* Had she been wrong to let the issue drop after his death? Was that why Joey had withdrawn, because the hurdle was still there?

"Joey is just . . . stubborn," she faltered. "The chair never really mattered."

"Did Frank believe that?"

"There wasn't any need to keep making him—"

"But Frank thought so."

"Just stubborn."

"Frank knew, Carolyn."

He seemed to be growing on the other side of the table, towering in the darkness. Why didn't the lightning flash?

"He has to feel strength coming out of himself, and Frank knew it," he said in that prowling voice of his. "Stubbornness isn't strength. Stubbornness is the ally of weakness."

So sure of himself, like Frank.

"Strength, Carolyn. The boy needs a man."

Needs a man. A man.

Lightning. Blazing white. White-white. Studio white. Not the white of Joey's voice, but the lucid white of irrefutable realities. And in it he leaned across the table, white face flawless with power, arrows darting from the corners of his dusky lips, flying from the centers of his eyes. And whatever he saw of her in that protracted blaze frightened her, because she read her own capitulation in his slow descent and iron grasp. Up she came, whether by choice or levitation, onto the table, warming lustily to his rough caresses under her skirt, the squeezing of her flesh, white and rippling, turgid, dewy, a primitive heat and scent rising from their deep and urgent lovemaking, pounding, pounding, pounding. . . .

15

B etrayal.

That was what he woke up thinking. His mother had betrayed him. Why? She knew about the chair and how much he hated it, and after Daddy died it was never supposed to happen again. But it had. She had let it.

Why?

Something had changed. As if Daddy had come back. *Just wait till I get this coffin lid off!* Up, up, out of the metal box. *Joey, you're going to sit in the chair and that's that!* Arguing with his mother. *He's just being stubborn, you've got to break a child's willfulness, Carolyn. He's deliberately chosen the chair because he knows how important it is, and if he can defeat us there he can hang onto all the fears and insecurities he thinks are protecting him.* She had believed it then. But after he was dead, she had let it go. No mention of the chair at all. Instead, she had talked to Joey directly about his fears and it was more like they shared them, because she had lots of them too and sometimes they even talked about Chip, but whatever they talked about it was never, never, like everything would be all super if he just sat in the chair. Once she had said they were making each other worse, that she wasn't helping him to deal with people. But he didn't see how that was true, and anyway it had nothing to do with the chair. And now she was acting like before. Only it couldn't be his father who had changed her. It must be his uncle. Uncle Luce had made her change her mind. But how? He hadn't known about the chair. Not until yesterday.

Joey grew chill under the covers, remembering the terrible look of deadness and joy. That was the moment when his uncle knew.

He had slept for fourteen hours, fitfully at first, aware in the encroaching night that the people were gone, leaving behind a silence that roared at first and gradually guttered out like a drowning candle. The deeper sleep had come in almost total silence, empty and absolving, perhaps taking on form with the faint pulse of lovemaking on the breakfast table downstairs and rising in incessant throbbing dreams to its own climax: betrayal . . . betrayal . . . betrayal.

Sitting up, he suddenly realized that the sun was gleaming off the baseboard opposite the window. It was never on the baseboard when he got up. His mother hadn't called him for breakfast, and she must be gone to work by now. Maybe she was angry. Sometimes she let him sleep until she was ready to leave, but she always said good-bye. She must be angry. And then he thought he hadn't heard the car go out. He just couldn't have slept through that. She must not have gone to work—that was it. She wasn't angry. Maybe she was even sorry for having betrayed him. She had stayed home to make it up to him.

He slipped out of bed and ran barefoot to the top of the stairs. "Mommy?" The echo was so quick it smudged his voice a little. She was gone. He knew that now. The house was empty.

He fled downstairs, pattering here and there and ending in the doorway to the garage. The Escort was missing and the

house was empty. His uncle and his mother had both left. Together. And now he was really worried. He had ruined everything, disgraced his mother, embarrassed the family. No one
was ever going to talk to them again. No one was ever going to
talk to *him*.

"Mom? Mom?"

Through the house, angry, frightened, opening and slamming doors, eyes smarting, throat aching.

"Mom!" Demanding. "Mommy. . . ." Breaking into little
sobs of frustration.

Finally there was just one door left. The white one. To the
white-white room. The studio. Upstairs. He didn't hesitate until
he got there.

"Mom?"

He said *Mom*, but he knew already who it was going to be.
Uncle Luce had not gone with her after all. Just a tiny part of
Joey wasn't sure—the same part that feared abandonment and
shared hope—and so he opened the door, and there was Uncle
Luce, and the whole room was like the inside of a piano now,
all wires and hammers strung from ceiling to floor and wall to
wall so tightly that they began to hum and groan the moment
you moved—the air moved—incredibly eerily, like a billion bees
waking with a dangerous murmur. But the thing that took his
breath away with a double whammy was that in the very middle
of the room, the very middle of the spider web, his uncle
sat . . . on the chair.

"Hello, Joey."

It was all Joey could do to keep breathing.

"You must be hungry."

Joey shook his head abruptly.

"Your mother wanted to say good-bye this morning, but I
thought it was best to let you sleep. She said she'd never left
without saying good-bye to you before, but I told her it would
be all right."

I?

"Is it all right, Joey?"

He nodded obediently.

"I thought it would be. We had a long talk about you last

night. I said I thought it would be best if I talked to you alone today."

I.

"Oh, Joey, how I misjudged you. You have a will of iron and a secrecy to match. I never knew anything about this chair business." He smiled a forever smile that seemed to keep on going like a chasm opening. "What is it *exactly* that you don't like about this chair?"

Something in the word "exactly" found a matching resonance in one of the thickest piano wires, answering with a groan.

"Is it some kind of pain or just a fear?" his uncle posed. "You couldn't have picked a worse heirloom to be intractable about. It's like being allergic to mother's milk, Joey. The chair is the mother's milk of this family."

He got up then, meandered around a lattice of wires, circled behind Joey's shoulder.

"Pain . . . or fear?"

"Both."

"Really? That *is* bad. Of course, both are imagined. It's all in the way you look at things, isn't it?" Joey couldn't answer, couldn't say it wasn't. "You have to change the way you look at things sometimes. If you want to grow up, you have to put your childish fears aside."

"I don't want to grow up."

"Ah, but you want friends, you want to fit in."

"*You* don't fit in," Joey ventured timidly.

Lucien laughed softly. "Do you want to be like me?" And that was when the joy in his eyes went to deadness again. "Sometimes a boy needs to be made to overcome childish notions. Your father knew that."

"My father's dead."

"And I'm his brother, your uncle. Your mother and I talked about that. A boy needs someone to help him. It's fallen to me."

Joey began to shake his head slowly.

"You've got to sit in the chair, Joey. It's the only way."

Faster now. Turning his head almost full profile, right, left, right, left.

"Remember what I said that day at the studio when you

117

asked if I was a magician? I said I like to expose things. Illusions are my specialty. You've got an illusion, Joey."

"No!" The heavy wires buzzed, as if shocked.

"I need to know what happens when you sit in the chair, so I know how to deal with the illusion."

"I'll tell Mommy!" he threatened classically, and the room added a curious, flat, metallic ghost to each syllable.

"Your mother understands, just like your father did."

Joey shook his head fiercely.

"She's agreed that you need me to do what has to be done. If you won't sit in the chair voluntarily, I'll have to make you."

"She wouldn't say that."

"Well, to be exact, she said, 'I know I'm not strong enough to help Joey in this, so I promise not to interfere.' She was talking about overcoming your fears. About the discipline necessary to overcome your biggest fear—"

"You're lying!"

Softly. "Well. You can ask her. You can tell her when she comes home. Tell her I made you sit in the chair. But what she'll want to know is . . . Were you afraid?"

"I *will* tell, too!" Joey maintained, uncertainty in his voice.

And then his uncle, using the tone that resonated the bass, rumbled, "Sit in the chair, Joey."

The rest was pantomime. Maître d' seating a guest. Father Lucien sharing the Last Mile, firm grasp on the collapsing prisoner about to be electrocuted. Pas de deux. Pirouette. All fall down.

In the chair.

Joey was probably screaming.

He couldn't tell because he was underwater. Gone was the ceramic tunnel as white and twisting as the snow tunnels of Little Two Hearted Lakes. Gone was the horned satyr of that transport, and in its place was a vague, dumb thing dancing slowly like a balloon in a sluggish wind. It was much bigger than a balloon, though. And it hovered in the gluey greenness at the bottom of wherever he was. There were noises like the groans of his uncle's piano wires, a mighty concert of a single sustained note that made Joey think he was listening to the center of the earth. Every bone inside him seemed to resonate with that note. His teeth ground and his flesh vibrated on its skeletonlike loose clothing. The dancing thing came closer, waving playfully, its arms floating stiffly back and forth like an overstuffed Raggedy Ann. He tried to swim, to claw his way out of its path, but the distance between them steadily shrank. And now he realized he wanted air; he was *dying* for air! He had to go up. So he pushed off the ooze on the bottom, pushed like he had on Lake Erie, and this time . . . he made it. His feet shot clear and he would have risen, only he was caught after all. And if it wasn't the mud that got him, then what was it?

(Raggedy Ann.)

It was Raggedy Ann!

Soft fingers around his ankle, rising with him, faster, in fact, its face even with his knee and then his chest and then . . . *Just wait till I get this coffin lid off—*

Hi, Dad!

But still, a Raggedy Ann face . . . terrible . . . terrible . . . because his father's eyes were flat and round as saucers and his nose was just a hole like a triangle, his lips all crossed with grooves as if his teeth had chewed through.

Panic filled Joey like helium. Up, up, he went, dragging Raggedy Ann with him until he broke free of the surface. And just before he breathed he saw that it was Echo Lake. And one more thing—one more thing in that anaerobic limbo—paddling away from the spot in a green canoe, wearing a lethal expression of deadness and joy . . . was Uncle Luce.

Then he breathed.

The great searing breath cleared his head, banishing the nightmare. But now there was another, one he could scarcely sort out. His mother. Naked and lying on her back in her own bed. And his uncle, also naked, pale hands reaching up to cup and stroke her paler breasts, arms straight as suspenders down her sides as he buried his head between her thighs. His mother was breathing funny, her head jerking up from the pillow and a great animal sound coming out of her. Then her arms came up, beckoning, and his uncle writhed into them, flattening his

119

tummy onto hers and thrusting up and down. His mother began crying breathlessly, but she sounded happy (happy!) as she hugged his uncle with her legs, her arms. . . .

There was no water now, but Joey was drowning when his uncle let him out of the chair.

"It's fear," Lucien said. "Not pain. Just fear. That's all it is, Joey. You'll get over it. Illusions of that sort go away in time. When you face them."

If you face them.

Joey wouldn't, couldn't. He huddled against the headboard of his bed, teeth chattering, waiting for his mother to come home. He was not precisely in shock—unless a child's protective fantasies can be called shock—but he had stopped being eight years old. He was four again. That was before the chair business had gotten serious. He was four, and if he had been screaming and now felt hollowed out it was because Chip had been taunting him all morning, not Uncle Luce. Chip had broken his Fisher-Price Busy Box and eaten his strawberry Jell-O and finally tripped him when they were playing Army out on the lawn. He had a skinned knee, which he held with his left hand. His right hand became a fist and the thumb went into his mouth. Sometime around three in the afternoon he fell asleep.

When he awoke it was night and he was eight again. He was under the covers now and the sheet had been tucked in at the side of the bed. And that was good because it meant his mother was home. She had tucked him in without waking him. He wanted to go straight to her, to lie in her arms and pour out what had happened to him, but there was something funny about the room. He almost never got out of bed at night, especially if he heard a noise. Especially if there was something funny about the room. And there was. Both, maybe. Because he thought he had heard a noise too. Daddy used to call it "the dark ickies" and laugh. He had stopped laughing when Joey admitted to wetting the bed while awake rather than get up in the dark. That was part of the reason Daddy had always been mad at him.

The window was open and the leaves on the maple outside were chattering. Uncle Luce had told him he could understand

120

the leaves when they chattered. Joey didn't know about that. What he did know was that his uncle could stop in the middle of a walk in the woods and without looking tell him what kind of tree was rustling its leaves. He had never really liked the things his uncle could do, and now he was truly terrified of him. He had been afraid of his father, too, but this was worse. Uncle Luce was going to be *much* worse than Daddy. (But Mommy would stop him.) He thought maybe the sound of leaves chattering had been the noise that woke him.

And now he saw that something was standing at the foot of the bed.

It hadn't moved all the while he had been awake, and so his apprehension, like the realization, dawned slowly. But moment by moment it mounted as he stared at the gloomy outline, bigger than Mommy, bigger even than Uncle Luce. What did it want? Why did it just stand there? And then he thought, It's Raggedy Ann. All the terror of the chair flooded back then, fresh and insidious, but even that thought produced no change in the thing at the foot of the bed.

A rational suspicion came next, growing cautiously to a conviction, still held at bay by fear until he forced himself to edge forward on the mattress and touch the first of the presents piled there. A pillar of presents. Mommy had piled them for him to find when he woke up tomorrow morning. Mommy wasn't angry anymore. And with that sudden rush of relief he knew he had to go to her.

He spun off the mattress, pattered across the cold floor into the hallway, running now—Mommy, Mommy, Uncle Luce says I have to sit in the chair and you said he could make me do it and I want you to tell him that we don't need him any—

There was the noise again.

He was at the door of his mother's bedroom, and he really didn't need to drop down and peek through the keyhole. But he did. Even though he had already seen the flashes of flesh afforded him by the aperture, the ones that fit the animal sound she was making, the ones he had seen in the chair when his mother and his uncle did the naked thing together. And he knew it meant they liked each other and were close—as close as Mommy and Daddy—so . . . so maybe what his uncle had said

121

was true. She wanted him to sit in the chair. Could she have been that mad at him?

Maybe Uncle Luce had used magic on her.

It didn't matter. Because now Joey saw that they were agreed about him. This was what his uncle had meant about showing people things that had always been there. This was how he was showing him his il-lu-sion.

And the chair.

Maybe that was his uncle's magic too.

Because Joey understood now that it was taunting and threatening him. Showing him Chip first. And then the white tunnel—the ski trip. And his father drowned with Uncle Luce paddling away. And the naked thing. That was his uncle's way. Using the chair to scare him, to make him see that he was alone.

And he was.

16

She wasn't the least bit shocked at herself, Carolyn thought, driving to work the morning after Joey's birthday party. Sex was bound to happen again in her life—even that kind of circumstantial sex—and if she was surprised at all it was that Luce had been so passionate. His insight went well beyond good guesses, and he had a certain carnal rawness that wasn't at all unappealing. But she didn't love him, wasn't likely to in the sense she had known with other men. Having sex with Luce would be as functional as sharing a bathroom, once the arousal tempered down. She would go back on the pill and it would all be very therapeutic and businesslike.

A white-haired harpy piloting a green scow with engine knock slid past in the right lane and gave her the finger. Shit,

123

I'm asleep in the passing lane, she realized. She tried to move over, but the traffic was aggressive and stingy, as it always was this time of morning. She got horns and glares and self-righteous scrutiny. How dare you! Goddamn woman drivers! Pariah of the rush hour. It always got to her. Always made her feel freakish and alone. Like Joey. Joey had her personality, and if she couldn't lick it, how could he? She wondered how much of it was genes, how much environment. The genes were something she wouldn't blame herself for, but the role modeling—yeah, that was a guilt cruise. He reacted to the same things she reacted to, got scathed by the same nuances, found stress and anxiety in the same relationships. Was that basic training? And here she was back in the same pitfalls of the first marriage, no different, no better. . . .

It was a big red semi this time. Air horn blasting its rocks off up her tail pipe. What did they let them on the expressway this time of morning for?

Luce was going to be good for Joey too. Painful, maybe, but Joey needed to get away from her, needed to emulate a man. She didn't want to be around when the discipline took place. That was exactly the kind of thing she couldn't handle—hadn't handled. And Joey was going to come screaming to her. Mommy, why can't we live alone? That was going to be tough. She would have to make sure he didn't think she had abandoned him, stopped loving him, given up.

Grand River exit next. She gave it a creative move and hit the left pedal as a conga line of brake lights came on. Another horn behind her. All right already! Welcome to the hostility capital of the world, where vehicular homicide is death by natural causes. She snuggled to the right. Some ambitious but foolhardy bastard was out there on an ice-cream cycle already. Who ate ice cream for breakfast? He was going to be strawberry glaze if he didn't keep over. And then she felt a little envy for him. She was headed for the air-conditioned sterility of a windowless room, and he was out in the open air all white and free and jingling a bell. Maybe she should open a greenhouse, tote her azaleas down to Eastern Market on Saturday mornings.

Sinswicki was picking his nose when she shot through the

gate, and he tried to grin, which was all rather hideous. She parked and took the lift to her office. Screw the main assembly room. No need to posture anymore. Good old Walter Barths would have all the ducks in a row. The office she had given him wasn't going to wear out any time soon. Sleep well, your V.P. is on guard.

No, she wasn't the least bit shocked at herself, she thought again, with her hand on the doorknob. But she must have been. Else why think of it now—here—the moment she was entering Frank's office? And it was Frank's office again. She had told him that last week. Frank . . . I don't want it. All these phone lines scare me. Let's pretend the calls are for you. I'll just answer them on your behalf. And she did. Only when she answered she didn't say, "Just a minute, I'll get Frank." She said, "I'll have to consult with my operations vice-president, Mr. Nevus," or, "Let me check our requisitions on that, Kent, and get back to you." It would be Walter who called back, of course. Walter was a gem. If he understood her condition Jell-O, he never let on. A gem. But now she had her hand on the doorknob to Frank's office, and she *was* shocked at herself.

She went in, threw the switch, closed the door. Yesterday's mums on his side of the desk were already curling. "Frank, Frank, I told you they needed more water," she murmured. She had forgotten to water them herself, of course. She didn't really believe he could do it. It just helped to shift the blame a little. She put her purse in the tiny bathroom, glancing in the mirror. Still potato salad. Worse in the light of a sixty-watt bulb. She had fared better in the car mirror. A tan would help, she thought, and resolved to spend the weekend on the patio.

Her desk was as orderly and uncluttered as the pictures in an office supply catalog, and it would stay that way until the mail came in at nine-thirty. She hated to start a morning with yesterday's paperwork. Frank's side was a mess. Of course, she had *let* it be a mess, the way he always had. And she still told him about it. Just for the memory, of course.

Men were such slobs.

"Men are such slobs," she said aloud.

There was the cologne, paper-clip chain, comb, loose

125

change—it looked more like a dresser top than a desk. She had felt silly at first, leaving the things there. Putting things there. But, what the heck. . . . It's your office, Frank.

Her only worry was that someone might think she was crazy. That's why she put the stuff away at night and brought it back out the next morning. When they had a meeting in her office, it went away. No sense starting rumors about the CEO's emotional stability.

God, Frank was listening, and she had to tell him about Joey.

She sat down on her side of the desk and began to flip the Rol-o-dex—as if it had to make noise to work. I hear you listening, Frank. She made three phone calls, the innocuous kind, checking on deliveries, but afterward the office sounded just as quiet as before. She went to the invoice file for August; then she sharpened a pencil—all the pencils, actually—from the desk caddy. She sharpened the ones that were already sharp, just to make sure. She took out a tray full of paper clips, a stapler. The invoice file had a lot of paper clips in it. One by one she removed these, dropped them in the tray, stapled the invoices in their places. Damn it, Frank, I talk to *you*! I don't want to hear from you, so cut the shit with all the indictment.

Out loud she said, "A couple of things happened yesterday, Frank."

Can you believe this? You're nervous as hell, girl. You called on the dead to make life more bearable, and now you act like . . . like—

"The birthday party was a disaster. It was going along just fine until the presents. Lucien" —there, you've said his name, girl; tell him—"as a magician was a rave, and Bozo showed up plenty early, and the caterers had everything under control until the banner people put the chair at the end of the tent with all the presents on it. The chair, Frank. As in Joey-is-terrified-of."

Don't forget to tell him about the second thing, Carolyn. I mean, he's dead, you know, and why should he care about your sex life now anyway? You kept it in the family, didn't you?

"So he threw a fit. Wouldn't sit in it, of course. To tell you the truth, I hadn't thought about it much since . . . since the last time, you know? But I certainly wouldn't have sprung it on

126

him like that. It was a stupid oversight on my part. I'm not doing too well with Joey, Frank. I mean, letting that happen in front of all his friends and being too petrified to smooth it over or something—it was really stupid, don't you think? Definitely all my fault, so that's everything that happened yesterday."

You didn't tell him.

And then she turned around and saw Daryl Millman grinning at her from the doorway.

"Am I interrupting something?" He wore innocence like a vampire at a blood bank.

Hi-ho, way to go, girl. What do you say now? He was transparent as hell, and she had to assume he had heard enough to know who she was talking to.

"There's always a danger of that when you don't knock," she said curtly.

"Guess you didn't hear me."

Then she noticed his cigarette. She hadn't smelled it. Maybe he hadn't been there too long, hadn't heard.

"I was just talking to myself," she said, mustering a smile with difficulty.

She had stood up, intending to guide him out of the office, but he was coming forward now, fascinated by Frank's things on the desk.

"What do you want, Daryl?"

"The members asked me to come," he said.

"Did they say you should barge right into my office?"

"Hey. I knocked."

"Next time wait for an invitation."

He shrugged. "Sorry." Grinned.

"And what do the members want now, Daryl?"

He transferred the cigarette to his lips, reached to his back pocket. "OSHA rules ain't being followed." He laid a well-thumbed sheaf next to the cologne. "We need more ventilators. Air back there in the shop ain't got no oxygen in it."

"You mean back there where the NO SMOKING sign is?"

He stiffened a little but kept on puffing. "Back there with the paints," he said. "The fumes are bad. We need more vents."

"Did you talk to Walter about this?"

127

"He don't know that things have changed for the better and we've got rules to protect workers' rights now. He just says it's been that way since the plant opened and nothing has to change. Talking to Walter is like talking to . . . yourself." Grin.

The bastard knew. He was toying with her, threatening her: "Hey, everybody. Guess what I walked in on in the boss's office!"

"I seem to remember handling an OSHA air quality verification on that about a year ago," she said. "We had an inspection then."

"Fumes are worse now."

"Why would they be?"

"Just are." He looked a little surly. "You gonna do anything about it?"

"I'm going to talk to Walter."

"That's just a waste of time, I told you. I'll have to tell the members, if that's all you're gonna do."

"Tell them *what*?"

Grin. "How things stand."

Give him what he wants, shut him up. Except he won't shut up.

"How *do* things stand, Daryl? Tell me too. I won't know until I talk to Walter. You know he runs things in the plant."

"I guess I do. And I guess I know he won't do anything."

Damn you, Millman. Damn, I hate you and I hate arguing like this. Make me the bad guy. Make everyone hate me. Damn, damn, damn.

"I want to know his reasons, Daryl. What kind of president would I be if I didn't consult my own people?"

Grin. "Well, we'll find out all that, I guess. Let me know when you know."

He hesitated and leaned a little as if to peek behind the door on the way out. And the grin that followed was bigger than all the others, even though it was offered only in profile.

Oh, shit. You let him walk all over you, girl.

And then she had the door shut and locked. No one was going to interrupt this conversation.

17

"Joe-ey."

His eyes snapped open, and he knew without even looking at the baseboard where the sun had already reached that his mother was gone again. His sleep habits were all screwed up and he had lain awake most the night and, yes, he had heard the Escort go out this time, but it was just before his uncle's voice brought him all the way around—

"Joe-ey."

Uncle Luce was going to do it again.

Just like he said he would, he was going to make Joey sit in the chair. They had had a collie named Wendy once, and she couldn't tolerate sharp noises. Chip had shot caps around the house to make Wendy get all frantic—drooling and lathering

129

and pacing from one room to the next trying to get away from the sound. She had loved them, Joey knew, and she would never have run away except she just couldn't stand the caps. And so one day when Chip started to shoot them off she pushed out the screen door and was gone. That was how Joey felt.

He just couldn't stand the chair.

His mouth got watery under his tongue and dry at the roof and his legs felt twitchy now just thinking about it. Poor Joey. Like a Pavlov dog. His uncle was going to come for him when he stopped calling and Joey was already salivating.

He jumped off the bed and pattered to the door. No one in the hallway. He darted across into his mother's sewing room. There was a basket chair and a daybed, a sewing machine and an ironing board set up. The closet had shelves, and these were packed tightly with bolts of material. He went through into the sun porch, which was as bright and barren as an examination room. The playroom was out, too—Uncle Luce would look there first, probably. If he could just get past the white-white room and run downstairs, he could leave the house like Wendy had. Maybe he wouldn't *run* away, but he could stay away until his mother came home. The trouble was that if he went past the white-white room, his uncle would be waiting to surprise him the way Chip used to. Only, when he heard his name again it didn't come from the white-white room. It came from downstairs. So he wasn't going to get out of the house at all. He could only go up.

Up was the attic.

He hated the attic. It was webby and creaky and full of vague things. Even the doorknob was different. Green metal. It turned like you were twisting a hand against its will, and the door came open with a little pop, exhaling dried wood aroma and dust. He kept to the wall where the stairs wouldn't creak as he climbed up in his bare feet.

There was the feeling of a past boiled into the air which Joey sensed strongly here. He searched for it, not knowing what it was, thinking it must be still in the dead husks, the ambered glass and stiffened clothes, or in the locked drawers of brooding furniture. But the gummy resins and fragrances had long since bled into the air itself, a delicate echo only an alien of Joey's sensitivity might detect, and it was this that made the attic swim with maledictions. Sunlight exploded on the quatrefoils at either end and seemed to turn gray after getting in. But it was hot. Hot as if that little bit of sunlight had only been added to the boil like a pinch of ginger. Joey picked his way cautiously to the far end, and there, amid white and shapeless mounds and residues of lace, he crouched.

Silence lay thick as sediment in this attic, and he could hear his own rhythms, his breathing and pulse like some wheezing, thumping monster nesting in dust. He was hungry and he had to go to the bathroom. Sweat rolled down his squatting calves. The motes of decades disintegrating were tickling his sinuses, as if he were allergic to that past he sensed but could not locate.

"Joe-ey!"

It was chillingly different this time. Dogged by an insidious counterpoint, a buzz, ominous because he knew what it meant. His uncle was upstairs walking past the white-white room, and his voice had stirred the insane jungle of piano wires stretched from ceiling to floor and wall to wall inside.

And now he could hear the shoes, those black Red Wing work shoes his uncle always wore, coming straight down the hallway without any hesitation whatsoever.

The attic door opened and closed and up he came, one heavy step after another, unrelenting and so certain, as if he had been told—and that was the first time Joey thought it: that the chair had told him—but of course Uncle Luce was a *finder*, and finding Joey must have been . . . child's play.

"There you are!" A voice filled with wicked music. The thin, sallow face with the long, grinning teeth rose above the floor, rose and rose until his uncle filled the end of the attic. And even then it kept rising, hunching forward to permit the expansion. Joey's nocturnal eyes receded between the rafters until a long, bony hand found him and dragged him out.

"You've got to learn to mind me, nephew," Lucien said, this time with a peculiar savage grace. *Nephew*. It always meant something bad was waiting for him.

Down they went, like a cat carrying a mouse, down into the den where the patriarch chair had been returned. Joey began to cry, then to plead. "Please don't make me . . . please." And when he asked to be allowed to dress first, Lucien looked at his thin pajamas and smiled.

"What good will getting dressed do you?"

"I don't know," Joey said, in a voice broken with frustration. "Maybe . . . if I put on enough clothes, I won't feel it as much."

Lucien's curiosity was incandescent. He seemed to think about it a full minute before he burst into a laugh and shook his head. "No more stalling, nephew."

"I've got to go to the bathroom!" Joey whined, and he flexed his knees several times as though the pressure in his bladder demanded it.

Lucien probed him with a long stare, then brightened again. "If that's what you want. Get dressed first and use the bathroom."

He stood at the foot of the stairs while Joey scrambled up.

Anything to get away from the caps, Joey kept thinking, Wendy would do. . . . He raced to his room and shut the door. Then he grabbed his jeans and a T-shirt that said *Ann Arbor Art Fair* that his mother had gotten him and his new Pumas and a looseleaf binder, because it had a tapered edge, and the mouthpiece to his toy saxophone, because it had a tapered end, and his wood rocket model, because it had a tapered point, and then he rushed all these things down the hall into the upstairs bathroom where they would help him, because it was the only room besides the studio that had a lock on it, and when he had thrown the lock and wedged the tapered things under the door *there was no way his uncle could get to him!*

Uncle Luce was going to be very mad, but Joey was that desperate. He just couldn't sit in the chair again . . . couldn't . . . could not.

When he had set the lock and wedged the things under the door as far as he could push them, he sat down on the cool tile and cried very softly. There wasn't a sound from outside, but he had no idea how much time had elapsed. Probably his uncle figured he was still dressing—he was always very slow at dressing. It couldn't be too much longer, though. Pretty soon he would come like before, calling, knocking, then banging. It was a good door, a good lock, he thought. The wedges would help too. If his uncle pushed them out, he would be right there to push them back. But for a long time nothing happened. Until nothingness itself became an event.

Ah.

A trick.

Just like Chip. Maybe he'd heard the lock and the wedging and now he was going to pretend he wasn't there anymore, or didn't care, or maybe he was going to wait until Joey was curious enough to peek out. But Joey wasn't going to peek out. He absolutely wouldn't open the door until his mother was right there and he could hear her voice promising it was okay.

He thought he'd better go to the bathroom now. Once the action started, he wouldn't have time to go. So he went to the bathroom and then he got dressed. Lacing the red Pumas snugly on his feet always made him feel more secure, as if he could outrace any danger. These were pretty new—the successors to the ones he had worn that day in the Lake Erie marshes—and he could still feel the ribs of the soles whenever he pivoted suddenly. He was getting a drink from the faucet when he did just that—pivoted suddenly. He pivoted because he thought he saw something move in the mirror, something behind him, something that shouldn't have been there.

"For an eight-year-old you're very clever," Lucien said, as he sat up fully dressed in the bathtub.

Joey began to pant and wheeze.

"I was a very clever boy when I was your age. *Very* clever." The rush of false grace was back in his voice. "They all said that. Clever Lucien. I guess you come by it honestly. The thing about growing up, though, is that it makes you even more clever."

His uncle had been there all the time, and Joey wasn't sure anymore what was magic, what wasn't. He remembered the studio with the hands and how his uncle had gotten into the next room without passing him, and even though he knew the trick, the impression still lingered that it was magic and that his uncle's powers were without real limits. He felt sick to death as he ran to the door and started to pry the wedges out.

"You *could* run away," Uncle Luce said thoughtfully. "Like Chip did."

Joey sat down on the tiles then, his back against the door, his arms and legs rubbery, spent. "Chip didn't run away," he

133

said, scarcely aware of what he was saying. "And you know where he is."

"Do I? I know that you saw your mother and me last night." He was sitting on the tub rail now.

Joey didn't try to deny what he'd seen. He understood that he had invaded an adult world of privacy last night. But his uncle seemed glad about it.

"So now you understand that your mother and I are very close. She trusts me with you, Joey. I'm not going to let her down. I'm not going to let my brother down. You're a clever boy, and I'm going to see that you get over these fears."

"I'm not afraid anymore," Joey said as if he were making a promise.

"Good."

"No. Really, I'm not."

"I knew you could get over it."

"Just the chair," Joey said.

"That's the weak link."

"But if I'm not scared of anything else, the chair doesn't matter."

"Yes. It matters. It mattered to your father."

"Mom doesn't care."

"She does now. She thinks Frank was right about it after all. If a man's home is his castle, his chair is his throne, Joey." He got up, ambled into the corner of the room where the acoustics of his voice suddenly went as flat as stale soda water. "Of course, if you were really, truly not afraid of anything else, I suppose we could postpone the chair until you're older. As long as your mother didn't find out."

"I am." Joey brightened.

"You'd do anything else?"

(Wendy would do anything to . . .) "Yes!"

"You know where I thought you were hiding today? I thought you were hiding out on the roof. I suppose it was just the squirrels, but I thought at the time maybe you were getting braver."

The roof.

That was how he got him up there. As if Joey had suggested it. The deal was that Joey would have to cross between the sun porch and the playroom dormer. It was a steep pitch, slate-tiled, and when it was muggy this early in the morning you could see the rivulets on the shadowed side like moisture beaded on glass. "God's first breath of the morning," his mother used to say. "A yawn in the dawn," father had always quipped. Whatever you called it, it would be ten-thirty or eleven before it burned off.

Neither his mother nor his father would ever have permitted this, but they didn't understand about the chair. Uncle Luce, oddly enough, did.

"Someone had to put the tiles up there in the first place," he said to Joey when they got to the sun porch. "So I guess it's safe enough for a lightweight like you."

"They probably had ropes and things," Joey murmured.

Uncle Luce smiled faintly. "Well, you'll have bravery, nephew."

Joey retied his Pumas extra tightly as his uncle unlocked and raised the sash. The air that pushed in was so wet you could drown in it, and he heard the late August leaves chattering to no apparent breeze. Zephyrs moved through the trees on their lot like solar winds in far-off galaxies and seemed never to touch anywhere else. Joey only knew that when he clambered tentatively out the window onto those first wet tiles it was dead and still, like the hush before an aerial feat of death-defying odds.

He had barely edged away from the sash when he heard it come down with a slow hiss on his uncle's soft "Full speed ahead, nephew." A sharp click announced the lock and then, as if that faint vibration had started an avalanche, he was sliding, sliding. His thin body rippled toward the precipitous brink of a three-story drop to the sunken patio like a piece of paper. Telephone wires rushed toward him. He would have to grab them, whether they could possibly hold or whether they would electrocute him or . . . he got his tennis shoes under himself then and began to slow, catching, slipping, slow, slow . . . stop.

A very delicate stop.

There were his toes just over the eaves, and there was the top of the oak tree and the ground a million miles below. His heart was coming through his chest. If there had been anything in his stomach, it would be in his mouth now, because his stomach had shot into his throat. He could *smell* the emptiness that he hung over, a clear smell that pierced his brain like a swallow of cold water. And he could feel his uncle's eyes behind him, above him. There had been no cry, no sudden rush of the sash to indicate concern. And he knew that if he dared glance back, there would be the look of a hawk keening down on a doomed mouse.

Very slowly he moved one foot. A tile grated. He knew they could come off. Once he and Chip had tried to bounce a basketball from the sun porch to the playroom. A tile had come loose then. And sometimes after a storm there would be tiles smashed or fallen from where broken branches had struck the roof. And that gave him an idea. Because the replacement slate had been bound on with copper strips folded up at the bottom of each tile, and there was one almost within reach.

Inch by inch he began to test his small frame against the loose overlap of slate, edging sideways. The pair of copper strips bent over the replacement tile gave his agile fingers enough purchase to move upward several feet, and again, a yard or so away, he found another to support the added thrust of moving higher. He was shaking and tense, and the limit of his frail muscles was quickly being reached. His jeans were soaked through with dew now, and it was that minor decrease in friction which suddenly betrayed him, launching him on a bumpy water slide toward the lip of the roof. The Pumas, pressed flat on the pitch, squealed as they rubbed dry at last, and he froze at the edge for long terror-stricken moments before the aching in his neck and his bruised elbows forced him to try again.

This time he was going to make it.

This time he was going to reach the dormer—he was already on a level with it—and grab around the edge and clutch the sill and haul himself in and . . . and . . .

Except that now he could see the window, and it wasn't open like his uncle had said it would be. It was locked, and there wasn't anybody there. He turned his head slowly over his shoulder toward the sun porch. Empty. Closed. Locked.

It wasn't fair. Clinging to the edge of the dormer now, he began to breath hotly and vent little sounds of frustration. Uncle Luce had promised. He couldn't hang on until his mother got home, and he couldn't go back. He couldn't break the window because the effort of that would surely throw him off the roof. He couldn't do anything but hang on. And he couldn't do that for long.

But he did. Forever and ever.

Or so it seemed. And then the Atkinsons' grandchildren appeared, Julie and Carl, hiding behind the blue spruce at the property line. They were only four and five, but they were probably hiding from Barry, who was seven.

Joey started to shout.

He didn't make much sense, but then he didn't have to. The Atkinson children were looking, pointing. Fascination would yield to a need to communicate this phenomenon, and Barry must be close at hand. The Witherses' Llewellyn, Rocky, was barking two doors down. He should have hollered before. The whole neighborhood would be out soon.

And then there was a click—the analogue of that little doom he had heard half a roof and all of an eternity away outside the sun porch—and the rush of a sash going up.

"Time for lunch," Uncle Luce said soothingly.

18

Carolyn turned the Escort toward Franklin Village.

Mazey bird to tower. I have been a negligent mother lo these many nights. Joey, I'm coming home.

Half a dozen times she had been on the verge of calling him from the office the day after the party. Out of the devastation of that dismal afternoon and the wellspring of consolation and direction that Luce had provided, she had backed off as she knew she must, had relinquished Joey to an upbringing she could not provide. But the mother in her had balked every hour of the succeeding day, and if it hadn't been for the trauma of Millman's walking in on her while she was entertaining the walls she might well have yielded. And when she had found her baby

138

alive and breathing that evening—sleeping, actually—the house unscarred, the carpets unbloodied, she knew she had done the right thing.

"He sat in it," Lucien responded in a satin whisper to her only question. "He didn't like it, but he sat in it."

It was like labor pains. She was giving birth all over again. This time by omission. By surrogate. And she must preserve her rhythm, her breathing, while Joey left her body, her yoke, and the cord was severed again.

Mater absentia.

And in the morning (she was always stronger in the mornings) he was still sleeping, the pile of presents undisturbed. So she had done the hard thing again, leaving for work without so much as breaking out a new box of his very favorite Fruit Roll-Ups as a clue to how hard this was for her. Joey, I love you very much, but you're limping through life and I'm going to back off for a while. Say that, and she was finished. Say that, and he would know it was just another experiment, a crusade she couldn't maintain. He would not come to grips with his fears and isolation then. There would be no male figures in his life to show him how. Mommy would be back. Crippled, wrong-sex, frightened Mommy would stump back in on her crutches to aid and abet his unreasonable weaknesses.

The day that followed had been hell. One big grinning silence. Sinswicki hadn't even been picking his nose when she drove in. He was standing there, smiling intently, like he'd been waiting forever for this one moment of supercilious exhibition. The rest of the looks ranged from pitying to arch sneer. Walter's was the only one that didn't have judgment in it, but even there she could see that his jury was deliberating her stability. And Millman swaggered around like the cock of the walk (*prick* of the walk, actually). She fluttered around the plant, trying not to look intimidated, but she was. And the worst part of it . . . was that she couldn't talk to Frank.

Joey had his arms around her before she was all the way out of the car, and she gave him one uncompromising squeeze and then began patting him, saying, "Well, my little man is glad to see me, and I'm certainly glad to come home and find he's taken care of things for us," but she was thinking, This 'is bad . . . he's clinging to me like I'm a float ring from the *Titanic*.

"You didn't say good-bye this morning, Mommy."

Here we go.

"Or yesterday."

Lord, help me, Jesus.

"You didn't say good night yesterday either."

"I know, I know I didn't say good night yesterday," she soothed. "But you were asleep, and it wasn't that important. Was it?" He was looking hurt. "I mean I wanted to, but it wasn't as important as you getting your sleep."

"Yes it was."

She brushed his sandy hair back and took in his amber eyes as glistening as raw egg yolks. "You can't always have me right by your side, hon. What about when you go away?"

"I'm not going away."

"No, not for a long time, of course. But what if you go to camp or decide to stay overnight at a friend's?"

"I don't like camp, and I don't have—"

Luce was standing in the doorway to the garage, a fly swatter in his hand.

Carolyn smiled dryly. "Chasing dinner?"

"Dessert. Dinner was a foregone conclusion the minute I ran over a cat on the way to Farmer Jack's."

"As long as it has ketchup on it, Joey will eat it."

"I'm not hungry," Joey said petulantly.

"Something happen?" she asked Lucien as soon as they were alone.

His lean face looked absolutely commanding. "Wasn't that the idea?"

She wanted to say, You know what I mean, but Joey was back in the doorway.

"You know what?" she said. "I've been dying to see what your presents are. It's been two days, sport! You've broken the Guinness world record for patience. What did you get?"

"I didn't open them."

Again she looked at Luce.

"I hate them!" Joey exploded. "I hate birthday parties. I wish you'd never given me one!"

Lucien said, "I think your mother needs a few minutes to

140

shake the dogs off her ankles before she reenters our world, Joey. Why don't you go watch a little television?"

Carolyn's eyes flashed wide at the kitchen table. Then she looked at Joey, glowering at his uncle, and at Lucien, firm and self-assured, and she knew this was it: the old moment of truth with the three of them. It wasn't going to be a tug-of-war; if she opened her mouth now, it was all over as far as Lucien's control over Joey. She looked down at the floor, tried to smile a little.

It was a very long ten seconds.

She waited until Joey had trudged all the way upstairs on the way to his room, and then she said, "Hooray for me. A month ago I couldn't have done that. I would've felt like shit."

"Congratulations."

"I still feel like shit."

"An apron string gets untied, it always makes a mother feel like shit. Would you like a martini dry enough to pucker your navel?"

"What happened today?"

He bent slowly and kissed her on the mouth just lingeringly enough to part her lips. It was the first time he had kissed her in daylight, she realized, and somehow she felt faintly outraged. Here, in her own kitchen—Frank's and Joey's and Carolyn's kitchen—her brother-in-law was arousing her.

"If I tell you the details every day, you'll light up like an emotional billboard for Joey," he said. "He doesn't need that kind of sympathy. He and I understand each other. He may think he hates me, but deep down he knows that what I'm trying to do is right. And if you and I maintain confidence in it, he'll eventually accept the inevitable task of growing up. Trust me."

Trust me. Cheap words, followed by cheaper actions. His sensitive hands were cupping her breasts, drawing her up. It was a seduction scene from a B-grade movie, but she was stirred by it. As with anything Lucien did, there was a note of mockery in it, the playing out of a satire that made everything inevitable. He had his hands behind her knees now, feeling deeply into her thighs as they came up, seeming already to penetrate. The satirical element kept him just beyond reach. And that made her want him—want *something* she could never totally possess. She had been wrong about the sex becoming therapeutic and

141

businesslike. It wasn't going to be that way. It was going to get hotter and hotter. *Trust me.* He had her pants off, her legs up and spread, and he was driving her with elemental intensity. *Trust me.* She had given her body and her son. How much more trust could she have?

Joey heard her coming up twenty minutes later, and he wanted to ignore her, to show her how hurt he was, but he couldn't. She brushed his hair back and kept right on talking to him about what a wonderful boy she thought he was and how she hoped he understood how much she loved him and that was why she wanted him to do what his uncle wanted him to do, because a boy couldn't learn how to be a man from his mother.

So she knew.

At least she knew about the chair. Uncle Luce had said they wouldn't tell her about the roof and things like that. After he had let Joey back in, he said the phone had rung and that was why he couldn't come to the window. And he said it was stupid that Joey had yelled at the Atkinsons' grandchildren, because if an adult had gotten involved in it, it would have gotten back to his mother, and then—the next time—they would have to use the chair instead of substituting something to prove Joey's bravery. Joey wanted to tell his mother anyway, to throw himself against her knees and say how scared he had been when he started to slip on the roof and that if she didn't make Uncle Luce move away something awful might happen to him.

But she knew about the chair, and that was awful. That was the most awful thing of all. If she didn't care about the chair, how could she care about the roof?

"It would be very hard for me to raise you without him, Joey," she said. "He came here reluctantly, at my request, and I hope he intends to stay. The truth is he's apt to go soon and suddenly. Your father told me he was like that as a young man, that he came and went without a hello or good-bye. But he's older now, matured, and he's welcome here as long as he wants to stay. I hope you understand that, Joey. We need him."

She needs him, he thought.

"Now, what are we going to do about these presents?" she asked in a confiding whisper.

He thumped his foot on the bed rail peevishly. Her lips pushed forward a little then, like they did when she teased him or when he told her a lie and she saw through it.

"My, my, what will we tell all those nice people who spent their time and money picking things out for you?" she asked. "They'll be disappointed when they don't get a thank-you note."

He thought about it a minute. "We can send them thank-you notes anyway."

"I suppose that would do. But . . . you've got to mention what they gave you in a thank-you note."

He put his hands in his pockets.

She glanced around the room. "Maybe we could just peek a little—just to see, so we can write the notes."

He had shoved all the presents in the closet, but she looked under the bed first. She wasn't like Uncle Luce—a finder, someone who knew right away where little boys hid and where presents would be. Then she looked behind the door and behind his bookcase. Finally she opened the closet.

"Aha. Yes. Here we go." And she began hauling them out. "Heavy, heavy, hangs over your head. What do you suppose . . . what do you suppose is in this one?"

It was long and red with a white bow. He took it, shook it. Light. She read the card aloud. Melissa Spengler. Ugh! She was always writing notes to boys and planning parties. He bet she wrote a note this time, too.

" 'Dear Joey,' " his mother read. " 'I hope you like these and can wear them some time.' "

He tore the paper off slowly; it was practically like tinfoil and it came apart in bits.

"Ties," he said. "I hate ties."

His mother laughed. "The ties that bind. There's one girl who thinks you've grown up."

He didn't understand that, but she was handing him a second gift—this one blue with no ribbon—and he unwrapped it in a single swipe.

"Ocean Pacific," he said with a little more enthusiasm as he raised a green polo shirt. "Sweet."

The next one was an Encyclopedia Brown book and an action figure of Han Solo, no doubt bought on a child's budget with a child's allowance, but the next was a Walkman and the one after that was a Nash skateboard. The skateboard had no card with it. "I'm afraid someone's gone overboard on the spending side," his mother said. And then she gave him her gift, which was a tape recorder and a lot of clothes, and Uncle Luce's, which was a microscope. A microscope! Joey tried not to look pleased but his mother's lips were puckered out again and he grinned briefly. Then came a big green box with red ribbon. "No card again," his mother said, but he could tell by the little dryness in her throat that she had noticed the red and green and was thinking of the picture he had drawn of Chip with snakes coming out of his mouth. She had asked him about it that first Christmas and the Christmas after that, as if the red and green wrappings on presents would always remind her.

"Got to be a card in here somewhere," she said, going through the closet.

And when she turned back he had the thing open and he could hear her gasp.

"It's just Snake Mountain, Mom," he said.

She recovered in an instant. "Now who would give you that?"

"Don't you like it?"

"It's peachy." She exhaled a little laugh. "All I meant was it's too expensive for a birthday present. A few of your friends must have gone in together. You can ask when you get back to school on Tuesday."

"Tuesday? That's when school starts again?"

She knelt down beside him. "I've been meaning to say something to you about that, Joey. I mean, I know the party must have soured you a little on seeing all the kids again, but if you don't get right in there the first day, you'll make them think that what happened is a bigger deal than it was. I'm not telling you that nobody will tease you, but I can promise you that the best way to handle it is to ignore any remarks and act like nothing ever happened. I really do understand how you feel, hon—believe me, I do—but we've both got to stick it out, face people. I've been wrong to protect you like I have. So come Tuesday I'm going to let you walk on your own, and I want you to go without any argument. Okay?"

144

"I want to go to school, Mom."

She looked at him as though she must not have heard correctly. Surely he had said he did *not* want to go. Ever since vacation he'd been saying he didn't want to go back.

"I *want* to, Mom."

"Well . . . good. I mean, you should."

He was thinking about Uncle Luce. If he stayed home, he and his uncle would be alone in the house. If he went to school, and took it slow coming home, there wouldn't be time for anything to happen before his mother returned.

"Good," she repeated, staring at him. "Melissa Spengler was right, you are growing up. Look out, world, here you come."

"I'd rather go to work with you, though."

"Well, I've got wonderful news for you. Do you remember where we always go on Labor Day—the day before you start back to school?"

"The company picnic," he said as if she had announced his engagement to Melissa Spengler.

"That bad, huh?"

"I thought you didn't like to go to those picnics."

"Me? Naw. I *want* to go. Look out, world, here I come."

Joey was right, of course. She hated the picnics too. The company bought the beer and the hot dogs, and for a couple of hours they stood around a grungy grill on Belle Isle and pretended they had something more in common than making a living. Frank had loved it and firmly believed that they really were a family with common interests, efforts, and goals. The company owed its success to that attitude, he had maintained. Carolyn understood that it made good business sense. But she still hated it. That was why she wouldn't succeed where Frank had. That was why he had been stable and secure, a part of a successful family, whereas she barely spoke to her father, could not discipline her children, and at age thirty-six was both a divorcée and a widow.

Stop it! she told herself en route with Joey in the car. Once they all get plastered you'll look like Lee Iacocca to them. She hadn't looked like Lee Iacocca four years ago when Millman got drunk and made a pass at her, though. It was no big deal, except that she knew he hadn't done it *despite* the fact that she was Frank's wife but *because* she was. The big egotist. He wanted to cuckold the boss. He hadn't given her a second look when she was just the secretary, younger and available.

"Look, Mom."

Joey was pointing at a freighter upbound on the Detroit River. You could see it off the head of the island as they took the causeway to the bridge on the American side of the river, a big ore boat with a smug look on its bow and wheelhouse as it sidled toward the channel on the Canadian side, smoke sliding out of its stack like toothpaste.

"I see it," she said. I see it. That was why he needed a man. She never knew what to say when he got enthused about something boys seemed to like. I see it. Yup, that's a ship all right . . . wonder if she's gonna sink. How did you exploit a little boy's interest? What did you say to develop his interest in *things*? She didn't know what she should be interested in. I wonder how many people are on board? I wonder if any of them have wives and children and little houses in Toledo with azalea bushes all around? Whatever she imagined seemed to feminize the conversation.

She wished Luce had come. He had been working in his studio and said he might come later, but she doubted he would. Despite what she had told Joey about his uncle maturing from his free-spirit days, he hadn't really. Frank had said you could have breakfast with Luce and then not see him again for six months. No good-bye. No plans. Sometimes he would leave so abruptly you'd find a cup of half-finished coffee on his desk or the radio on in his room, his personal effects still scattered about. She might lose him any time. She might wake up and—presto— gone! It wouldn't pay to become emotionally involved with him, and she didn't think she would—not for herself, anyway. But what about her dependency on him for Joey? What would she do without that?

The island, Detroit's bid for urban sanity, was already looking like a staging area for Sodom and Gomorrah. Wisps of pearl-gray smoke stirred from hibachis and Coleman stoves around which stood beer-can-fisted vets and bikini-clad store clerks

146

tanned well south of their navels. Homemade signs on sweating coolers staked out territory, and picnic tables were drawn into circles like green Conestoga wagons. Normally you could ride the perimeter road with your eyes closed and tell by the smell where you were and what time of day it was. The deeply dredged-up river smell washing over the head of the island early in the morning, the clean cool mist of the fountain on a midday breeze, the dankness of the canals late on a hot afternoon, the yacht club serving prime rib at twilight, an evening's collection of organic garbage marinating along the beach—these were the countersigns of a grand tour. But today it was Kingsford briquettes and Match Light from shore to shore, heating up for the charred Coneys of the carnivorous and the barbecued-rib recipes of a thousand reunions.

Joey studied the freighter (silently now) when they rounded to the Windsor side of the island. A flotilla of bicycles, pedaling, gliding, pedaling, as if in concert to invisible currents, slowed them at the Dossin Great Lakes Museum, and then they were at the ball fields and the shaded picnic area they had used since the first Whitehall company picnic over a decade ago. Millman's red pickup was there already, along with a dozen hatchbacks, campers, and sedans. A yellow Frisbee lay on the wind, shimmering as elegantly as the bicycles now floating toward the lighthouse off the point.

"There's Bill Lunden's little girl, Joey," Carolyn said as they were unloading their cooler. "I think her name is Jennifer."

Joey gave her a look as white and blank as a marshmallow, and she knew he wasn't going to leave her side. What the hell, I'll just lean on his little head when they start to frost me. Be nice to have family backing. Mother and son at the emotionally disadvantaged table.

There wasn't any way she was going to feel less than a freak today, and she knew it—knew, too, that she might as well laugh about it. Hell, she had enough experience with her emotions to know that that was what she built her best fortifications out of. Laughter. Cynical, give-it-all-up laughter. Chuck-it-in-baby-you'll-feel-better-in-the-morning levity.

"Hello, Carolyn!"

Bonnie Blish calling. A nice formal hello to start things off.

So that was how it was going to be. Bellowed, yet. Like she might be hard of hearing. The sick lady. Talks out loud to her dead husband and thinks it's just an internal monologue.

Carolyn laughed, waved, said something inane.

They all came around like they'd rehearsed it. A nod, an ingratiating smile, a banality. Paying lip service to the pecking order. Staring a little too intently, eyes brightening perhaps at the too-easy laugh, an alcohol laugh, a Valium laugh. Even Joey knew how fake it all was, shrinking uncomfortably behind her the way he did.

The worst of it was the meal, though. Because when the tables were set and everyone seated and more or less waiting, she was supposed to make a speech. Frank had always made a speech. He had said wonderful things about labor and commerce and togetherness. But not Carolyn. Carolyn likened the sudden hush before eating to church communion and made some ass-hole remark about "God's hors d'oeuvres." I'm just killing them with my humor! Get out from under the table, Joey, maybe I'll do a little soft-shoe in the pickle relish.

And then Millman came up with the snappy, "Good bread, good meat, thank God, let's eat!" and everyone laughed.

Walter Barths started talking to her therapeutically after that, imparting an aura of dignity to the whole farce, and she just listened, following his lead, and that was how she got through the meal and how she survived the general table talk afterward and also—unhappily—how she got into the softball game.

Millman and Barths picked sides and she went to the latter by default. She had always been a terrible baseball player. The ball came at her like a moth, blurring and jumping all over the place. She held the bat cross-handed and minced around the place as if it were an open manhole. They put her on a foul line with a catcher's mitt, and she stood there literally with one foot in the game, one foot out. The thing that made it humiliating, though, was that Millman pitched.

He had thrown sissy stuff to the other women (except for Sandy Raddler, who had powdered one over the left fielder's head last year), but when Carolyn came up he got real cute. Hardly anyone had made an out—the scores in their annual games often topped fifty runs—but now he bore down with malice aforethought, giving it a lot of motion, spinning the ball, changing speeds, coming at her from the side. As if she needed help to look foolish. She went out on three pitches the first time, reaching for the third like she had a butterfly net just before it hit the dirt in front of the plate. Agnes Predamowicz—madam umpire—called a tick on a ball she came within a foot of the second time up and everyone applauded sarcastically. But Carolyn missed the next pitch by at least a yard, and as she walked away she caught sight of Joey hiding behind the backstop as if it wore a skirt. It seemed like all she was doing was walking. Walking to and away from the plate and carrying an absurdly useless piece of lumber. When she trudged up for her third spectacular, Millman waved the outfielders back.

"I guess we ought to give you four strikes under the circumstances," he sneered.

"Pitch the damn ball," Carolyn ordered, and whereas she had struck out like a jellyfish with a stick the first pair of ups, this time she went out swinging like an ax murderer in a vacuum.

That was when she saw Lucien sitting at the top of the bleachers. She saw him because she noticed that Joey had moved to the other side of the backstop where he could huddle on the ground away from the stands. Wearily she clambered up the empty seats to the top.

"Abner Doubleday sucks," she said, "and so does Millman."

Lucien smiled wanly. "Millman would be the pitcher."

"I really don't care about striking out, I mean I really don't care at all." She banged her knuckle off her knee. "It's just that Mr. Cool out there is bent on making me look like his soiled jockstrap again."

"Again?"

"Silly me, I guess I never mentioned that I'm just an ineffective, waffling, president-under-siege who can't face her union rep and who everyone thinks is—" She focused on him for the first time, shook her head. "I guess you can tell I'm having problems."

Lucien said as languidly as before, "Millman would be the union rep."

"I guess I ought to thank him for curing Joey of wanting to hang around me all the time," she said, waving coyly at the backstop.

Joey waved back. Once. Quickly.

Freddie Osmond popped up then, and she had to take the field. Millman's team had its biggest inning—eighteen runs. Millman himself homered twice. Carolyn was standing at the remotest point on the foul line, singing "Take me out of the ball game" to herself, when she had the godless luck of having the second homer hit past her. If she had conceived that a batter could actually aim the ball, she would have felt worse for the event. As it was, by the time she was done prancing after it, had picked it up and jogged it back within lobbing distance, Millman had circled the bases twice in derision.

"Buy me some Valium and arsenic . . . "

Something hostile and surreal was happening on her side now. She could see it in her teammates' haughty glances. Even bucolic Norma Sweeney folded her fat arms in disgust and Sandy Raddler sat on her glove. It was as if civilization had suddenly come to judgment in the innings of an asinine game. And now she really dreaded going up to the plate again. Dreaded it more when a rally started in their half of the frame and the bases loaded up and emptied and loaded up again and no one had been out yet. Maybe if she didn't move, they'd overlook her. But Joey was watching, dammit. She couldn't quit with him watching. Someone handed her the bat. Sudden silence outlined her. Silence so keen you could hear every step this time. She was walking on wood chips, but it sounded like potato chips. *Crunch . . . crunch . . . crunch—*

"Pinch hitter."

Lucien said it. He came up quietly behind her and took the bat from her hand.

"Hey!" Millman hollered.

Articulate union negotiator. Hey.

"You're ahead by eleven!" Freddie yelled. "Give us a break."

"We're ahead by eleven," Harold Winnaker repeated from second base.

Lucien settled into the batter's box, a leftie. It didn't seem to be an issue with him.

Millman scowled but prepared to pitch. Prepared. Because he had wanted to pitch to Carolyn, to humiliate her again, but now he couldn't, and so he would pull out all the stops on this intruder, fingering the ball for the right grip, stepping off the mound in a lunge as he windmilled and fired hard at the plate. And what happened next was equally unexpected. Because Lucien walked into the delivery, ripping the bat through the pitch and driving it straight back at Millman. It was a ferocious line drive and it caught him on the hip, handcuffed him, and spun him down.

The afternoon turned really ugly then, and it was a funny thing because Carolyn couldn't stop feeling better and better as Millman came hobbling in all threats and vileness while Lucien just smiled his mirthless smile and apologized in that magic voice of his that said everything and nothing at the same time. Almost everyone seemed outraged at Lucien, and Carolyn loved it. Take that, grinners all. The game was over, the picnic soured, the afternoon mercifully coming to an end. Oh, joy. And the other thing she noticed that put a cap on it. One last bit of redemption, vindicating her to the only person who mattered. Was that really admiration for his uncle she saw shining reluctantly from Joey's eyes?

19

Tuesday. Joey's turn.

He hadn't seen a single classmate since the party, and now he would face them all. But that was better than what he faced alone at home with Uncle Luce. They hadn't been alone since the day he had gone out on the roof. Bad enough that his mother had left for work ten minutes before he left for school. It would have been twenty if he had waited till the regular time. Twenty minutes for the conversation to get dangerous again. Yesterday Uncle Luce had gotten even with the people who were making fun of his mother. He had done it in a neat way that made them unsure it had happened, but Joey knew better than anyone that it was deliberate. Uncle Luce had been a clever boy, and when you grew up clever you got even more clever. And strong. And you could find things. And there was no hiding from you.

"A little early to be going to school, isn't it?" his uncle had asked.

(No hiding anything.)

"I think we go earlier this year," Joey had said, and the way his uncle smiled made him start to crawl inside. As if a lie was wonderful. As if it kicked down the door to the game they played. As if Joey had suspended all the rules.

"Why don't you take your skateboard?" his uncle had asked softly. "That would get you there faster."

And home faster, too.

Joey left without it. Left on a dead run. But it was a long way, and he slowed to a walk at the curve in the road. He had taken the bus in kindergarten and first grade. Last year he had taken the bus or walked with his mother and the Witherses. Now he could walk it alone, Mommy said. And he would walk it home, too. But very slowly.

He didn't see anybody from his class until he got to Kohn's Confectionery Shoppe. That was a block from school. Then he saw Alicia Morgan chewing a lemon Gummy Worm and watching him from the steps. She always looked at everyone like they were standing in her private universe, but he stared back and she spun a quarter turn away after a few seconds. She did that to show anger or to hide a smile, usually. He wasn't sure which one it was this time.

Everybody pretty much looked at him with the same scorn as he passed through the doors and got in the third grade line. But the excitement and distraction of the first day back were going to save him. He would get the three-second stare while they remembered and sized him up, and then Andrew Harrington would step on the back of someone's shoes or Billy Duquesne would make farting noises and no one would pay any attention to him anymore.

Mrs. Ardmore, tanned and smiling, was at the door wearing a green carnation when the safety brought them to the room. Joey had met her at last spring's orientation, and she seemed to take a special interest in him. He thought it was because she had been told he didn't adjust well and because he had drawn the picture of Chip. All the teachers knew he was a loner. He thought he might like her anyway.

There were apples cut out of red construction paper with their names on them, one to a desk, and she sat them down and told them how good it was to see them and what they were going to do that morning right up until it was time to go home at eleven-fifty.

Eleven-fifty!

Because of course they only had a half day of school—everyone knew that—just like it had said in the bulletin the school mailed out, just like they had discussed at the spring open house, just like it was every year. Everyone knew. Except Joey. So now he was pretty surprised (shocked, actually) to find out he got to go home early and be with Uncle Luce.

He had never liked the glare and the hardness and the coldness and the dryness of Formica, tile, and green chalkboards, but now the room got rosier and rosier, because it was a sanctuary, a sanctuary, and Joey didn't have a doubt in the world about how wonderful it was. The murmur sounded like friendly voices at the end of a long, dark tunnel. He could see the light, hear the voices, but he couldn't quite reach them. And he was running out of time. I'm late, I'm late! screamed the white rabbit inside him. And won't Uncle Luce be savage! But that was the wrong fairy tale. Because the deadline was eleven-fifty, and that gave him ten minutes to get home where at the stroke of twelve he would be turned into—turned over to—the chair! No, no, that was wrong, too. What was the right fairy tale?

"Joey?"

Oh-oh. Mrs. Ardmore was calling him—had been calling him—to tell him to turn the lights off and pull the drapes. He hadn't been listening, but he hurried to do it now, and the room started to get really crazy then, because it was already ten-twenty—where had all the time gone?—and kids were moving about, laughing and chattering as they went to sit up front, and the slide projector was shining a picture of Colorado on the screen while the white light coming from underneath shone up Mrs. Ardmore's face, making her nostrils look really big and throwing huge shadows on the ceiling. The picture of Colorado was from her vacation. She had about a hundred of them. The kids watched the slides, but Joey kept looking at the clock. Ten-thirty already. He wouldn't go home, he decided. He just wouldn't go. So where would he go? Think. And now it was ten-forty. He would hang around the park in back of the church until maybe four-thirty and then start home. Great! Who's afraid of the big, bad wolf? Not I! Wrong, wrong, wrong. He was very afraid. Because now Mrs. Ardmore was calling his name again and asking him to open the drapes, and he did, and that was why his blood stopped moving, because it was five minutes to eleven and right outside the room some very, very black clouds were boiling like mad.

So he wasn't going to hang around the park.

Not unless the storm passed. Rain, rain, go away. . . . This was punctuated by a torn sky—white wound blazing—and a long chain of concussions. *Tick, tock, tick, tock,* eleven-thirty and all is hell. Joey moved about with agitation as the storm grew. He wanted to erase the boards, dust the almost-brand-new-used-only-once erasers, empty the nearly-virgin-screwed-only-once-by-a-skinny-Eberhard pencil sharpener. He wanted to stay forever. But no one lives happily ever after. Eleven-forty-one. Oceans were falling outside. Lights and laughter inside. Joey was somewhere in between. A frenzied moth palpitating between panes of glass. Half an inch from destruction, half an inch from salvation. Only, the panes of glass were really a watch crystal and he was trapped inside waiting for the tick that would spring the case open and deliver him to—

Eleven-forty-nine!

"Children, we can't let you go home in this storm if you're a walker. Bus people may line up. No pushing, please. Walkers, please sit down."

Salvation.

Sanctuary.

A stitch in time saves—

"Oh. Joey. Your uncle is waiting for you at the door."

The correct fairy tale was Little Red Riding Hood.

Joey didn't appreciate the full insidiousness of it, but he

understood the journey and the peril and the fact that he had been intercepted by the wolf. His uncle just happened to have the skateboard and it was raining midnights and traffic would murder anyone who tried to skateboard home on the yellow line in the middle of the road—which was exactly what he was going to do, because *he would do anything to keep from sitting in the chair*.

What he didn't appreciate was that the wolf (conjugated: *lupus, lupine, Lucien*) was going to chug along behind in his black Fury with his brights on just to make it tougher on oncoming traffic, and so that he could whip up and rescue him—the strange, weird, isolationist kid who might do or say anything—in the unlikely event that a police car appeared.

"Right on the yellow line, Joey, like a tightrope. Nonstop. Even if a car passes. Even if cars pass you both ways at the same time. And when you come to an intersection, you can't stop."

"What about the traffic lights?"

"If you stop, it doesn't count. Crossing against the lights takes a lot of courage, but it's dangerous. Are you sure you want to do this?"

He nodded reluctantly in the light from the dash. It was so dark you needed the lights on, and the rain flickered like tinsel in the high beams.

"Ah, nephew. One of these days I'll choose something so frightening to you that you'll pick the chair. And then you'll be a *real* boy and we'll all live happily ever after."

That was Pinocchio.

Joey got out at the first intersection. The light had just turned amber, and he scampered across, hitting the yellow line on the other side with the skateboard. He wasn't all that good at it. Oh, he had used the Witherses' board before, and like most kids under sixteen he had an instinct for running computer games and employing anything with wheels, but still he didn't have that much control. Especially in the dark. Especially in the rain. The street shimmered with reflections and oily voids that smeared objects and scattered shadows. Already his clothes were pasted to his thin frame, the rain driving on his face and on the backs of his outflung hands in a hurting way. Thunder boomed malevolently at discovery of so fragile and foolish a

mortal running the storm's gauntlet. It was the audio counter-
part of his uncle's expression of deadness and joy.

He had to concentrate very hard. The yellow line . . . the
yellow line. Most of the time he could barely see it. But he could
follow it, somehow, in the absolute darkness where the road
dipped. He could catch it in bits and pieces in the glare of lights
(the old now-you-see-it-now-you-don't). And in the lightning
he could glimpse it vividly—the lightning which for one terrible
millisecond seemed to dry him out and crackle down his spine,
exploding with bowel-ramming force and grumbling away. It
was a serve-and-volley storm: flashes that tore scabs off the soul,
pulverizing thunder that left bone fragments in the flesh. Joey
sped on, small and insignificant and hammered, expending all
his energy in a kind of mad rush that left no statement, no sound,
though on a quiet day you would have heard the roaring of
plastic wheels on asphalt, the chatter of bearings, the pad of a
thrusting foot, the oscillating voice of a child in terror.

A car came at him, flirting with the curves, touching a soft
shoulder here, violating the line between the legs of the road
there. The driver was guessing where the lane was or perhaps
driving a memory. The headlights owled through the inkiness
and blazed over him, and he would have veered off but at the
last instant he heard the second car, felt it swishing alongside
him going the other way. Both cars were honking frantically, a
twin Doppler effect marking the symmetry of a certainty, that
there wasn't a breath of margin for error. But the thing that got
him were the lights.

The traffic lights.

Nonstop, or it doesn't count, Uncle Luce had said, and he
knew the old black Fury was there perhaps a block or so behind.
He caught the first light on the green, and the next, but the one
after that was red.

He tried to slow, to time it, but it hung there like a drop of
blood in the storm. Cars swished in both directions beneath it.
Lights were coming up behind him, too, silvering the rain in
front of him. He thought it might be his uncle, swooping close
for the final judgment: You stopped! We'll have to use the chair
now. And that was when they came to him again. The pictures.
Right there with all the thunder and the downpour and the

157

hurtling cars and the blanching yellow line, they pushed into his brain unbidden, coming, he knew, from the chair. The rain was pounding through his body, filling his shoes like lead weights, and he was sinking into the street just as his father had sunk into a lake. He saw his father reaching up to his uncle in the canoe, and his uncle trying to get him to grab the paddle. The paddle kept twirling and dipping in his uncle's agile hands—now you see it, now you don't—so fast, so fast. And then he realized that Uncle Luce wasn't trying to get his father to grab the paddle. He was trying to *keep* him from grabbing the paddle.

Uncle Luce was helping his father drown.

And Joey was drowning.

He had almost come to a stop, but now he surged out into the intersection, gliding awkwardly into a chorus line of lights. The first behemoth slid by too startled to react, but the next swerved violently, and another dug into its brake linings, and then another. The will-o'-the-wisp human flesh of a small boy pirouetted and dipped with death as a partner. It was a *danse macabre*, and the careening coffins somehow saw him, missed him. There was the single brief dismay of a car horn sounding, and then the whole company seemed to collapse upon the stage with one great cry of calamity.

But a small boy escaped.

20

"Name it. Red Lobster, Chuck Muer's, London Chop House—my boy *walked* to school today and *I* let him, so that's two reasons to celebrate. But no McDonald's, okay?"

"A and W," Joey said.

Carolyn rolled her eyes. "No restaurants that are more than fifty percent ceramic tile. I want to be able to tell the dining room from the john."

"Chi-Chi's."

"Stucco and porcelain. I'm offering you chandeliers and you're asking for gas lights. Gas, period. Okay, okay, Mazola corn oil, here we come."

She decided to take the van for no other reason than she felt expansive. It had been a red-letter day at work—the best since she had threatened to sell out to Sony. No one seemed to remember that she was the great white mother who spoke to the dead, and Millman had limped around like a tin man with a rusted gonad. He didn't get much sympathy either. The more ominous the noises he made about a possible lawsuit, the more everyone was amused. All in all, the grins had been foolish and easy grins today. A lot of stress never happened.

"Where's Uncle Luce?" she asked.

Joey shrugged.

"Can't go without Luce. My hero. My assassination batsman. He's definitely a cause célèbre—" She saw from Joey's long face that it wasn't the best news he'd heard this week, and she gave him a soft right cross that stopped short of his chin. "Listen, sport, we haven't been this close to rock stable in a long time, and the team is kind of thin without him, don't you think? I mean, we're a family and we've got to count heads morning, noon, and night or else 'together' becomes 'alone' again—listen to the girl. I should've given that speech yesterday at the company picnic."

"I don't know where he is. He was pounding on something a while ago."

"Pounding?" She looked at him carefully again and saw that he looked washed out. It wasn't just the forever paleness of his face or that flatness of his mouse eyes in the dimness of the living room, it was his voice. Deeply fatigued. The day had been a strain on him. How was school? hovered on her tongue, but she didn't want an answer in this mood, didn't want to know. Not yet. "In his studio?" she asked about the pounding.

Joey nodded.

She went upstairs, called through the door. No answer. She tried the handle. Locked. It had annoyed her the first time she realized he had gotten a key made and unfrozen the ancient mechanism. But then she had thought, Well, why not? A man. An artist. Used to privacy all his life. Probably didn't want Joey messing around where he worked. She called again, then went downstairs to tell Joey that they would have to go alone. He took it well.

"Hey, some storm, huh?" she asked when they were on their way to Southfield in the van. She would have gone to the

Chi-Chi's in Bloomfield Hills but it was too close to the lake Frank had drowned in. Enchiladas and bad memories. The Southfield location shared parking with Toys 'Я' Us, but they weren't going to eat in the parking lot. "We lost power downtown for twenty minutes."

"It stormed out here, too."

"Yeah. Figured it did. What do you think of Mrs. Ardmore?"

"She's nice."

"Oooh. 'Nice.' Much better than 'old fossil.' " She glanced across, got the smile she wanted. "Any cretinous little scholars get on your case?"

"No one said anything." He answered hesitantly, not sure it was what she meant.

No, they didn't say anything. Just frosted the hell out of him. My little boy, so fragile, run over by a herd of Lilliputians on his first day of third grade.

He turned on the radio and she didn't try to engage him again until they were seated at a table and he had downed half a basket of corn chips.

"More ceramic tile," she said, tapping the inlay on the table. "I always feel like I'm eating off a cutting board here."

"Have some sauce, Mom." He pushed the jar forward that said HOT.

"Ah, you little rascal. Think I don't remember last time?"

"You ate it," he observed, with a glee that reminded her of Chip.

He ordered something minimal—the chips were what he wanted—and she had the Mazatlán. As soon as the waitress departed she said, very seriously, "Now, tell me everything that happened today."

He sat on his hands and straightened up and pretended to be searching the table for something as he rocked back and forth. "Mmm. We looked at pictures."

"And . . . ?"

"Mmm. We cut out our names."

"And . . . ?"

"Mmm. I got to pull the drapes."

It was a game they played where she got three *And*'s and he got three *Mmm*'s. She had never tried for a fourth, but today she sensed he was holding back, that there was something else hiding behind that innocent, high-pitched monotone. "And . . . ?"

He leaned sideways over the edge of the table, smacked his lips together. "Mmm." Almost a whimper. "Mmm. Uncle Luce drowned Daddy."

End celebration.

Things were caving in inside her. The imp of victory turned malignant in her soul, and she just looked at him for a moment with no emotion at all, thinking he hadn't said that, wishing he hadn't said that. But she knew he had, knew every nuance of what he felt—how awkward it was—and then the pain began to drip into her eyes, and her mouth worked in slow motion as she tried to deal with it.

"Joey, that's an awful . . . awful thing to say."

Fear came into his face, and she saw that he really believed what he had said and that he felt trapped by it. He was a sick, sick child.

"I saw it, Mommy."

"No, Joey. You couldn't see it. How could you see it?" She was clutching her napkin, balling it up like it contained the smear of accusation.

"I saw it in the pictures."

"You mean the ones you think come from the chair?"

He nodded.

"Is that what happened today? You sat in the chair?"

He shrank back in his seat, and a face she hadn't seen since he was four or five appeared, mouse-tiny, smooth, offering nothing. He had sat in the chair, and he hated it so much that now he was slandering the person who made him sit in it, who would go on making him sit in it if Joey couldn't discredit him. She should have expected this. But it was so cruel. He wasn't four, he was eight. He knew how mean false accusations were. How many times had she held him and they had discussed the slanders and gossips of others aimed at him.

"It's obvious you don't like your uncle, Joey."

"I did see it, though. I saw him take the paddle and push—"

"Stop it!" That got them a few stares, and she dropped her

162

voice. "This is very cruel—to me, to Uncle Luce, and to the memory of your father. You're talking *murder*, Joey, do you realize that? You're saying your uncle murdered your father, and that you know this because of pictures in your mind. At the very most, you want to believe it, Joey. But it's totally false, and you have no right to say it."

The expression on his face frightened her now, because she had never seen it before. He looked like a gremlin, lips stretched at the corners by some unidentifiable force, brow knit like chain mail. His eyes, riveted on the table edge, sought something far away, and she wondered for an instant if there could be anything to the pictures he said he saw. Of course not. They came out of his subconscious. He had an iron will no one knew was there but which she understood. His imagination was stronger than reality—not so unusual for a child—but he was past due to accept things as they were. Frank had called it simply "stubbornness." It was more than that, more even than the complexity of fantasies and strategies for survival that fed it, but Frank's prescription was valid. Joey had to step over the hurdles, be forced over if necessary.

Her eyelashes beat back tears but her voice was cold. "Joey, I want you to understand. Uncle Luce is in charge while I'm at work. That's not going to change. So you might as well quit fighting him and start cooperating."

The Mazatlán came then. A half dozen moist and tangy ingredients meticulously blended and served steaming to win the most discriminating palate. And she didn't taste a thing.

She found the clothes he had worn to school in the dryer along with his red Pumas just after Joey went to bed. She saw the new skateboard, streaked with rust where the wheel hardware had run, leaning upside down against the staircase a few moments later. Joey had gone skateboarding in the rain. In a thunderstorm. Why?

She resolved to ask him in the morning, if she remembered. And that almost guaranteed that she wouldn't. Because she hadn't remembered to ask him if he had found out at school who had given him the skateboard or Snake Mountain, and she almost never remembered to follow up on things that had to do

163

with relationships or talking with people. She was missing a gene or something. The same one her father and mother had been missing. It was the gene for *security* or some damn thing, and it meant she couldn't be decisive with people, couldn't stop looking at herself and feeling like she was forever dancing naked in front of the Supreme Court. So how could she think about others? She did better with children becuase they weren't as judgmental as adults and she didn't have to worry about what they thought of her. She just kept giving and giving to them, and pretty soon they were weak and helpless, if they were like Joey, or spoiled and tyrannical, if they were like Chip, and the only answer for them then was some sort of belated discipline or structure, and that was where she fell apart. She couldn't role-model that.

God bless Lucien.

Only she wondered what Joey had been doing out in the rain while Old Luce was guarding the nest. Maybe Joey was too much problem for both of them. Maybe he needed a psychiatrist. Doc, we've come to see you because Joey here went out in the rain. . . .

She went upstairs and took a hot bath. Lucien had come down while she and Joey were in the living room, and they had chatted briefly during an ABC special on the oil industry in Texas. Joey never moved the whole time but remained glued to the TV as if the state of the economy in Fort Worth was fascinating him. When Lucien retired to his studio she had sent Joey to bed.

She never knew when Luce was going to come to her room, but she felt tonight that she needed to talk to him, to get a little hysterical if she wanted, to decide about a psychiatrist for Joey. The arms around her wouldn't hurt, either.

He came more often than not, and she had resumed adding erotic touches to her nocturnal preparations. Her first husband had been a "boobs" man, Frank a garter-belt-and-nylons aficionado. Accents, she understood, turn men on. But Lucien didn't seem to care what the fetishes were. It didn't matter, except for the surprise itself, and he would fondle her at varying rates and with unpredictable force or tenderness but always climaxing with a passion that devoured her whole.

She snuggled into a lavender lace braselette and lay down on the bed. The lamp and the TV stayed on. Channel fifty gave her news at ten and Jackie Gleason reruns at ten-thirty. At eleven she switched to anchorman Bill Bonds on seven, but the same news she had seen an hour before now seemed ghoulish and cynical. She hit the remote OFF, doused the light, and slid under the covers.

It was late. He obviously wasn't coming. She loosened the lace braselette, freeing her breasts, thinking she would rouse herself in a few moments to take it off completely. And the next thing she knew she must have dozed off because she could smell the English Leather he sometimes wore, and she came all the way awake just as his silhouette knelt over and his hands feathered slowly down her kneck onto her breasts. He gripped them boldly, plucking her nipples erect with his lips.

"Howdy, stranger," she said, locking her arms around him.

He came down on her in the embrace she wanted, and for half a minute they just melted into one another. He always seemed to know. Take me soft, Lucien . . . take me hard, Lucien . . . feel me deep . . . tease me . . . console me . . . stroke me with your breath. . . .

Tonight she wanted to talk, and he waited.

"What are you working on?" she began.

"Extreme lust," he whispered sibilantly against her neck.

"Joey said you were pounding—no puns, please."

She could feel him smile. "I've discovered wood," he said. "Wonderful stuff."

"Yes. They tell me they're building houses out of it now."

"I'm not building a house."

She exhaled in a little rush as if to un-dam her frustration. "We tried to find you earlier to celebrate Joey's first day back. We ended up at Chi-Chi's."

"My loss. I was slumming at Taco Bell."

"It wasn't much of a celebration."

He didn't react, waiting for her to strengthen the cue.

"Lucien, I think maybe he needs to see a child psychiatrist."

"What did he do that was so terrible?"

"It's not what he does. He doesn't do anything. It's the way he thinks. The things he says he sees." She took a deep breath.

"I don't want you to be angry at him over this, but . . . he said he saw you drown Frank."

Not a ripple above her. Lucien remained dead calm.

"He was exorcizing his own ghosts, of course," she went on. "I don't know why exactly. Maybe because he's all twisted up inside about his father, and because you came along and made him sit in the chair the same way, and because he feels guilty about Frank's dying when they weren't getting along. Maybe he just tried to juxtapose everything. I don't know. That's why I think he needs help."

"Sounds like we've stirred up the conflicts that had to be stirred up."

"You don't think he needs a psychiatrist?"

"I don't see any change that would call for one, no. A psychiatrist would bring these things up for him anyway. It's a step forward, isn't it? You can pay someone sixty dollars an hour to listen to him, but then nothing gets solved until Joey can sort it out with his environment, with us. The psychiatrist is a digression, an intermediary for people who don't have a clue to the answers—and, of course, when you're all done with the commercial interference, you're left with its stigma. You still have to recover from the psychiatrist."

These were Frank's sentiments. Again. Maybe she *was* trying to hire out the problems that eventually had to be solved at home. She had always done that. Run away. Postponed. Transferred. Avoided. A psychiatrist couldn't live your relationships for you. No running away for Luce. He was the kind who stood fast. The pinch hitter.

"Joey must be giving you a very rough time," she said absently.

"That was to be expected. We had to let each other know how strongly we feel. Now he knows where I stand, and I know where he stands—and sits. It's all very candid."

"That's something I never was."

He stroked her shoulder. "If you want a failing, it's that you couldn't enforce."

Feeling sorry for myself again. Thank you, Lucien. "No, I'm not an enforcer."

166

"But now you're stronger, and he'll become stronger for it."

"How do you know?"

He ran his index finger slowly, stiffly down her front and slid it into her vagina.

"Because of the bold way you've opened yourself up."

It wasn't what she meant. How do you know Joey will get stronger? was what she meant.

"You're uninhibited now; you've never been so free and lusty," he said.

True. True! Even though he couldn't know. And to hell with all this motherhood. Joey was going to survive.

He had three fingers in her now. Three strong, sensitive artist's fingers playing nerve endings and succulent ridges, engorging her flesh as if each touch carried its own orgasm. His other hand flowed over her like a soft steam iron, raising goose bumps on her thighs, her hips, and stiffening her nipples till they ached. And he was stiff, his body, his erection, brushing down her wide-flung form while his tongue did what his fingers had done. She lost it all then—time, train of thought—all but an intense consciousness of rushing currents, surging euphorically, thawing, melting, liquefying whatever had been turgid and throbbing seconds before, abating with a final tingling at the extremities, the last involuntary outposts of pleasure, while his molten lava surged into her womb. Spent and adrift she lay welded to him, thinking dimly that nothing could be more perfect, and failing to attach any significance to the distant sneeze of a small refugee from the day's storm.

21

Three-eleven A.M. Joey awoke without urgency from the same dream that had been repeating for the past several hours. In it he wandered through empty rooms, opening doors and calling for his mother. Distant thunder came from somewhere within the house, only no matter where he went it never got any closer.

He blinked his eyes, knowing she wasn't there and that he was in his bed in his room in the night. Blinking got rid of the fuzziness that made shapes move in the dark. But when the room stopped ghosting, one shape remained.

It was blue and black. He couldn't see the eyes, but if they were in those sockets at all, they were staring down on him—had been staring down—and something that must have been a grin thinned a shadow beneath them. He thought he could just make out his uncle's quill-like hair flaring back, his face pan-cake white, his eyes diving like a hawk's. Uncle Luce had come to drag him along a sickeningly familiar, agonizingly repetitious, one-way, dead-end, doesn't-this-just-make-your-stomach-churn path to his favorite piece of furniture. All roads lead to the chair. It made a sticky lump start to throb in the back of his throat and a dry ache stab behind his eyes. He wanted to stamp his feet in frustration, but his legs were too rubbery, his feet too numb. And that was when he really woke up—right to the roots of his soul—because he realized suddenly who it really was.

Long-dead Chip.

Chip of the air.

All the way from the Erie marshes. A long crawl. Joey knew it was the marshes because he could smell the old reedbeds and all the bubbly stuff that got caught in the edges. Except that he had allergies and the first frost was a long way off yet and sometimes *any* sharp smell went wherever his imagination went. This one was English Leather, he discerned at last. Chip didn't wear English Leather. Chip wore nothing at all. And then the whisper came like a rope unwinding, and he knew that he had been right the first time.

"There is nothing as innocent as a little boy's sleep," his uncle said. "I can't tell you how sad I was when your mother told me what you accused me of."

Joey's heart was kicking through his chest under the sheet, and still there wasn't enough blood to reach his scalp or his feet. She had told! His mother whom he trusted and confided in. He opened doors and called her in his dreams, but she wasn't in the house anymore. There was just distant thunder in the house. And pounding. She was somewhere else. With Uncle Luce.

"Do you know what slander is, Joey?" The shadow loomed a magnitude larger. "It's when you tell lies about someone. Like saying your uncle murdered your father. That's a terrible lie." The whisper turned into a croak. "A real shocker."

Joey wanted to deny it, but even if he had gotten his mouth open, nothing would have come out.

"You've really upset your mother. I had to come here like

this because I didn't want to upset her more. And because I couldn't wait. Most of all because I couldn't wait, Joey. I want to hear it from your lips. I want you to tell me everything you told your mother. And anything you didn't."

Anything you didn't! But if Uncle Luce *believed* it was a lie, how could there be anything more than what he had made up?

"Tell me, Joey."

The words came now, tumbling like shallow water over sharp rocks, a soprano of desperation.

"I didn't want to see it. It was when I was on the skateboard in the rain. The chair showed me you in the canoe with the paddle and I didn't want to see it and all I said to Mom was that it showed me the pictures of you drowning Daddy. I didn't want to see it."

"The chair showed you this?"

"Yes."

"But you weren't sitting in it."

"It always shows me things like that. I know it was the chair."

"Fascinating." The word became darkness without a ripple. "Fascinating," he repeated, and again it was like a long-ago voice at the light switch saying, That's amazing. "Did you tell her about the skateboard?"

"No."

"But still, you told a terrible lie about me." Somber inclination of the head. "Saying I drowned my own brother. Maybe you saw me trying to help him with the paddle, not push him away from the canoe. I can understand your resenting my disciplining you, but I thought you realized I had your best interests at heart."

"It was the chair," Joey insisted plaintively.

The shadow receded a little. "Well, Joey, I can't say that your slander has hurt me. The truth is that it's shattered your mother's confidence in *you*. For her sake, I'm not going to tell her that you haven't been sitting in the chair or that you caused a traffic accident yesterday afternoon. But I hope you understand just what awful things might happen if you ever talk to her—or anyone—like that again."

Joey understood. He understood that his uncle and his

mother were too close for him to separate. He understood that he had no friends to talk to and that the world regarded him as a "troubled" child. He understood that the chair was alive and that it was far better to risk whatever his uncle put before him than to enter its unpredictable realm of horror. And he understood about his uncle and the pictures—because he had not told his mother about the paddle pushing his father away from the canoe, and he had not said anything about it just now. How could his uncle have thought that was what he saw, unless it had really happened?

22

Day two.

The third-grade line was rowdier than yesterday. Andrew Harrington was stepping on toes and making fake punches while he thumped his chest. Billy Duquesne had brought a rubber to school, taken from his father's closet, and most of the boys and all of the girls thought it was a balloon. Joey stood at the end of the line, noticing how quickly everything had changed.

The shine was off the tracking area of the hall. You could see where the tiles shone near the walls. The shine was off the faces that had been so attentive yesterday, too, and the chatter was louder, though less excited. Neither secretary smiled at them through the office window today. One was typing, the other on the phone, and even Mrs. Ardmore's tan seemed to have faded overnight along with some of her energy. Joey noticed her red hair and freckles, which is what he had noticed most at spring orientation. People who had red hair and freckles didn't keep tans very well.

"Hello, Joey," she said when he came in. She had said hello yesterday, too. Ms. Farthing back in first grade held the record for the least "hello's"—six all year. Mrs. Ardmore didn't talk to him again until midmorning.

"You look a little tired, Joey," she said when they were drawing their houses.

He tried to open his eyes wider and he sucked his lower lip in and kept on coloring the roof white—because that was what it looked like when it was slippery on muggy days—and when she asked if the white was snow he just shrugged.

"I like winter too," she said.

It was the last thing anyone said to him. Or maybe he wasn't paying attention, because he was thinking about the end of the day. What if Uncle Luce came? It wasn't raining and he had no reason to, but what if he did? Joey would have to line up with the walkers, and even if he somehow snuck out, his uncle would come in looking for him and then the principal would know and they would see to it that he never got away again.

He noted each car that arrived during cleanup. The Kellys' station wagon came first. He could see their cocker spaniel yapping at the passenger window and the driver's side was nothing but sun glare on the windshield, but Mrs. Kelly must have been smoking a cigarette because he spotted the plume twisting up from the roofline. More wagons came, along with a van and a couple of four-doors. All late models, shiny, brightly painted, paneled and chromed. No black Fury. No old, sheenless, creeping mystery car kept alive somehow by a sorcerer. But Joey remembered yesterday's last-second malicious surprise and kept watching.

When the bell rang they trooped out to the foyer in parallel lines. Uncle Luce was probably waiting to step out suddenly from behind the showcase or the column, he thought. But he didn't. And when he was actually out the door and the line dissolved, he thought maybe it was the flagpole where he would see him. He broke into a run, the red Pumas biting into the pavement, spitting it out like he was on springs. Nothing could catch him now. He was flying, he was unpredictable. Even an uncle who knew where little boys hid couldn't tell what they didn't know themselves yet. He was just going to keep running, that was all. Run and run and run until his trail was so mixed up nothing could follow, could know.

A block past Kohn's Confectionery Shoppe he turned right instead of left, then a block farther on he hung another right, then left, left, right. Block after block after block. No one could possibly know, not even—

He was there suddenly, sitting on a bench in front of a church, pretending to read a newspaper. Joey's lungs seemed to die first, collapsing into his stomach where the air rose and fell in ponderous upheavals. He didn't think anything, feel anything, until the man brought the paper together to turn the page and he saw that it wasn't his uncle. Of course not. How could it be?

He walked now. Walked and breathed in the last exhalations of summer on the day after a storm that had brought out the final virility of the earth. The grass that had been curried all season around the houses was so green it looked like plastic. The not-quite-rotten smell of ancient flowers penetrated his allergies, and it was the pungent note of apples within this skein that drew him to the mill. Apple cider and donuts. Suddenly the world was soft again.

It was a long, rambling structure—the mill—rooted in the flank of a hill. It sat in the sun like a big baking apple, and the decades of red paint that did as much to hold it together as the weathered wood itself were a medium-rare hue, except for a few unpainted outbuildings as charred as well-done steak. If you crossed the brook at the bottom of the hill you were in the parking lot, and if you browsed above the brook and behind the mill you got to see the waterwheel that ran the press and also the donuts moving like washers along an assembly line. The cloying tang of cider was in your lungs back there and the savory smell of the donuts permeated skin. Joey browsed.

His mother had never permitted him to come here alone. The crowds, particularly on weekends, came from everywhere and anywhere. They came in Mercedeses and on motorcycles, wearing suits and dresses or leather and iron crosses. But the bees that swarmed thickest near the waterwheel and the fermenting apples kept most of the few customers at bay this day, and Joey stayed there, checking the clock he could see through a rear screened window. He didn't care whether he was supposed to be here or not if it kept him from being alone with his uncle. Uncle Luce was going to care a lot, though.

The first thing he noticed when he got home at four-thirty was that the garage door was closed. It had been open when he left, and usually it stayed open all day unless everyone went out. And even if his uncle had gone out, his mother would have opened it coming home. Maybe Uncle Luce was out looking for him. Worse yet, his mother might have come home early and they were both looking.

All she had been through with Chip, and then Daddy drowning, and when she had finally let him go off on his own, he did this to her. As much as it chilled him to think that his uncle had set out for him alone, he hoped she wasn't with him, that she didn't know he hadn't come home. He jumped up on his toes to peek through the garage windows in the folding door, and through the gloom he could tell that her car was gone. Uncle Luce's was still there. With the door closed, it meant they had gone off together. *I'm sorry, Mom. I didn't mean to.*

He trudged up the front porch steps to wait, and just out of frustration he fisted the door petulantly, a solitary blow to let the spirit of the house know he was locked out. Only he wasn't. The door popped open and a little of the atmosphere—his mother's houseplants, the dampness of the vestibule—came out to greet him. Anger and frustration fled, leaving him blank and impressionable to new clues.

Maybe his uncle was here after all. Maybe his mother *hadn't* come home yet.

He pushed in, closing the door slowly behind him.

"Mom?"

The refrigerator hummed distantly like something on a relentless journey—like the engine of a train moving through time and events that its sometime inhabitants could not possibly understand. *Jump aboard if you can, but don't interrupt. We're traveling, you know. Can't you feel the movement? Don't you hear the rush? Don't you know it's all changed since you were here last?*

And then he saw the white ribbon.

It began in the center of the step that led up from the vestibule and lay perfectly flat all the way up the hall carpet. *Rushing, rushing. Get aboard, if you can. Things have been happening, and we haven't time to fill you in.* Joey was already walking forward, caught up in the momentum of the house. The white ribbon striped the carpet and turned to the right where the T came. *Almost there now, keep coming, keep coming. Can you feel the excitement?* He saw where it went, saw in an instant what it meant.

He spun around, but the red Pumas must have been hitting the ribbon as he ran because he could feel the slip, as if he were in one place and the silk was whizzing out from under his feet. Somehow he kept his balance, sidestepping. And then he was flying. Nothing could catch him now. Not even an uncle who knew what little boys would do. Down the hall and into the vestibule. Both hands on the doorknob, leaning back, yanking—

"Hello, nephew."

Uncle Luce stood on the porch, serene as marble. He hadn't been out looking. He had been waiting. Sitting in a white web, waiting for Joey to vibrate a thin white strand. It had all gone according to plan, even the flight.

Joey wheezed like a pack-a-day octogenarian.

"Good thing your mother went to have her hair cut." He backed Joey inside, casually but firmly closing the door. "Imagine how she'd feel if she came home and didn't find you when you were supposed to be here. I'd have to deliver you to school and pick you up each day. Sometimes you don't think at all."

Joey stumbled up the step into the vestibule. "I—I was just playing . . . everybody plays after school."

"Let's play Chair."

He began to whimper as his uncle fastened a hand to his shoulder, turning him toward the den.

"I didn't mean to be late . . . I won't ever do it again."

"Yes." The voice was sad. "You will. You'd cheat and lie and steal to avoid sitting in that chair."

"I wouldn't. Honest." He shook his head wearily.

"Do you love me, Joey? How many times have I died in your dreams the way your father must have?"

He turned him around, their eyes locking: ice vs. egg yolk. Joey's face was incandescent with fever, his hair spiked with sweat, his puffy lips moving but emitting only a lame denial.

"I didn't want him to die."

He saw the chair coming as his uncle picked him up, its knobby blackness resolving into carvings, the red and green silk cover a meaningless tangle of Eastern deities as smooth as coiled lizards. Uncle Luce had him around the knees and he was dropping now, the treachery of air conspiring with gravity and a foretaste of destination. He was rocketing down into a pit whose granite bottom would tear him apart, whose walls would collapse in on him while eyeless things howled the thrill of everlasting death.

Only this time . . . it didn't.

23

"Glory be to blazes, I am hot shit," Carolyn said into the mirror. She said it in an undertone, completely awed by the new entity there. But the hairdresser, who had treated her with an air of pomposity, broke into a belly laugh and reached for her cigarettes.

"If you looked any younger, you'd be jailbait," she concurred.

Five-inch locks formed a crescent around the base of the chair, and a fine cross-hatching shaded the pastel yellow sheet draped over her shoulders.

"I can't wait to be carded," Carolyn murmured.

She had wanted change, and change she had got. The strain

of the past few months had continued to imprint, and she could no longer stand to watch her face become oatmeal without a fight. She had discarded her dowdy clothes, but the frumpy look had remained, aided and abetted by a little cynical extension to the line of her mouth and a heaviness that seemed to emanate out from beneath her eyes to her jaw. It didn't really stand out yet—actually it made her a wee bit sensual, she thought—but it was going to keep sagging until her face was all fleshy dunes and a great sloppy mouth. And her hair had started to look like a gigantic cowl—Sister Carolyn—framing and emphasizing the whole thing. So, change.

Vanity was not her failing, but she stared at her reflection again in the shop glass and in her own car door and rearview mirror. She was tempted to stop at Horning's Gallery to see what might catch her eye or what eye she might catch, but it was late. Joey would be a basket case. Time to go home and rescue him from his own salvation. She made one quick detour to Baskin-Robbins for a half gallon of Pralines 'n Cream. Hard for an eight-year-old to hate his mother while he garbaged out on P 'n C. He might even speak to her in an hour or two, she thought.

"Joey?" she called as soon as she got in and was pawing a couple of ice cube trays out of the freezer in order to cram the ice cream in. "Luce?"

And even as she called out, her senses were feeding her a steady flow of negatives. No lights. No TV. No dishes on the table. No movement. No windows open. What the hell was going on?

"Joey!"

And then her heels were clattering across the kitchen tile, digging into the hall carpet, passing the dining room, the den. Oh, God, the den! She stared in, unable to comprehend the subversion there.

Joey was grinning at her. He was sitting in the chair, grinning like his mind had snapped. And she took several numb steps, still searching for the nuances of meaning. It wasn't until she stared directly at Luce reclining on the brown leather couch that she got the proper cue.

179

"Behold!" he said, gesturing with a swan's grace.

"Surprise, Mom!" Joey grasped the arms and rocked back and forth. "I've been sitting her for hours and hours."

Her eyes went back to Luce. "A half hour anyway," he affirmed.

"It doesn't bother me anymore, Mom. I can sit in it anytime."

She let her own smile come.

"It doesn't show me pictures anymore, either. It's just a chair." He wriggled some more. "See?"

She had enough presence of mind to joke about the pictures. "All out of film," she said. "Chairs do that. You got one that didn't have any cartoons."

"It's just a chair now," he repeated.

She went over and hugged him awkwardly; he wouldn't let go of the arms. Her eyes misted at Lucien, but he preempted her gratitude with a nod. The relief she felt was damn near postorgasmic. All this time. All this stress. How ridiculous that a thing as mundane as sitting in a chair had become such a phobia!

"Seems to me I can smell Pralines 'n Cream in the freezer," she said, to excuse her sniffling.

Joey laughed. "You can't smell ice cream."

"I can. I can hear it too. All the little pralines thumping around inside the carton." He laughed a startled syllable of delight it seemed she hadn't heard in years. "What a coincidence, just when we needed something to help us celebrate."

He bounced in the chair, braced himself as though to spring.

"No. Just stay right there. I'll bring it and you can enjoy it *in* the chair."

And he did.

They all did.

She couldn't remember him ever eating in the chair since the awful time as a baby when he had nearly strangled on the strained peas. But now he ate as if he had a cast-iron stomach, ate and chattered excitedly about how easy it was and how he wished he could have his eighth birthday over again and even how "sweet" it was when Uncle Luce had hit the line drive at the picnic. Nothing succeeds like success, she thought, and clever Luce, more nonchalant and sure of himself than even Frank, had succeeded.

She would have to find a way to thank him, but it wasn't until he commented on her hair that she got the inspiration. "Bold and sexy," he said.

Sexy is as sexy does. Bold, too.

She went out right after dinner and rented or bought the things she needed. The last place she stopped was a novelty and gift shop where she picked out a card with the old Mae West line, "Why don't you come up and see me some time?" and a well-endowed model on the front at the top of a ladder holding her skirt down with a little "Oh" of surprise. When you opened the card the skirt came up over her head, revealing a lot of everything.

Back on the home front, Joey and Luce were watching Bill Cosby and eating popcorn. In the den, reserved chairs only, of course. She couldn't recall Luce so leisurely before either. She wrote *10:30 p.m.* after the Mae West line and slipped the card under his studio door. At nine-thirty she put Joey to bed and took a long hot bath. Then she retired to her bedroom, where she was busy as a beaver until ten-thirty.

He tapped lightly just as she gave the bedspread a final shot of Wild Cherry from the little can of Essential Oils. Then she opened the door and stood there with her hand on her hip, making sure he got a full measure of the black nylons and garter belt and the fact that she'd shaved everything from the neck down.

"When I get a haircut I don't fool around," she said.

She thought he blanched and swallowed hard, but the red bulbs she had installed over the bed made everything look puffy and stark, and the glow from the adult videocassette she had rented did nothing to mitigate this as she closed the door.

She had lip gloss on and tiny bell earrings, and when she kissed him suddenly on the mouth there were moist sounds and a faint tingling. A wave of frangipani wafted up on the heat from her breasts as she spread the lapels of his robe and pressed against him. He grew erect instantly.

"Mmm, nice party favor you got there, stranger. Does it plump when you cook it?" But she had her finger on his lip to stop him from answering, replaced quickly by a flick of her tongue. "I'll do the rhetoric, stranger. I'm just full of hot, hot gratitude to tell you about."

She led him to the bed, tugging off his robe and handling his penis like a leash. The couple in the video were already exploring each other in whatever ways could make their fingers disappear. And then she spread-eagled him and straddled him backward, offering him all the animation of unshaven joy she could while performing miracles of sensuality she had never really thought about before.

Until that blanch and swallow at the door, she had not been sure she could pull it off. Despite their previous intimacy and the bold carnal things they had done, she had always felt acted upon, seduced. Now she was light-years beyond passive. But that swallow, that slight drain in Lucien's face, had told her what she needed to know. She could arouse. She wasn't going to be rejected. Silly fear. Silly as Joey's chair thing. And she went to work, exciting herself for the power of what she was causing.

In the end he took her again and again. The ecstasy was overwhelming. She had made him into a satyr, and she fell asleep as sated and secure as she had ever felt.

24

The morning sun tore slivers in the apple-red drapes and set the den awhirl with motes. It made the chair look brooding and ponderous by contrast. The longer Joey stood barefoot in front of it, the more ominous it seemed to become. Maybe yesterday had never happened, he thought fleetingly. Maybe he had forgotten how to sit in the chair. And that made something cry out loudly inside him, as if in outrage that his secret terrors might get loose again. It was a silent scream, the kind that stopped the voice in your head, and before it died he had impetuously whirled and fallen into the lap of the patriarch chair.

And nothing happened.

It was just a chair.

Teak.

Silk.

Carvings.

Embroidery.

Inside was stuffing. Probably a lot, since it was solid down to the floor. There were faces on the arms that he had never noticed until yesterday. You had to be sitting in the chair to figure them out, and he had never sat there that long, of course. The reason you had to figure them out was because they were so dark and because they seemed to be stretching like taffy about to pull apart. You couldn't tell whose faces they were, men or women. But their mouths were open as if they were screaming silence the way Joey's soul had screamed silence.

He heard an upstairs door open then, and a few moments later his mother's legs appeared on the stairs. She looked funny because she had black nylons on beneath her robe.

"Trying it on for size again?" she said when she reached the doorway.

"Yeah." He rocked a little. "Still fits."

"One size fits all, Joey. It's yours forever now."

He liked that.

One size fits all. He said it to his uncle at breakfast when they divided up the scrambled eggs, and Luce just grunted while his mother laughed airily. He said it to Andrew Harrington when they were playing musical chairs in gym and they both went for the same one. He said it in art when they made Indian bonnets out of construction paper. No one gave him much response, but he didn't mind. It was his little reminder of the chair. An inside joke, a shibboleth, a cry of victory.

He came straight home after school, and he would have gone to the den first but his uncle called to him from the kitchen. "I want you," he said. It sounded peculiar.

Joey went slowly into the kitchen. His uncle was leaning back against the sink, arms folded, a blank expression on his face. Nothing in the room seemed out of place, but still Joey sensed something different.

"I want you to go into the garage, nephew."

There was no emotion in this, unless you counted the word

"nephew." Joey wanted to ask why, but then he thought maybe it was the fact of the command that was important. Like a test. He went to the door, put his hand on the knob, looked at his uncle, opened it.

He couldn't see anything out of place there either.

Maybe he was supposed to *do* something there. He took a step in, and that was when he saw it glittering from the other side of the van. He had just seen the gleam over the hood when the garage-door mechanism engaged and light poured in, emphasizing the chrome.

"A ten-speed!" he exclaimed reverently, dancing around the bumper of the van.

"One size fits all," said his uncle behind him as he struggled to mount the frame.

"A ten-speed!" he repeated.

"Twelve."

"Twelve, wow."

Wow. Antecedent of *sweet*. The awe was too genuine to be trendy. And the anticipation was too keen for gratitude at that moment. Joey was off, soaring down the drive into the street. He knew nothing of Shimano brakes and Campagnolo derailleurs, nothing of adjustments and tensions and torques. The thing glistened and meshed effortlessly and, even if it was a little big for him, he could still stay on the seat when the pedals bottomed out. So it was his, forever and ever, and he set out to put his first miles on it, but he only got to his first curve when he met his first car and almost had his first accident. And that was bad—or maybe good, depending on how you looked at it—because the car was an Escort, and you know who the driver was.

"Joey!"

She was out from behind the wheel before he even got the bike out of the hedge he'd ditched in.

"Mom, look!"

"Joey, do you realize I almost—"

"Look what Uncle Luce gave me!"

"Joey, listen—" She expelled her breath sharply, gave up trying to counter his deaf and blind joy with the gravity of what had nearly happened. "Uncle Luce got you that?"

"Yeah. Sweet, huh?"

"Don't you think it's a little big?"

"I can handle it, Mom." He could see she wasn't convinced, that she was weighing out limitations and prohibitions. "I used to ride Corky Miller's all the time. Heck, I rode it when I was seven, don't you remember? And I know all about bike safety and everything. And this bike's got twelve gears and"—he checked the back—"a reflector."

She took hold of his shoulders. "It's a beautiful bike, Joey. I'm glad you got it. But we're going to have to talk about this. Luce never mentioned—"

"It was a surprise."

"Definitely that."

"He prob'ly gave it to me because I sit in the chair now," he said earnestly. "I can do lots of things now that I sit in the chair."

She looked at him in a funny way.

"Please, Mom, I'll be careful. Let me ride it."

She started to shake her head "no" and ended by nodding as she spoke. "You can ride it for a little while if you stay out of the street." There weren't any walks in this section of Franklin Village. Just small estates and grounds. Roller-coaster roads. "You can ride on the flat straightaway at the other end of the block. No hills. I'll let you ride there for now, if you promise to pull off whenever a car comes. Promise?"

He promised and she returned reluctantly to the Escort, watched him remount, and followed him slowly back up the street.

For almost an hour he circled and weaved along the asphalt strip she had banished him to, worrying about the argument he knew she was presenting to his uncle—that he wasn't old enough for a twelve-speed, that it was too dangerous. He wondered if Uncle Luce would argue for him very much. He didn't deserve a bike, especially after what he had said to his mother at Chi-Chi's. Uncle Luce was right; he should keep things about the chair to himself. The pictures still seemed vivid, but everyone always said what a good imagination he had. Maybe—just maybe—his fears had made them come, made them seem real when they weren't. He was confused about that, but it seemed that everything he had believed about the chair was false now. And he welcomed the discreditation. Probably the dangerous things his uncle had let him do had caused the change. Uncle Luce had said he'd get braver. And he had.

When he saw the Escort coming slowly down the street again, he thought he had lost the bike. One size did not fit all. But she pulled over and smiled and said she guessed he'd earned the privilege and that sometimes she forgot how quickly he was growing up. Then she said that the reason she had come home early was because there was a trade show banquet and she had had to change her clothes.

"I won't be home till late and Uncle Luce is going to take you to a movie, sport," she said. "You've really impressed him. Give me a kiss and pedal on home—*slowly.*"

He clambered off and smooched her on the cheek and clambered on again, and she didn't pull away until he was all the way back to the drive, where he waved.

A bike and a show!

Uncle Luce had really gone to bat for him, the way he had for his mother at the picnic. He didn't know how he could have thought those things about his uncle. He had grown up a great deal in the past twenty-four hours. Conquering the chair and now the bike.

He wheeled the twelve-speed right up to the kitchen door, taking note of the crisp chatter of the crank—a wet-marbles sound that had a special clarity on a new bike. His uncle would probably be in his studio, but Joey looked for him in the den first and, of course, lingered a moment to study the chair. Lingered and crossed boldly to it and turned and dropped and—

Lights, camera, action!

Take a shot of Joey, here. That's it. Would you mind telling us, sir, how you conquered this chair? Did you use a safari or did you hunt alone?

Well, I took my uncle along. We always hunt together. Had some pretty scary adventures, too. But now that we've tamed the chair we're turning our attention to raising and breaking wild bikes. Nothing wilder than a good twelve-speed.

Do you use a special saddle?

Saddle? Heck, no! I ride 'em bareback. One size fits all, ya know. Why, I broke one in up there on the plateau before supper—

Supper. They had to eat before the show. Or maybe they wouldn't. Uncle Luce skipped supper lots of times, and Joey wasn't very hungry. He grabbed a banana from the bowl in the kitchen on the way upstairs so that he could say he didn't need to eat, and then he knocked on the door to the white-white room.

"It's open," his uncle said mellifluously.

Joey could hear the buzz in the piano wires, ghosting after the voice inside like awakening bees. And, in fact, the first thing he saw upon opening the door was an immense piano.

It was almost twice as long as any he had ever seen before, with almost twice as many keys. He could see where it had been added to at either end, an old black upright that his uncle must have brought up in pieces or had moved in during the day. He understood now about the pounding and the distant thunder of his dreams. Because as he watched, the piano started playing itself, impossible notes on the deep end—muted, croaking— and the farther to the left the keys went down, the less Joey heard and the more he only felt the sounds.

"What do you think of it?" Uncle Luce's voice was almost obliterated by a low, ominous resonance.

He was inside. Inside the piano. And Joey laughed. He was tuning the piano from inside, making the keys go down and thrumming the wires. And as Joey continued to stare, the top of the thing began to thump and thud like a coffin lid (*just wait till I get out of here!*), rising up slowly until his uncle's burning eyes and serene smile were upon him.

"A most extraordinary instrument," he said, his lips very red in the shadow of the lid. "Deeper, longer than anything ever built. One hundred and fifty-two keys. Even bats can't hear the highest notes. But I can. I can just hear them in the tips of my fingers if I keep the hammers down. Come around back. You can climb up on the seat and I'll lift you in."

Joey scampered around the piano as he had danced around

the van to claim his bicycle just an hour and a half before. The piano *was* deeper—big enough to hold God knows what. But it was to remain God's and Lucien's secret. Because Joey did not clamber upon the seat to be lifted in. Because the seat was the chair. And if he had just sat in it downstairs in the den, what was it doing up here?

25

Flash-frozen Joey. His soul was cracking into bits of fractured ice as the room vibrated to a single mammoth chord. Groaning, shrieking. The primordial sound of a universe gone mad as it reawakened and staggered to life.

There was no doubt as to the authenticity of this chair. The red and green silk cover with its serpentine knot of deities was like an indelible stain of something else—something Joey had never seen but knew was there beneath. And the faces were yawning and ghoulish, emerging from some ectoplasmic flow, still soft, still molten with the boneless agony of creation. He could feel the arms already, rising up around him like snapping dogs.

Yesterday was gone. Today was before and after yesterday. Today was a millennium.

"I had to do it," droned out of his uncle as awesomely as thunder. Not distant thunder. Rumbling stuff, breaking all around. "Your mother was very, very worried because of the things you said. You can see how I did it for you. Otherwise you would have had to visit a psychiatrist. And if he found out what you'd been doing, then we couldn't avoid the chair anymore, could we? So I had to do it. And anyway, maybe you can sit in this one too. They're exactly the same. One size fits all."

Joey shuddered without tears. He was standing in a white-white room holding a banana peel, listening to a man inside a piano, whose eyes peered at him from under the lid, whose voice coiled around wires and vibrated through his shoes.

"You know I can't," he said brokenly. Of course he did. He wouldn't have made the second chair if he hadn't believed they were different.

"Why don't we put them together, Joey? Why don't I mix them up and you sit in whichever one you choose?"

Joey shook his head.

"Well, then."

Well, then.

What?

They went to the show.

101 Dalmatians had been rereleased, and Joey sat mesmerized by the flow of electrically charged dogs filling every avenue of escape. The dynamics of animation brought them onrushing into his lap or performing pinwheel reels to a cacophony of howls. His uncle bought him popcorn that stuck halfway down and left his throat burning. Shock over the chair seemed to have shut down his salivary glands, his attention span, his hope, and his brief, victorious joy. The only thing he really noticed was his uncle's face. In the flicker of the screen it looked lavender and silver.

When the show was over, they strolled out of the theater and down the street to an ice-cream parlor.

"I recommend the double banana split with the cherry cluster," Lucien said.

"Vanilla's okay," Joey answered. He felt vanilla.

The ice cream unstuck his throat but seemed to line his

191

stomach with permafrost. His uncle had a malt. They ate inside while the night continued to gather. It almost seemed like they were waiting for something. The malt went on forever, and when at last the straw bottomed out it kept sucking at the blisters of foam in an annoying way.

"That was good," Lucien said, lifting his head slowly. "Are you done?"

Joey had been done for fifteen minutes.

"Well, then."

They left the ice-cream parlor, and his uncle turned them away from the theater and the parking lot where the car was.

"What we need is an adventure this time, nephew. Something with an element of surprise. And it just so happens that across the street here we have a lumberyard. Lumberyards at night are great places for adventure. This one has an oak tree with a magnificent rack just outside the front gate. You could climb that oak, cross over the fence, and drop onto that pile of cedar posts. Then you could have an adventure."

Joey couldn't see the cedar posts in the dark. The only thing that was really clear to him in the soft light of the street was his uncle's face. It was still lavender and silver.

"Instead of the chair?" he asked.

"Instead of the chair."

"For a week."

Lucien laughed through his nose. "What a bargainer you've become. A week."

"How do I get back out?"

"That's part of the adventure."

The oak sat on a wide apron of grass between the yard and the sidewalk. For all the security provided by the towering fence crested with barbed wire, getting in didn't seem to be a problem. The idea seemed to be to keep a thief from getting out with appreciable amounts of lumber. His uncle wouldn't leave him there indefinitely, Joey reasoned. If the owner of the lumberyard caught him inside in the morning there would be too many questions, and if they weren't home before his mother returned there would be a search.

They crossed to the apron, where his uncle's fingers went around him like iron laces, lifting and offering him up to the

192

mighty oak. There in the breezy underskirts of a half dozen dark limbs Joey heard the last breath of summer and the first wheeze of fall. The crotch of the tree had a cool, moist smell, the sediments perhaps of timid night things that had sheltered there. He moved easily on the broad thigh extending over the fence, and it wasn't until it began to dip toward the cedar posts that the leaves sibilated a warning and the branch bobbed once in benediction, allowing him to drop three or four feet onto the pile.

The roar of shifting logs was so deep and instantaneous that he knew at once it had been unavoidable. Virtually every post was moving. Instinct told him to scramble as his feet went out from under him. He *ran* up the tumult. Ran and lost height but somehow—feet flying, hands thrusting—managed to avoid being pinned under the cascade. His palms were skinned, his left knee ringing with pain where a cedar end had grazed it, but he was whole and unbroken. The problem was the roar. When the cedar logs stopped moving, the roar went on. And Joey, breathless and faint, was mesmerized by the flow of electrically charged dogs filling every avenue of escape.

There were three of them actually, and they were not Dalmatians but Dobermans. He caught the flash of fangs and the refraction of amber eyes just before he turned and again struggled to climb the vastly wider, dismayingly lower jumble of posts. The roars were feral and carnivorous, but they told him which way the dogs were moving. His own cries were as diminutive as a doll's by comparison. He reached the apex and threw his arms up at the oak branch a million miles away, flexing his knees, shouting for Uncle Luce, even though a rational part of him was already whispering deep within his mind, Your uncle knew about the dogs . . . he planned this . . . you won't have to explain it to the owners in the morning because you'll be dead and your uncle will make up some story about how you got in here. Two of the Dobermans were testily working their way higher now; the third was bounding up.

Joey went down the opposite side, given reprieve only by the occasional yelp behind him as a canine paw misstepped in the frenzy of the chase. An orange sodium light somewhere beyond the fence drew murky outlines for him, and he got to the bottom just as the lead Doberman reached the top. A single glance caught the animal coiled as if to spring the entire descent, then actually leaping a good quarter of the way down and miraculously recovering on the flanks of a pair of posts. There were perhaps only four or five seconds left when Joey saw the hole.

It ran like a tunnel into the heart of the lumber pile, eight-footers stacked unevenly end to end with breathing room to dry out. Joey squeezed in, at once enveloped by a strange muted feeling and the redolence of pine resin. He had gone only six or seven yards when he saw the other end, saw this and heard behind him the scuff and pad of the first Doberman. And suddenly the narrow opening exploded with the tight repercussions of a roar. Joey squirmed around while continuing to back in. Amber coals soared toward him. He could hear the second and third dogs now, the sound channeled to him by the acoustics of a lumber pile so that he wasn't sure which end it was coming through or what he might be backing into. And that was when he felt the slash at his elbow. Twisting reflexively, he saw that it was a shaft split from a board. It was a long stilettolike piece, and the suggestion of a weapon was not wasted on him. He snapped it off, gripping it with both hands. He would go for the eyes, he thought, but the teeth were on it in a literal flash, gnashing off the point before he could move. He lanced tardily and this time the savage snap caught the shaft solidly. Splinters needled into his hands as the Doberman jerked and released, snapped again, catching and wrestling the shaft back and forth. Joey's heart leaped with the connection—a shark on a fishing line, a jolt of electricity felt through a handful of wood. The bloodlust will surging into his frail arms from just inches away terrified him to faintness, and the sickly smell of resin touched with the Doberman's fetid breath made it even more unreal. Each assault seemed to boil a little more air out of the passageway. And now the creature had the shaft again and was heedlessly bashing the narrow confines to gain room. Joey never saw what slipped. He only knew that he was falling backward without the stick, anticipating pain and the ultimate agony of being torn apart, when he heard the boards clattering loudly, briefly, and then the light and the dog in front of him were gone and he was crab-walking out of the pile into the relative coolness of the night.

But that left a duet of single-minded viciousness to contend with, half of which was backing out already from the front of the collapsed tunnel.

The fence was within range. If he ran to it and climbed, he would probably make it to the barbed wire. But that wouldn't be high enough, and there would be no recourse from there. The other choice was the ladder. The trouble with the ladder was that it was attached to a two-tiered loft whose depth and breadth promised stairways and dead ends. Once committed to the second tier the dogs might trap him, and they were just insane enough to spring off that porch directly on top of him if he tried to return down the ladder. The choice was really *now* or *later*. Joey ran to the ladder, his half-formed thoughts only the instincts of a boy born to flight. Long-lived rabbits thought that way. Methuselah mice.

He had a dozen rungs beneath him when the rails were jarred completely out of his hands. The lead Doberman had sprung, slamming full tilt against the frame. For an instant he felt himself paddling wildly in the moat of space. If the second animal were to reach him then, his red Pumas would have peeled off the rung like the skin of an apple. But he had the moment's reprieve, enough to clutch the same rung with both hands and resist the lazy undertow of a free-fall. By the time the second jolt came, he already had a foot on the platform. And then he saw what the cynical core of his instincts had already known: the Dobermans knew another way up.

They actually collided as they broke for the interior beneath where he now stood. What was it, a ramp? steps? The danger had been so imminent, so intense, that the few seconds of sanctuary seduced him, and there on the edge of a twenty-foot drop he suddenly felt that they would be a long time reaching him. He had forever to rest, to think, to feel relief. It was a short-lived illusion. Flailing nails shattered his torpor. The staircase was in the middle directly in front of him. What could he throw? What were his weapons? There was absolutely nothing. Except the second ladder.

This one was not attached to the structure but lay flat along the same axis as the lumber. He couldn't see its end, and what he could see wasn't very long. The strategy, like the instinct for flight, was only half formed, but there was the fence and here was the ladder and if he could just have a minute or two he might actually get it off the second tier and clamber down it and move it to the fence and—

He jumped forward, grabbed the first rung. It was heavy. Rung after rung came out of the shadow, the rails roaring sluggishly along the boards and counterpointed in the pauses by the insidious flail and thud of hurtling mayhem fixed so irrevocably on his mutilation. What happened then was a sequence of actions that created and carried its own momentum. Joey triggered it, was part of it, but did not actually conceive or believe in its outcome. First, the ladder began to tip. The balance point went over the edge of the platform and the whole thing began to slide and swing upright until the invisible end banged into an invisible eaves, dropping it into place where Joey stood. He did not mean to jump. He meant to swing around on it, to climb down despite the certainty that the dogs would spring after him. But now the first one was rushing out of the shadow, feral eyes, harrow teeth, lean silhouette lunging in the trajectory that would end with Joey in its jaws, and Joey himself lunged in that final delay, forcing the ladder away from the edge, accepting the ride into space that would end disastrously but add two or three seconds to his mortal preservation. The Doberman hit the ladder too—hit and hung and fell to the ground in a heap. But Joey did not fall. He rode the ladder into the oak tree, where startled branches pushed back, slowing and deflecting the flying staircase against the fence—straddling it, actually—delivering a mild contusion or two to his braced forearms as it teeter-tottered him into a pair of strong, sinewy hands. And his uncle said:

"Gotcha!"

26

She got home from the trade show banquet some time after one-thirty. The speeches had been as dry as a mouthful of tablecloth, but the afterglow down Jefferson Avenue from Cobo Hall was a kick. Somehow she had wound up in a hole-in-the-wall where the lights looked like distant galaxies, the floor was gummy and invisible, and the smoke suggested a fire in a botanical garden. But after the airless sterility of the banquet it was like CPR, and she had hit it off well with the little cadre of auto supply execs she had found herself with. It hadn't bothered her to be the only woman in the group. Hell, she liked the odds.

"Well, President Whitehall, consider me sober enough to know what I'm doing and drunk enough to be forgiven," said the eligible and distinguished-looking CEO of a competing firm in making a pass at her.

"I never rush into a merger like that," she said.

"Maybe we can study the situation now and then."

He liked her tight organization and assembled lines. But what the hey, she hadn't gotten her hair cut and paid one-five-oh and eighty cents for a garment of blue taffeta just to show off her expertise on mums. Notwithstanding, they seemed to be impressed with her company and the fact that she ran it. So what if she was the only white woman in the bar? One of the banquet execs she had yakked away the night with was black. And after a few drinks everyone was the same color anyway.

She stood now in the foyer and the house seemed very stiff and formal, as if she had come from the rubber walls of a play-room into the hard angles of a tomb. Her maternal sensibilities sharpened—how many times since Chip's disappearance had they quickened in the night out of fear for Joey? And they had always been wrong, these presentiments of disaster. But there was inevitably a first time. Chip had only disappeared once.

She took off her shoes on the way up the stairs and left them by the newel post on the landing. Joey's door was shut tight. She turned the handle as gently as she could, but she need not have bothered.

He was sleeping like the Grand Canyon. The wind in his little lungs respired heavily—a touch of asthma. He was going to be a colossal snorer, this one. Holy Van Winkle, but he was out! He must have been exhausted. No wonder, though. All the excitement of the last two days. It was terrific to see him so peaceful. Dream victories, Joey. Dream bikes and silly chairs. She still had not asked him who had given him Snake Mountain or why he had skateboarded in the rain. No matter. Best for-gotten now. Live the present while it sparkles. He wasn't going to need a psychiatrist. Good grief, will you listen to him snore? How late had they been out? Must have been a double feature. It was going to take cannons to wake him up in the morning.

Wanna bet?

She heard the first reverberation at five-ten. It was a solid sound as masculine as thunder, the kind that enters your bones

198

with a jar. She might not have awakened fully then except for the cry that accompanied it. The cry was pure child. She had heard it a thousand times from taunted children on the verge of tears and an inch from laughter. It had a poisoned brio to it—fear and joy and pain. The second cry and reverberation came just as she sat up.

From another part of the house she heard the toilet flush, the bathroom door open quickly. She struggled out of bed, a slight hangover rebounding from her head to her stomach. By the time she got to the hall Lucien was at the door to the studio, his hand rattling the knob. He slept in the studio. How had he locked himself out? She was standing there in her nightgown, head pounding, not thinking at all. From within the room came a third tandem of the same sounds, and the whimper and wheeze that followed were rending increments.

"Joey!" she shouted.

Lucien turned crisply, his face faintly luminous in the dawn. "It's all right, Carolyn. I'll handle it."

"Joey?" she called loudly.

"Really . . . he's all right. It would be better if you went back to bed and let me do this."

"Do what?" She rapped smartly on the door, called. There was another chunking sound, followed by that unearthly reverberation. *Buzz, buzz, buzz.* "Break it down."

"Carolyn—"

"Break it down!"

He hesitated just a second, then wheeled back down the hall to the bathroom.

"Joey, what's the matter?" she demanded, pounding on the panels. "Are you all right?"

She didn't like the looseness of his cry—that joy again, an aberrant sound like the one she had heard herself making at Frank's funeral. Sans *buzz.* And then Luce was back with whatever he had brought from the bathroom, kneeling at the lock. She couldn't see what he was doing, but there were metallic scuffs against the disturbing rain of thuds from behind the door and almost immediately it opened, exposing an incredibly long piano and a jungle of wires all groaning and shivering with Joey's sobs. She damn near decapitated herself dashing around the end of the instrument, but what she saw took her breath away.

Joey had a hatchet, had a chair, had a fit.

He was dancing around the thing, in and out, striking awkward blows with the hatchet, each accompanied by that little, deranged thrill sound, as if he was absorbing electric shocks with every contact. The atmosphere was as charged and palpable as Frankenstein's lab in mid-thunderstorm. Wires everywhere in blue-black silhouette, the sound of insane events coiling up and down them like oily whispers in the bowels of hell. Lord Jesus!

"Joey." Lucien said it softly. Taking the hatchet away on the upswing.

Joey stopped. He stood there as calmly and quietly as if he had just arrived. In a way, he had.

Carolyn turned him gently toward the door and led him back to his room. He was soaking wet. Sweat and urine. She didn't try to bathe him. Just changed his pajamas. Tucked him under the covers and sat with him until she felt sure he was going to rest.

It didn't seem to be the time to talk, and she didn't think he could at that moment, but as she was leaving he said, "It's the chair, Mom. It's back. I had to do it. It was telling Uncle Luce wherever I was going to go."

She watched him another moment, then retreated slowly down the hall.

The studio door was still open. She found Luce kneeling by the chair, examining the gashes.

"Repairable," he said. "Hard to destroy teak."

She looked at him in horror. "My God, Luce, how can you be talking about that chair? I hate the thing. If it weren't for Frank, I'd—"

"The chair isn't the problem, Carolyn. Joey made it into something it isn't. The problem is in his head, and therefore the chair has to be the solution."

"No." She flashed him the hardest look she had ever given him. "The solution is a psychiatrist."

"Bad choice."

"Maybe." She seemed to bristle again. "Didn't you see him? He wet his pajamas, for crying out loud."

200

"Maybe he wet them in bed."

"His bed is dry."

"I'm the last one to tell you he hasn't got a problem, Carolyn. But he really has improved. This is a mild setback really. He was half asleep. It was probably a nightmare that confused him—"

"Oh, no." She shook her head vehemently. "I tucked him in around one-thirty and I thought he was sleeping soundly, but he was probably awake then. Awake and just lying there waiting. He got the hatchet and he waited the whole damn night for you to get up and go to the bathroom, and then he locked himself in here and . . . and *damn it, Luce, he was practically in shock!*"

"Did he say anything?"

"Yes. He said the chair was back."

He cocked his head, studied her. "I lied to you, Carolyn. There are two chairs."

She felt more stricken by that than the whole trauma of the dawn. Luce was the linchpin that was holding her together, making it possible for her to deal with her life.

"I built a second one. I thought that if I showed Joey both and he sat in the one I made and saw it was all right, and then I switched them and told him he was sitting in the real one, he'd have to accept a victory. And it worked. But he changed back. He started to fantasize that he'd only been sitting in the one I made."

"His fantasies are sick."

"No. He just didn't have the courage to accept reality yet. Almost but not quite. If I'd waited a little longer, he might have overcome this phobia permanently. A boy grows by fantasies. I should have told you what I was doing in the first place, but I've spared you the details of his vacillating progress thus far."

"Progress?" She looked at the scarred arms of the chair. "You can't repair everything, Lucien. I'm going to take him to a psychiatrist. Joey isn't made of teak."

REVELATION

27

Shock. Temporary death. Joey kept one foot on either side of the line between shock and reality, like some nocturnal creature flirting with the terminator between night and day. He didn't want to let go of the light. His mother inhabited the light. But if he surrendered to the darkness, if he became part of it, there would be peace of a sort.

It was a seduction no one in the house understood. So he was going to see the psychiatrist. Because there were moments when he was sliding into darkness.

She took him the very next Tuesday. That's how much of an emergency case he was. She had stayed home with him on Friday, sent him to school Monday, and now Tuesday she had an appointment for him. It took a month to see the dentist.

"We were really lucky, Joey. Dr. Coker is a nice man."

"Will he give me a shot?"

"No. He just wants to talk to you."

Everyone wanted to talk to him. Almost everyone. Uncle Luce didn't talk to him until just before he left on Tuesday morning. His mother told him to get in the car while she finished up in the bathroom, and that was when Uncle Luce came. He put his hands on the doorsill, smiled, and said, "The chair is fixed, Joey. I can always fix the chair."

That was all.

Joey saw him staring down from the landing window as they pulled away a few minutes later. He knew he hadn't hurt the chair enough. Probably nothing could do that unless he burned the whole house down. His uncle was warning him against telling the psychiatrist the same things he wasn't supposed to tell his mother. *I hope you understand just what awful things might happen. . . .* But he wouldn't tell. No matter what, he wouldn't tell.

Dr. Coker's waiting room had a yellow beanbag chair, some toys, and a lot of *Ranger Rick*s. It also had some big chairs, a glass table, pictures of clowns on the walls, and one gleaming stuffed fish. Joey thought he knew already what Dr. Coker looked like. Doc Samuel, who gave him checkups, had a stuffed fish on his wall, and he wore glasses and had hairy hands.

Jiminy Cricket was singing "When You Wish Upon a Star" out of floor speakers in each corner when his mother went in to see the doctor by herself. A pretty woman behind a desk asked him about school and had he been to camp and did he have pets, while six more Walt Disney songs played, and then his mother came out and he went in. It was a soft room this time. The carpet was like a mattress and the curtains made the bright sunlight into the color of Bambi. A tall man came forward then with black-rimmed glasses on and stuck out a big, hairy hand.

"Hi, Joey. I'm Doc Coker and I'm glad you've come to see me."

He led Joey to a pair of overstuffed chairs by a fish tank and they sat down. Joey stole a couple of glances at the doctor's face but pretended to be interested in the fish. It was an okay face, he thought, a little like one of the clowns in the other room. It had a beard like the hobo clown and a nice smile and twinkling eyes behind the glasses and no hair on top.

"Looks like Baxter has taken to you," the doctor said. "Baxter's the one with the yellow fins."

"Fish don't care about people," Joey said.

"No?"

"Fish are dumb."

"I guess you're right. But some of the children who come to see me like to pretend." There was a little pause, as if Joey should say something. "Do you know what I do?"

"You solve kids' problems."

"Well, I try. But I really just help *them* do the solving. Know how?"

Joey shook his head.

"By listening. They tell me whatever they feel like telling me, and sometimes I ask questions about things that are interesting or that I don't understand and sometimes I make suggestions. That's about it."

Joey didn't understand how that solved anything, but since he wasn't going to tell him about Uncle Luce, he didn't think it mattered.

"Now, I don't know a thing about you, Joey, but I'd like to, if you want to tell me about yourself."

Of course he knew about him. Mother had talked to him for a long time. She had come here to tell him.

"Some children like to start with their friends."

Joey didn't have any friends, so he made one up. Alvin, he called him, like the chipmunk. Doc Coker listened for a while, eyes twinkling. Then he asked Joey if he had any other friends. He thought about it, shrugged. Then it was, Do you want friends? And then, What's your school like? And then, Tell me about your house. And when they got all through the house, the doctor started to get a little too close with, "Tell me about your furniture."

Joey told him about the furniture in his bedroom.

"And the rest of the house?"

He must have balked a little then, because Doc Coker shifted his feet and said, "You don't have to tell me anything you don't want to, Joey. But your mother said that there was a chair you didn't like."

Joey fidgeted. Rocked his feet.

"Is it like the chair you're in now?"

He shook his head.

"Did something happen in it?"

Fidget. Rock.

"What's it like to sit in it?"

Stop it, stop it!

The doctor stopped it. "It's perfectly all right if we don't talk about the chair today. Would you like to tell me about your toys?"

Joey named as many of his toys as he could think of.

"Ah. Your mother must love you very much, don't you think?"

Joey nodded.

"And your uncle too? Does he give you presents?"

Shrug.

Doc Coker pursed his lips and pushed his glasses up the bridge of his nose. "Do you know I've got a whole room full of toys? Not as many as you, perhaps, but a lot. Would you like to see them?"

"Uh-uh."

"No? You could play with them. I don't mind if children play with them."

"I don't want to play with them."

The doctor scratched his beard. "Do you know you're the first child to ever turn me down? Usually they play and I watch." He spread the hand that wasn't scratching his beard on the air. "But that's all right. Maybe you'd like to draw. I've got lots of paper and the biggest selection of crayons you've ever seen."

Joey didn't want to draw. He wanted to go home.

Doc Coker glanced at his fish. "You know, I haven't really asked you about your family yet? How could I forget something as important as that? I must be getting absentminded."

But he wasn't absentminded. That was just a trick to make Joey say what he wasn't supposed to, he knew. The questions got dangerous then. Dangerous and faster. Part of the reason they came faster was because he gave such short answers, but he wanted to get it over with, and maybe if he answered them quickly and was very careful, then maybe he could get out of here. Only they seemed to go on and on.

"Tell me about your:

MOTHER

"Are you ever afraid she'll go away?"
"Sometimes."
"Has she ever left you?"
"No."
"Do you remember her when you were very small?"
"Yes."
"What was she like?"
Shrug.
"Did she ever leave you then?"

CHIP

"Do you miss him?"
"Yes."
"What do you miss most?"
"Playing."
"What do you think happened to him?"
"He drowned."
"He drowned?"
"I think so."
"Why do you think that?"
"Because."
"Do you ever dream about him?"
Fidget. Rock.

FATHER

"What kinds of things did you and your father do?"
"We went skiing up north once."
"Tell me about it."
Shrug.
"Was it fun?"
"No."
"Why not?"
"I don't like skiing."

209

"Did he make you go?"
"No."
"Why did you go then?"
Shrug.
"How did you feel when he died?"
Glad.
"Did you feel guilty? It's pretty normal to feel guilty."
"No."
"Do you ever think about him?"
A lot. Shrug.
"Do you wish he'd come back?"
Never. Nodding yes.

UNCLE LUCE

"Tell me about your uncle."
Tune out.
"Do you get along with your uncle?"
The fish tank was breathing.
"Are you glad he's living with you?"
Fidget. Rock.
"Does your uncle treat you the way your father treated you?"
Stop it! Stop it!
"What kinds of things do you do with your uncle?"
I hope you understand just what awful things might happen if . . .
"What's it like when you're alone together?"
The chair is fixed, Joey. I can always fix the chair.

"I'd like to see him on a weekly basis, Mrs. Whitehall. There are some conflicts here, and it may take a while to get them all out. He's obviously shifted some bad feelings he has about himself and others onto this chair. He misses his father a great deal, I think, and he resents his uncle's displacement of him in the household. You need to distract him from focusing too narrowly on those around him. Might I suggest that you get him a pet? Perhaps some fish."

28

The clouds were all funny and the sky seemed to be breathing like the aquarium. Joey felt sick. His mother kept telling him he was all right, that it was just the stress of the first visit, but in her face he read the running fear he had seen when his father died.

"I've got to drop you off, baby," she said in a squeezed-off voice. "I've got to go to work."

Preemptive storm clouds gusted in like sharks out of rhythm with the speedy school of fleece higher up. The whole thing took on the somber hues of a sunset, sinking like purple and plum and fire to the bottom of the earth. By the time they reached Franklin Village it was midnight at noon. The house rose like a

211

shipwreck, Captain Lucien at the helm, staring down from the landing window as if he hadn't moved since they left. She took him in, delivered him to the keeper of the chair.

"He's a little upset, Luce," she said. "I think he'll sleep if you can get him to lie down."

Lie down? Nay. Sit down. The whine of the departing Escort was already like the faint cry of the upper world heard in recession from a nether place. A great, dumb silence filled Joey's head like the airy hiss of a seashell. He could not speak. Whatever denial came out would tremble like a lie.

"Nephew, nephew, you told."

"I-I-I d-d-didn't."

Long stare.

For just a second Joey thought his uncle believed him, that his inarticulateness had spoken eloquently enough.

"Well, then, you'll only have to sit in the chair once," Uncle Luce said.

Revelation.

Eight-year-old Joey Whitehall, scion to the name and the privileges of the patriarch chair, was about to penetrate its oldest secret. Because when he was down within its grasp and the howling like a million cats reached its climax, reaming out his skull, infusing every nerve with a terrible resonance, he experienced the exquisite agony of kinship on the brink of annihilation that put him in touch with the faces. They were so stark, so ghastly, it was incredible that he hadn't recognized what they were before. Yawning ectoplasms gouged deep into the wood, now gashed here and there where he had struck them with the hatchet. Teak eyes murky with pain. Teak features heat-warped by the hell from which the tree had sprung. Flesh of teak, twisting with the grain. Bones of teak, bonded to eternity. They were children. Ancient children. And in the lightning-ravaged moments of extinction that threatened to transpose Joey forever, he saw two that were not so ancient. The first was unfamiliar except for the hauntingly recognizable eyes. They were his uncle's eyes. They were also little Bobby Bastard's. The second was wholly familiar. Grotesque distortions notwithstanding, he would know this one with the last essence of his soul. And he remembered then that he had known in a way that night four years ago that this was where *he* had gone. The Lake Erie marshes had had nothing to do with it. No question who this one was.

No question at all.

29

Petting a fish is like fondling a bladder, and they tire so easily on walks and hardly ever fetch right, thought Carolyn. Of course, they don't often make messes around fire hydrants but, hey, who needs scales? We want scales, we buy sheet music. Give me something with hair on the outside of its nose instead of in and a good old tail wafting about, a pet that maybe uses the neighbor's lawn in the dead of night or at least poops in the dark in a litter box.

The whole wall of aquariums at Fins & Furs was weedy and waving, a sickly yellow-green broken here and there by the tawdry iridescence of a neon light. Her aversion to fish reinforced, Carolyn migrated toward the cages of fur. She had grown up with dogs, a succession of terriers and setters that should have been a link between her and her father but never were, and which through accident, injury, or flight never lasted long. Dogs were still painful. She dismissed them in favor of the next display, a carpeted pen acrawl with kittens. There was something irresistible to maternal instincts in the subdued mews and diminutive ranging of the tiny felines. They had a Montessori world to romp in, and yet from her perspective she could see the limits. The one she chose was the last one she saw. He sat atop the scratching post, a gray capstone of aloofness.

Smoke, she dubbed him and took him home to Joey.

That is, if you could say that Joey was really home. He lay on his bed as lifeless as a potato curl, and his eyes had the gloss and set of a china doll's.

"Joey? You okay, baby? Look what Mommy brought you."

He didn't look until the kitten was crawling over him, and then it was with slow awareness and lethargic alarm. She had seen that look on a sloth, reacting with pathetic dullness to danger in its somnolent world.

"A kitten, Joey. It's yours."

He regarded it as if it were a caterpillar. His hands were balled, and his fetal curl unlimbered not a jot. She wondered if Lucien had thought to feed him. Little boys played themselves into exhaustion sometimes. Maybe he had taken out the stress of the psychiatric visit in an energetic bike ride. She stroked his eggshell brow. A little warm, but what did that mean? The elastic life signs of a little boy, one minute pouring out vitality, the next shut down in a rush.

"His name is Smoke," she said.

The kitten snuggled and curled in the hollows of Joey's body. Smoke from a dead fire. Something was very wrong. She knew it bone-deep now. Very wrong. The psychiatrist wasn't even close to the root of this one. Might never be. She stroked her son once more, a totally giving reassurance, feeling nothing, like the final caress of lovemaking bestowed in a state of numbness. Only this numbness was not euphoric.

"He's in shock," she said to Lucien as they sat in the breakfast nook. This was the same alcove they had made shameless love in, the same table she had sprawled all over, her underwear stretched around her ankles, pounding loins with this man, the

215

brother of her dead husband but a stranger really, and the memory seemed reproving somehow. She was old enough to know her own self-centeredness, to understand that when the urgency of physical passion ebbed, it was her dignity that would take priority, her self-esteem and libido. But their relationship was changing too. They were not as close. "It's as if he had a car accident or something," she said about Joey.

Lucien blew on his coffee, stirred, blew. A month ago his hand would have been across that table on hers, the commanding glitter of his eyes softening, music in his throat. "A psychiatrist is like getting hit by a car," he said at last. "Every week, same car."

The words were worn and together with the stirring made the kitchen seem lifeless. Like wind against a loose shutter in a ghost town. Beyond the kitchen loomed a house that seemed to belong to the night. Turn a light on and you borrowed it back for a while, the way you borrowed a music box idyll when you lifted the lid. Shut the lid—extinguish the light—and it became a dead thing. The ballerina froze in ceramic death, the house petrified into a carousel suspended at full gallop. It frightened her now, this sense of animation hanging in shadow. She slept with a light on more often than not because she hated waking in the night, sensing the arrest of motion, the not-so-subtle meshing of a sinister gear, and the final echo of a shriek lost in the walls of the house. It was the friction of a huge brake. Metal on metal, sparks flying, an oily, charred smell rising in protest. What hand was on the brake? It seemed to get tardier and tardier, as if soon she might wake up and whatever was going on in the void of night would continue unabated. And then she would be part of it. Forever.

But the morning came and she would hit the deck—aerobics, makeup, teeth, breakfast, a few chin exercises while she brushed her hair. Joey and Luce (and Smoke meowing now) would help her impose reality on the house; then off to work, where she would borrow factuality from the unforgiving traffic, the phone, the grinding sounds of the shop, and the smell of paint. She tried to be real, to match the fabric. She smiled, chattered, joked, and gestured in the face of her isolation and schemed to get rid of Daryl Millman. For a while the bustle would work. And then the door to the office would be closed and the phone wouldn't ring and the sounds of the shop would cease for some reason. And Frank would say, "How's Joey, Carolyn?"

She would try not to hear him. The shop would start up again, but his voice was there now and she would know once more that she was *not* part of reality. She was somewhere in between reality and the tin acoustics of a house in the middle of the night. And she would struggle with that; she would try very hard not to hear what he said next. She would bang a file drawer, call the weather, shift pencils. And then her dead husband would say, "He hasn't been to school all week, Carolyn."

Which was true. Even though she wasn't listening. Even though she was busy now trying to find last week's dash molding inventory. Why hasn't Joey been back to school? He sat home all day. In shock. Semi-shock. Pseudo-shock. Trauma, disassociation paralysis neurosismelancholiastupor . . . *Hello, Mrs. Gaylord? This is Mrs. Whitehall. Joey won't be in again today. I'm afraid he's still suffering from that ear infection.* When your border with the world is hemmed with lies, you are in trouble.

Why wasn't she making him go to school?

Why wasn't Luce helping her?

And that was when Frank's voice started to change. First off it popped like a bad radio signal. It might have been funny if this were reality, a little like an adolescent clutch slipping as a young man's vocal cords marinated, or maybe someone choking on misdirected pastrami. But this wasn't reality. This was a voice that was in her head. Presumably she directed it. Subconscious dialogue. So why was it popping? And why was it beginning to sound like a faraway song . . . gathering . . . washing in and out?

Pop-pop-pop.

W-DIE is on the air. The spectral chorale will now haunt you with . . .

Can't hear the damn thing. Whispering, yet. Like the ocean's persuasion in mother-of-pearl cornucopia. And it *was* persuasion, or some kind of insistency. And suddenly it slammed into her like a wave, lifting her out of the chair and pinning her to the wall. Her gorge rose in her throat and turned to ice water and kept rising until it flooded her skull and she felt she had established personal contact with every hair on her head. She was practically on her tiptoes.

It lasted no more than five seconds, but she stood there for five minutes, letting the chills race up and down as if all her blood were in an elevator car and her veins were express shafts. Her panty hose felt like a cold rubber glove. This was a modern office with indirect lighting, Dupont Antron carpet, and butcher-block panels from Forest City. Primal forces had no right to trespass.

Cut that shit out, Frank, she said in her head, and even unspoken her voice trembled. Frank was not some subconscious extension she had hung onto and scripted with her own conflicts after all. Frank was outside. Buried. Risen. He had a vantage point the living could not have, and he was trying to orchestrate something. There was malevolence all around her, and the only thing she could see was Millman's little piece of it, but it was much blacker and fouler than that. It was old and grave-sprung and it could destroy physics if it wanted to, the way it had done with her this hour, and, oh, God, she had better understand it quick, because Frank was warning her and it had to be about Joey, because dash moldings didn't mean a thing in eternity, but the family did. Frank's thrust had always been the family. So, fly for the fortress and *defend!*

Ladybug, ladybug, fly away home. Your house is on fire, your children will burn. . . .

Joey was born burning.

Conceived in sterility, carried in a used womb, he was not firstborn to Carolyn. Conflict and conception were one. But she wondered if she even understood the roots of that. What was the kindling of his fears? What kind of fire had raged in his cradle? Whatever it was, she thought she could still feel its embers when she put her hand on his brow. It was two-twenty by the time she got home, and Joey's fever was one hundred and two point six.

She called Doc Samuel. He was going to give her the take-Tylenol-and-wait-till-tomorrow-morning bit, but she wanted someone to see Joey now. She argued with the receptionist, the nurse, and finally—after she insisted on holding—Doc Samuel's imperturbable southern voice came on. He listened to her. There were probably patients backed up to the foyer and she could hear a baby crying, but he listened to her. She was beginning to feel like an ass even before he spoke. She told him about the psychiatrist and could Joey possibly be reacting psychosomatically to that, and all the while her voice, weary from arguing with the nurse and the receptionist, got weaker and weaker (a selfish, hysterical ass).

Yes, it was possible Joey could be that upset, he said, and it was a good reason *not* to bring him in. He'd had enough doctors for a while.

"Sounds to me like you're handling the situation just fine for the moment, Mrs. Whitehall. Why don't you try to bring the fever down with Tylenol? If it goes up suddenly or hasn't broken by morning, I want you to bring him in. He probably picked up a bug going back to school, but if it is a phantom thing it might go very fast."

That was what she really wanted. Someone to tell her she was doing everything right. You're a good mother, Mrs. Whitehall.

She got the Tylenol, gave him a full dose, and began a vigil that would last the rest of the day and into the night. He slept fitfully, awakening suddenly at odd moments as abruptly as if someone had shaken him (or called him). And as the day died, letting go the sounds of traffic, neighborhood children, dogs, she began to hear the voice of the house again. Was this what Joey was disturbed by? The hum of the refrigerator cycling on and off, the distant posting of seconds coming to attention with a faint click of heels, the sense that each one accumulated like energy compounding, like a spring coiling up in the dark of the earth beneath them and that soon the house would tear from its foundations with a great wrenching of nails and thudding bricks as it began to spin? And finally there was that faint, almost ultrasonic note. It came upon her in a way that made her know she had been hearing it for a long time without realizing it. Far away but getting clearer in the stillness. Plaintive . . . organic. Joey's lids were fluttering to the pulse of it. She stroked his brow for the umpteenth time and went to investigate.

It didn't take long to find—not far away at all. It was coming from the studio, and she realized before she got to the door that it was the kitten. "Smoke," she called, more as a way of alerting Luce that she was coming in. She hadn't seen him all evening, but she hadn't heard his car go out either.

"Smoke?" This time with the door open.

Luce wasn't there, but the kitten was cowering in the farthest corner of the room, its pitiful mews evoking soprano screams from the thinnest wires strung thoughout. She thought it was this that had frightened the poor thing, and the cruelty of it—*someone* had closed the door—made her see the studio for the first time as something more than eccentric. Lucien was unstable. It was the very nature of his art. A lack of predictability. She was glad they were drifting apart. One of these days he would do what he had always done. Presto chango! and he would be gone without notice. That moment would be the beginning for her. She was ready for the test. She had needed him after Frank's death, but now—

"Here, kitty." The kitten mewed as she picked it up, and there was that ghastly echo. "Poor Smoke." Its heart was going like a vibrator, and it began to squirm as she moved toward the hall. What she hadn't noticed was that the patriarch chair was still close to the door, behind the long piano. And as the open doorway come into view and she drew abreast of it, the tiny creature made a surprising surge from her grasp and shot along the wall out the opening.

Tomorrow she would notice the raised window in the downstairs bathroom. She would call and call and call. She would post a LOST KITTEN notice on the corner stop sign. But like Luce someday would be, Smoke was gone. Joey's fire remained.

30

He was cooking just fine when she made breakfast. One hundred two point six on the button. The bacon sizzled sadistically, popping and crackling the way Frank's voice had.

Joey wouldn't eat it.

"I'm taking him to see Doc Samuel," she told Luce. "He said if the fever didn't break by morning to bring him in."

Luce nodded, raising his brows in an effusive way that was somehow condescending.

"You don't believe he's sick?" she asked.

"I think he's a very willful little boy," he said slowly and softly. "Give him enough variables and he'll postpone the hard business of facing reality indefinitely."

"And the doctors are variables?"

He let her question stand as a statement.

"Well, he's got a fever and that's real, and a fever can kill, and I don't see how I can ignore it." She said this tremulously, struggling for logic and confidence.

"Is it real?"

"Of course it's real. Even if he caused it himself, it's real."

"If he caused it himself, he can stop it himself."

Lucien stirred his coffee, blew, stirred. It was beginning to annoy her, this teasing calm in the face of insoluble problems.

"But what if he doesn't?" she demanded. "What if he can't?"

"He can. Survival is his strongest instinct. It's all a grand tantrum, a bluff. And it works as long as there are people around him who go on dealing with the symptoms and the side issues. He needs to run out of digressions. But that's not going to happen. The professional-help merry-go-round runs forever, as long as you keep putting coins in the slot."

She knew that was true. At least the part about the professional-help merry-go-round. Specialists made careers out of your plantar warts, your allergies, Aunt Sarah's arthritis, Uncle Ed's insomnia. Counselors ensconced in high-rent suites with indirect lighting and soft music would listen to you indefinitely and offer textbook advice from the remoteness of academia until you got the strength and the courage to follow common sense. *You* were the expert. And this terrified her.

But the thing about Joey's will . . . that was something else. If only she could be sure what was bothering him. The fears went back too far. Before he could even think in an abstract way. Before self-consciousness. Born burning.

One hundred two point six, steady as she goes. She took it again just before they left for the doctor's.

"Ninety-nine even," Doc Samuel said, looking at the nurse's chart. "Not abnormal at all for a little boy."

"It can't be." Of course it can. Hysterical mothers come in here all the time. Some of them forget to shake down the thermometer, or maybe they can't read it. One hundred two point six as steady as a clock, that's kind of suspicious, don't you think? Maybe he was sticking it in a heating pad.

What he said aloud was, "Well, let's take it again, and let's have a good look at him while he's here. Fevers are deceivers."

Ninety-nine even. Fit as a fiddle. A little fiddle.

It didn't go up again until psychiatrist day. But this time he made it to one hundred and three. She took it at his insistence and then she got the Tylenol, gave him a full dose, and said, "Do you want breakfast before we go to Dr. Coker's?"

The amorphic wax of childhood immediately transfigured in his face, and Carolyn saw for the first time the vanguard of the young man he would become. Joey's eyes veneered, his jaw came forward, the slender little neck leavened.

"I'm not going," he said.

"Joey, you're going."

"I'm not!"

"Tie your shoes."

"No! I'm not going!"

"You are, Joey. We've made the appointment, and we're going even if you blow smoke. That's final."

He began to scream then, the primal screams of an infant unobliged to honor civilization or the conventions of a society. He fell to the floor, kicked off his shoes.

"You're acting like a baby," Carolyn said, though she could not hear herself and he was acting worse than a baby.

When she tried to pull him up, he grabbed the sheers hanging over his window and ripped them down.

"Joey!" she cried. He had never done anything like that before. Angered, she took one of his shoes, cupped his heel in her palm, and tried to slip it on him. To her surprise he brought the heel down sharply, pinning her fingers to the floor. She stared slack-mouthed into his eyes. He had tried to hurt her. He had deliberately tried to hurt her.

This time she took him by the shoulders and squared him around. Animal defiance scintillated back at her. "You're going, Joey!" she shouted.

And that was when he hit her.

223

"I hate you!" he screamed and struck her on the breast with his fist. It thumped into her with predictable anemia, but what she felt was as hollow and as bruising as a wrecking ball. And he would have hit her again had she not grabbed his forearms.

It was all caterwaul and thrashing now while she stood there stupidly, holding his arms as if she had grabbed the undersides of a bulldozer's levers and was trying awkwardly to steer it.

"Joey." Lucien's voice erupted like the hum of a heavy dynamo behind her. "I want you to stop."

There was a sudden purging of vitality in Joey's struggles, whether depleted by fear or obedience. He continued to palpitate but seemed to have lost his coordination.

"Joey," Lucien repeated, *"I want you to stop."*

Joey stopped.

It was all Lucien's voice now. The combatants, leaden as pilings in the wash of a resonant sea, wheezed and perspired as he told them what to do. Joey stayed; Carolyn went downstairs with Lucien.

"Why don't you let me drive him to the appointment, Carolyn?" he offered. "I promise you he'll do what I say and there won't be any need for force."

She regarded him blankly, her mind still struggling to leave the scene upstairs and catch up to this second surprise.

"The tantrum is for you," he augmented. "He knows it will work on you."

"It wasn't going to work," she said weakly.

Lucien didn't respond to that.

"I . . . I thought you didn't want him to go for counseling."

"Do you want me to pout about it? If a psychiatrist is what you think is best, I'm offering to help."

She made no move, unable to sort out the relations and motivations that had stunned her, and he slipped her purse strap off the newel post and onto her shoulder.

"Quickly, now," he said. "Don't give him another round."

He pushed her toward the door and she found herself moving, half persuaded, relieved to be told what to do. "You're sure?" she faltered.

"I'm sure."

"It's . . . it's Coker. On Telegraph."

"I know."

The next thing she knew she was backing out of the driveway and someone was playing "The Entertainer" on a piano at the Witherses' and the garage door was coming down, as if Luce didn't want her to change her mind and drive back in.

When she was gone, Lucien got into the old black Fury next to the bay she had vacated and turned the key. The engine grumbled to life, sounding trapped in the closed garage. He unlocked the passenger side. Then he went back in the house, passed directly upstairs, and said to Joey, "That was good. But this time I *want* you to go to the psychiatrist. If everything works out, you might never have to sit in the chair again. So put on your shoes and go wait for me in the car."

She started crying before she got to the end of the block. She hated women who cried. Forget all that bullshit about a healthy release and men being too egotistical to cry; the other side of that coin was an irrational, emotional, chauvinistic stereotype she disdained. Your son tried to damage you, girl! God, that hurt. It wasn't that children didn't strike out or say they hated you or lost control—Chip had, often enough—it was the fact that it was Joey. Joey had never been like that. Joey was restrained and considerate and caring, always. Momma's special baby, eh? Boy, are you an idealist!

And Lucien. She had misjudged him too. What kind of fantasies have you been living?

The real world honked at her through a glass darkly. Tinted windshields. There was always a glass barrier. Hello, world. Wave at it. But never the lasting touch, a sense of permanency. Alice in Wonderland. Her life was a mad metaphor going madder.

It took her twelve minutes to reach the John Lodge Expressway. That was when she heard the radio crackle. She reached out to shut it off. It was off.

Pop-pop-pop.

Oh, God, no. Not now. Not here.

Pop, crackle . . .

It hit her like Joey's punch, hollow and sickening in its portents. Intravenous antifreeze began to flow into her skull as it had that afternoon in the office. And, as before, its message washed in and out but carried with it the ominous certainty of disaster. *For God's sake, Frank, tell me what it is! Don't haunt me! Help me!*

She never saw the truck: a big eighteen-wheeler Meijer's Thrifty Acres job barreling along the inside lane. But she caught a flash of red in the mirror just as the air horns let loose, mournful as eternity, blasting her upright in her seat. She crossed the lane, the emergency access, and climbed the embankment all in a matter of two or three seconds, furrowing to a stop that locked her seat belt and rattled her teeth. A Doppler effect of air horns pronounced the whole event past tense and, oddly enough, restored her perspective like a slap in the face.

E.T., phone home, she told herself, and, righting the car, she headed for the next exit. Sixteen minutes had passed since she had pulled out of the garage.

The service drive was a bottleneck and the U-turn that threaded the overpass moved according to the charity of the drivers heading the other way, and they were mostly as charitable as sounding brass. It took her nineteen minutes to feed back onto the Lodge where it became Northwestern and to traverse Franklin Road to the loops of picturesque asphalt ribbon that wound her neighborhood. "The Entertainer" had become the even more ubiquitous "Heart and Soul" on the Witherses' piano, but all she heard was the rumble of the garage door as she pressed the opener. The smell of exhaust was sickly sweet before she even set the hand brake, and then she shut her own engine off and heard the Fury snarling softly and realized it was gloating away. She knew without seeing him that he was there. This was what Frank had been trying to tell her. With a shrill cry of rage she flung her door open and dashed around to the other side.

Joey very often locked the doors when he got in a car, and she was already calculating what she could use to break the window—a trowel, the rusted shovel hanging from a crosspiece between studs—but it wasn't locked and she yanked it open, snatched the key from the ignition, and pawed the limp, reclining form of her child across the front seat.

She dragged him from the garage like a rag doll, hoisting and then carrying him to the lawn. His skin had become dusky, his lips tinged blue, but he was already coming around. Lucien opened the house door into the garage, saw them, rushed out.

"What happened?"

She threw him an indicting glance but continued to chafe Joey's hands and stroke his brow. He was blinking now, his pupils undilated, a little color beginning to trickle into his cheeks. Carolyn cuddled him, emitting a maternal sound, half sob, half laugh. "Are you all right, baby?" she repeated over and over, and he was, and he said so.

"Of course he's fine," Lucien said, "but Joey and I have a little deal, and it all depends on us going to Dr. Coker's. So we'd better be on our way."

"He's not going," Carolyn snapped. "You left him in a closed garage with the engine running. He damn near died."

Lucien's face took on a semblance of shock and remorse. "I left him . . . ? The engine was on? But . . . well. He looks fine. And I'd really hate for us to have to cancel our deal. I think Joey must have turned the engine on." He knelt by the youngster, engaging him with a solemn look. "Is it too late for us to keep our *deal*?"

Joey looked back and shook his head—No, it wasn't too late. It was very clear what deal Uncle Luce meant.

"Did you turn the engine on, baby?" his mother pressed, leading him into the house. "Did you start the car?"

Joey nodded yes.

31

Y ou're doing very, very well, Joey." He said it to him the next day, after his mother had gone to work. "Admitting you started the car kept your mother from falling apart. She needed to focus on you, Joey. That's all that keeps her together sometimes—focusing on your problems and mistakes. So I let her. It would have been all right if the garage door was up. The truth is, I forgot to raise it."

Truth? Little boys lost in fictions do not perceive truths. They perceive cause and effect. And Joey was deep into a sunlit nightmare whose signposts he could not read. The citizens of his imagination were all of equal rank. Where could he turn? To what fund of knowledge or experience could he refer? Could he compare the distortions of his environment with an unknown world beyond the hedges of childhood? A hideous home is more home than a stranger's heaven. He was half an orphan, growing up with a mother he loved but could not trust and an uncle with whom she had betrayed him in a house whose axial furnishing beckoned him to be tortured. That was his normalcy. That was bedrock.

He did not think of Uncle Luce as trying to kill him. The nature of the beast was violence and magic and recklessness. In a way, his uncle was a shining path; because if Joey could ever conquer the chair, he would win. And he *had* dreamed that. Oh, yes. He could see himself master of the chair, its power his servant. Sometimes the dream was so vivid he was tempted to throw aside the reality. But he had sat in the chair, and its voice was alien. And that was why, when his uncle offered him another ultimatum, he barely protested.

"You really are amazing, Joey. You didn't even have a headache after yesterday. I think your lungs must have secret passages for storing air. Have you ever tried to hold your breath and time yourself?"

"No," he answered dully.

"Good. Then that's what we'll do today instead of sitting in the chair."

"But you said I didn't have to anymore."

"I said, 'If everything works out.' It didn't. I'll bet you can hold your breath for five minutes, Joey. Let's make that the goal. You hold your breath for five minutes, and no more chair. Ever."

"Ever?"

"Of course, I've got to be sure you're not cheating. It's easy to cheat when you're holding your breath. The only way to be sure you're not breathing is to be underwater. . . or to use a plastic bag."

They found one in the kitchen that a three-speed fan had come in. Joey knew as much about the perils of a plastic bag as he did about carbon monoxide poisoning. There didn't seem to be any danger at all in doing what his uncle said.

"We'll have to use duct tape to seal it tight," Lucien said. "I'll gather it in the back and put a piece on, and you signal me when you want it off."

Oh. The signal. That was what they had to plan. Not that

229

it mattered. It was just a plastic bag, and anyway five minutes didn't sound like such a long time. "How will I signal?"

"Just say . . . one size fits all."

"Okay."

Lucien turned his wrist. "I'm going to use my official Casio F-Eighty lithium battery alarm chronograph to time you. There. It's set. The tape is in the drawer. The bag is"—he opened it and set it atop Joey's brow like a chef's hat—"on your head. You take some deep breaths, and when I say 'now,' hold the last one while I get the bag down."

Joey hyperventilated the way he did when Doc Samuel asked him to.

"Now," his uncle said.

The last breath rushed in like a swallow of ice water while his uncle started the stopwatch, and then the bag came down over his face, Uncle Luce's hands stroking the air out. It felt warm and funny but he kept his mouth tightly shut because he already wanted to breathe. He heard the tape rip next and the plastic crumpling as it was gathered at his neck. When it stopped crumpling he thought he could hear his own pulse: *one size fits all . . . one size fits all.* The plastic was the thick kind and it made everything streaky on the outside. His uncle looked like a badly drawn cartoon and his voice actually sounded closer than it was, counting off the seconds, as if the bag itself were some kind of giant eardrum.

"Fifteen, Joey."

Fifteen? How many did that leave?

And now he wanted to breathe very badly. Very, very badly. "One size fits all!" he tried to shout but only got half of it out because the mechanics of respiration didn't allow for more and because the bag went into his mouth when he inhaled.

"Twenty-five," his uncle said.

The next sound Joey made was starved for substance, driving blood to his face and tears from his eyes but only the barest squeak from his throat. His hands clawed weakly at the plastic and grains of sand were starting to fall in his head.

"Don't give up, nephew!"

. . . ne-f-u . . . ? The word had the faint insistency of an alarm, but it was too far away to heed, to remember. His hands

230

felt more like they were spasming than clawing now—heavier, heavier. He had staggered against the sink, and in his final dim coherence he saw a gleaming thing in the drain rack, saw and understood and clutched it. He felt as though he were gripping it like a vise, but already it was sliding out of his hand. He raised it as high as he could, point downward, and plunged it toward his mouth.

The serrated edge of the steak knife caught his neck and entered the plastic where it was stretched taut. Air siphoned in. He took it in a long palsied gasp. It went down like ice cream, scoop after scoop. On the sixth or seventh gulp he began to cry.

"You didn't make it," his uncle said.

32

It had been an accident, Carolyn knew. Even though you had to think about that other thing. Suicide was a real possibility these days, even among very young children. You read about it all the time. Sometimes it was the stress, sometimes it was a fad, sometimes it just seemed like kids were so spoiled and weak that they killed themselves in a giant tantrum over the slightest frustration.

Joey had thrown his first giant tantrum.

But it would be stress if he ever—

Why was she thinking this? It had been an accident, plain and simple. You didn't try to asphyxiate yourself while you were waiting for your uncle to drive you somewhere (Oh, no? How about to the psychiatrist's after you had just thrown a screaming blue fit to avoid it?), and besides, Joey didn't even know about carbon monoxide poisoning (That's what he said, this kid of yours who has probably seen five thousand deaths on television), and anyway, he must have known it wasn't going to work (So maybe it was a cry for help, not to mention it almost did work. If it hadn't been for Frank . . .).

Yeah. Frank.

She thanked him aloud, but he had faded back into the files and the butcher-block pattern of the office panels today. There was no question in her mind of his psychic reality. Whatever the living were composed of, you couldn't kill it all by blocking a vessel to the brain or contaminating the code for cell reproduction or glutting the lungs with water or even rending flesh into useless pieces. There were subjective realities whose momentum would rally in the air, and that momentum, whether perfume or poison, could still effect the echo of a will. Sometimes it was strong enough to communicate. Especially if there was someone like herself, whose dependency had been great enough. But she was stronger now—dear God, she was actually blaming Joey for his behavior rather than herself! And it wasn't to bolster her that Frank had come so forcefully the last few days; it was to warn her about Joey.

Too bad he couldn't fire Millman for her. But that was the thing about Frank's priorities. The family had always been his consuming motive. And then she felt the first gleam of the idea: Why couldn't Frank help her fire Millman, or at least further discredit him?

It wasn't an incandescent burst as ideas went. She dismissed it, mused over it, dismissed it. It was a hell of an amusing fantasy, if nothing else. But by degrees she talked herself into the simple mechanics of preparation and enactment, and at four o'clock she called Millman to the office.

He took his sweet time, swaggering in at last with a cigarette dangling from his lips. Same fucking cigarette he had been smoking for the last decade, she thought. He wasn't quite grinning like he used to before the Labor Day baseball game, but his lazy blue eyes still smirked contemptuously. He was a caricature, the shallowest of men, secured to his environment by mundane definitions and menial relationships: union rules, blue-collar pecking order. So how come he still made her feel like an aristocratic tourist ill at ease in a Balkan wilderness?

She closed the door behind him and sat down in one of the two chairs facing the desk. Millman, a little struck by this, took the other. But she didn't turn toward him. She remained facing the desk.

"Frank and I just wanted to have a little talk with you, Daryl," she began, noting with satisfaction how his eyes jumped with interest and near triumph. "I think it's fair to say that we haven't had the best of relationships. We think it's time to clear the air"—she gestured toward the clear air behind the desk— "and bury the old ghosts."

Millman's eyes never left her. He sat expressionless except for the keen alertness implied by his rigidity.

"Of course, Frank isn't really there, as you can see," she went on. "I mean, not necessarily in his chair. But he's there, all right. I guess you think I'm a little crazy for saying that—I mean, that's what you blabbed all over the plant—but Frank has never really left the office. And he knows what you've been saying, Daryl. That's one of the reasons he wanted me to ask you in, because he knows, and he'd like you to stop telling people bad things about me. If you do that . . . if you do that, Daryl, Frank will do something good for you. Do you know what he'll do?"

Millman sat still as death.

"He'll put in a word with God for you. That's right. God, Daryl. You know?" She twirled her fingers. "Because Frank travels regularly from . . . from *there* now, you know—heaven, I mean. Every day from heaven to the office and back again. Except Sundays," she added thoughtfully. "So if you really do repent, things could be a lot better for you in the long run. Talk about a pension plan! I mean, the way you're going now, Daryl"—she gestured helplessly, wagging her head, and that was when the phone rang.

It rang because her foot had pushed the floor mat over the button that triggered the dictaphone transcriber. It was simple to record a ringing phone that way. Simple to cut it off with your foot at the same instant you reached across the desk and lifted the telephone receiver.

"Hello," she answered. Pause. "Oh, Frank. Yes, he's here." Pause. "He hasn't said whether he repents or not, Frank." Pause. "Okay. I'll put it on the speaker phones."

She laid the receiver down and toggled the speakers that rerouted a phone conversation for room consumption. Frank's voice immediately boomed forth.

" 'Our Father, who art in Heaven, hallowed be thy name . . .' "

It was simple to push the foot pedal again, triggering the tape Frank had once made when Chip had been required to memorize the Lord's Prayer for Sunday school and couldn't find it in his Bible. Frank had known the prayer and recorded it on the dictaphone for Carolyn to transcribe later. Hallelujah tape file! She had always been a meticulous record-keeper.

" '. . . thy kingdom come, thy will be done . . .' "

The thing about running the dictaphone through the phone speakers was that it added the tinny acoustics of a hereafter to Frank's voice. It really didn't matter that the cigarette between Millman's fingers had burned down to his flesh, or that Carolyn picked up the phone receiver and bobbed it at him in benediction as she encouraged him to repent, the union steward was on his feet and sidling toward the door. She could see the words colliding in his head. You're nuts, lady. He's nuts. Only *he* was dead, and Millman couldn't sort that out. The look of Neanderthal intensity he sported was worth diamonds and rubies. He was out the door on " '. . . on earth as it is in heaven.' "

Carolyn cut off the dictaphone. " 'Give us this day our daily bread,' " she said with true gratitude.

It didn't matter what Millman did now. If he was as alarmed and confused as he looked leaving the office, he might even quit the company. And if he went on being vindictive, relating what had just happened to him in her office all around the plant as she expected him to do, he would raise serious doubts about his own sanity. Everyone knew he was out to get her. At the very worst, she could simply deliver the tape to him in front of the others, exposing him as having been duped. One way or another, that thorn was out of her side. One thorn. And if it hadn't been for what she feared was happening to Joey, it might have actually meant something to her at long last to be free of his intimidation.

Long after she arrived home she caught a glimpse of what Joey didn't want her to see. "Where did you get that cut on your neck?" she demanded, after taking hold of his jaw and exposing it to the lamplight.

"The kitten scratched me," he said promptly.

The kitten was gone—had been gone—in a puff of smoke. But here it came out of Joey's mouth, a damnable lie, as easily as telling her the mail hadn't come. He had said he hated her, struck her, lied to her, all in twenty-four hours. That might fly with Doc Spock, but she knew her son, and right now he was possessed by Dirty Harry, Jr. Worst of all—and she feared this from the bottom of her being—was *what* he was hiding. First the car engine going in the closed garage, now this. Could she doubt it now?

Her little baby boy was suicidal.

33

He went with her to Burger King for breakfast. He had a ham and egg croissant. She had a coffee. At eight-twenty she rushed him through the last of it and got him back in the car. Then she took him to Dr. Coker's without saying a word.

It was a dirty trick, but he didn't protest. Uncle Luce had *wanted* him to go the day before yesterday, so it was probably okay with him. He didn't know when his mother had called to make the appointment, but there wasn't any receptionist, and he thought the doctor was there early. He must be really sick now, for the doctor to come in early.

There was a Burger King cup steaming away on Doc Coker's desk. Maybe they had been at the same restaurant together. He had probably used the drive-through, though, because the sack the coffee had come in was sticking out of the basket. The coffee was black. Daddy used to say only people who snored and people who ate midnight snacks drank coffee black. Joey thought Doc Coker might do both, because he wheezed a little and he was fat. He could smell mouthwash, too. There was a narrow door on one wall and Joey thought that it was probably a bathroom. Doc Coker had probably rushed in early and used mouthwash in his bathroom while his coffee cooled. Joey was noticing all kinds of things about Doc Coker, but the doctor wasn't noticing anything about him at all. But that was because he was a psychiatrist, and you had to tell them everything yourself.

"Oh, hello, Joey."

He was shining his glasses now. He probably did that in the morning. Ms. Farthing used to say she had to wipe the night off hers in the morning.

"I was just going to feed the fish here. Would you like to do that? I think Baxter has taken a—"

He stopped. Probably remembering that Joey had said fish were dumb the last time he was here.

"So, how are things going?"

"Fine."

He nodded, squinting as he inserted his face between the frame arms of the glasses. "Let's sit down."

There were three chairs in front of the desk. Joey took the one with the most upholstery.

"That a good one?" Doc Coker asked.

"Mmm-hm."

"Feel free to take any one you want. Try them all if you like."

"This one's fine." The chair. They were going to talk about that today.

"I like the yellow one myself. More support." Joey didn't say anything and the doctor asked, "What do you like about that one?"

Joey started to shrug, then said, "Nothing in particular." Particular. That was a good word, the kind grown-ups used. He didn't like being talked down to like a baby.

"Is it like the chairs you have at home?"

238

"Some."

"How is it like them?"

He shrugged "Big. Bulgy."

"Is it like the one you don't like to sit in?"

"No."

"How is it different?"

What's it like to sit in it? was the way he had asked it last time. Joey hadn't answered him then. But that was because his uncle had warned him. "It shows me pictures."

"What kinds of pictures?"

"Bad ones."

The doctor took a quick sip of his coffee and set the cup in a drawer. Joey thought that was funny.

"Well." He smacked his lips, wheezing. "Where do you suppose the pictures come from?"

"Inside."

Doc Coker looked at him, then nodded as if that was important. "Does it bother you that your mother and your uncle want you to sit in it?"

"I hate to sit in it."

"And your father, did that bother you?"

He nodded.

"Do you ever miss him?"

Joey thought about it a minute. "Once," he said.

"When was that?"

"On Father's Day last year, Reverend Terrey got all the kids up on the altar and asked if they loved their fathers. I missed him then."

Doc Coker glanced toward the drawer with the coffee in it. He locked his hands together on the desk and Joey thought that was to keep himself from reaching for the cup, or maybe because he had just said that about church and it made Doc Coker think about praying.

"Why was that chair so important to your father, do you suppose?" came next.

"Because of hair-itage," Joey said. That was another good word, but he had never really understood what it meant.

"Heritage?"

"A seven-year-old gets it on his birthday."

"Ah."

"But not just everyone. You have to be a boy, and you have to be first. Then you get all the money and the house and everything."

"Is that how your father got it?"

Joey shrugged. "I guess." He had never really thought about it before, but that must have been how. His father was the firstborn. His uncle was second. That was how it had been with him and Chip. And when Chip was gone—was dead—it went to him; only with his father it didn't happen that way, because when his father died, he left Joey. Funny how he had always known that but never saw what it meant before. If Chip had had a boy son, Joey wouldn't have gotten the hair-itage. Unless the boy son died too, maybe. Then maybe it would have gone to Joey anyway. And with his father it must have worked the same way. It went to Joey instead of Uncle Luce because Joey was alive.

And all at once he knew, saw with that sleeping level of the mind what he had never seen before. *Uncle Luce would be rich if Joey died.* It was like undressing and finding out someone was watching you. It was like being in the white-white room and hearing the terrible music that groaned in all the wires and the long piano making notes that either croaked like something deep in a well or screamed so high you only felt it.

"How do you feel about getting the heritage, Joey?"

He shrugged.

"Are you glad?"

"It's okay, I guess."

"Does it ever scare you?"

"When I sit in the chair. Then I'm scared." He was rolling his palms on the upholstered leather arms where he sat now, listening to them hiss. He wanted to tell Doc Coker what scared him when he wasn't in the chair, wanted to tell him about the roof and the skateboard and the lumberyard and the plastic bag. But the piano wires were groaning in his head again, a deep, ominous rumble that rose in volume but never changed, like a squadron of fighter planes in an old war movie.

"Do you ever think of ways to avoid being the heir?"

"What do you mean?"

240

The doctor put his hands behind his head and leaned back. "Do you ever think of things you might do to avoid being the heir?"

The air. How did Doc Coker know about that? Chip had become the air. Maybe the doctor knew all about the chair after all. Maybe he just wanted Joey to tell him. If he already knew, then it wouldn't matter if Joey told him the rest. "I don't want to be the air," he said plaintively. "Chip is the air."

"Your brother is the heir? Do you think he doesn't want you to become that, is that it, Joey? You think he might be mad at you?"

Mad? No, no, no. Chip wasn't mad. What did that have to do with anything?

"Joey, have you ever tried to hurt yourself because you thought maybe your brother was mad at you?"

"Chip's dead."

"Sometimes people go away or die and we still act like they were right there."

Joey quit rolling his palms and tried to listen very hard, as if that might cause what Doc Coker was saying to make sense.

"If we think they want us to, we might even try to harm ourselves. Sometimes it seems like that's the thing to do and that in a crazy way it might make us feel better inside. But if we hurt ourselves—really, really hurt ourselves—why, we might not be around to feel better."

Suicide. He was talking about suicide.

"Do you know what I mean, Joey?"

Joey nodded.

"Good."

"It's quite possible he did try, Mrs. Whitehall, and I don't want to underestimate that. You should keep an eye on him, be supportive, and above all *listen* to him. But these events often are more experimental than intentional. Children don't understand the consequences of suicide. In Joey's case, he may be feeling guilt about displacing Chip as the family heir. The fact that it was a disappearance no doubt has left it unsettled in his subconscious. Chip is still very real to him. Joey's resistance to the chair was probably a rejection of a role he saw as usurping a

241

brother who was still around. No matter that it was forced upon him. Down deep he doesn't want to be the heir. He feels he has deposed his brother. He feels his brother is angry and wants to punish him. There's some guilt and fear mixed together here, and that's why he's carrying out the punishment himself. I don't think he really wanted to hurt himself as much as he just wanted to let off some guilt and thereby lessen the fear. The chair is a barometer of this, and while I'm not suggesting you force him to sit in it, I will venture to say that when all the conflicts are settled in the past, he'll sit in that chair with a sense of real legitimacy and vindication."

"But he was afraid of the chair *before* Chip disappeared," she said with marked frustration.

The doctor blanked for a moment, recovered himself. "Child's fantasies, perhaps. Chip may have played games of dominance using the chair as a symbol. That may be why it's such a focal point to Joey now. Shall we set up the next appointment for Monday, Mrs. Whitehall?"

34

His mother took him home as before, went to work as before, leaving Joey with his uncle as before. But that didn't matter to Joey. Uncle Luce had said he *wanted* him to go to the psychiatrist's, and besides, Joey had it all figured out. He was going to hop on his bike as soon as they got home and steer clear of the house until his mother came back. Except there was one thing he hadn't counted on.

"Lucky as ducks," his mother said, on the heels of a roll of thunder. "We barely made it before the monsoon."

God took a flash picture of the house then, and before they could even get up the walk, enormous drops of rain began to splatter like water balloons. Ducks go out in the rain, Joey wanted to say, but he saw that his mother was right: the storm was an ugly one, bearing down on the earth with the speed of a dark comet, reeling off flash after flash.

"Of course, *I've* got to go right back out in it," she said, "but at least I delivered the future President of the United States home safe."

Safe.

That was a matter of grave uncertainty. Mercurial Lucien, himself grown to adult size in the shadow of a firstborn who had abdicated too late, alone with another pretender who had ascended unjustly. Clever Lucien, whose patience had been thwarted by the accidents of passion and the failures of accidents, now pressed by threatened exposure. Artistic Lucien, membered in a dynasty where blood ran thicker than water, soon to coronate himself with pigments of the former. The long shadows of his destiny were squeezing out the light. Joey was here, and "now" ticked like an overwound clock in the den where Lucien had just reinstalled the chair.

The first thing said was, "You shouldn't have gone, nephew."

Joey's voice had no air in it at all as he opened his mouth to protest, and the sounds that came out were like the soft roll of dice on green felt. "You told me I could," he tried to say, and it didn't matter how the words died, because his uncle was already burying them.

"You kept your mother from taking you the other day, so you must have let her take you this time. I told you what you had to do and you didn't. I gave you a choice."

Again Joey opened what felt like a foam rubber mouth and this time managed, "I-I didn't tell him." Doc Coker, he meant.

"No? Nothing? Not a word?" Cynicism flashed from his uncle's lightless eyes and shallow smile.

"About us. About the chair."

"I don't like it when you lie."

Joey started to cry. The response was all but conditioned now. The bankruptcy of communication with his uncle, the inevitability of the chair, were enough to overflow his banks.

"What *did* you talk about?"

"Suicide."

"Really. Why?"

244

"I don't know."

"What did you say?"

"Nothing. He just said I shouldn't do it."

"Well, well."

Joey thought he heard him leave the den, but he kept his head down, sniffling, cowering, as if abject surrender might soften the unmerciful. And it wasn't until he heard the ratchet whir and the mechanical meshing of the instrument and smelled the mellow tang of oil that he brought his eyes back up, void of strategy, smooth to the imprint of fresh terror. "I think," his uncle began, dropping into the cane chair opposite the couch, "I think we've escalated a step here, and that it's only poetic justice that your penalty should have some small element of the suicidal about it. Russian roulette comes to mind. You spin the chamber and put the barrel to your temple and pull the trigger. It's not very risky because there's only one bullet."

The phrases were chrome-plated like the gun, but Joey understood his uncle perfectly. The links were falling in place in his child's mind, and the revelation he had acquired in Doc Coker's office glided smoothly against this new obscenity. His uncle wanted him dead. The chair wanted him dead. And if he killed himself—if he fell off a roof or skateboarded into a car or got torn apart by dogs or suffocated or shot himself in the head— his uncle would get the chair. A magician and a magic chair. They were doing things to him together. And if they succeeded in what they wanted, it would seem like . . .

"Suicide. The ultimate test, Joey. I think I can promise you that this one will make a man out of you. Five chances to be a man, one that you won't care anymore. Either way, you win. You won't need to sit in the chair after this."

"No," Joey said softly.

Vexation and uncertainty dropped like a cloud over his uncle's face. "No?"

It had surprised Joey himself, that little syllable bottoming out at the end of a long fall. As if he had finally said "yes" to the chair. The wild dream of becoming its master was teasing him, betraying him. He was as terrified as ever, but he had a different feeling too, equally irrepressible. "I won't shoot myself," he said.

245

"Of course you won't." The carved composure of Lucien's smile was suddenly ruined by the sagging of his lip, as if his mouth had been gashed, like the teak faces Joey had gashed with the hatchet on the arms of the chair. "Hardly any chance at all. But a little. Enough to make you a man."

The outrage grew a few degrees hotter, fueled by his uncle's uncertainty. "You'd cheat. You always cheat."

"What kind of insurrection is this?" Lucien growled, jerking forward.

Joey was trembling, but he couldn't stop now. All the rationalizations, the ambivalences of their perverted relationship, collapsed together, replaced by cynicism and a small but unquenchable fire. Bitter insights darted up like cinders, the kind a child hides under a callus until infection brings them to the surface.

"You lied to me about the roof and about the bag, just like you lied to Mommy about the car in the garage," he accused. "You grew up with the chair and you know how to use it. You used it to find me and you made the pictures happen to scare me so I'd do the other things. You want me to kill myself, but I *won't*! I won't! I . . . ."—he broke into a quavery kind of gasping as he backed away.

His uncle had a dusky look, but he made no move to stop him. And Joey charged out of the den, stumbling up the stairs, sobbing brokenly all the way to his room, where he slammed the door and threw himself on the bed.

In a little while he heard his uncle's step on the stairs. There wasn't any lock on the door, no way he could stop what was going to happen next. The steps changed to soft, even falls on the hall carpet and ceased just outside the room. But the handle never moved. Instead, his uncle's voice came through the panels, caressingly intimate, chillingly blunt.

"I'm going to let you get away with this tonight, Joey. I'm going to give you time. You need it to sort out the terrible things you've said about me. You'd better think deeply about what you said. And believe me, it would be a mistake to tell your mother. You know she couldn't handle it. I'd just have to take over. Tomorrow I'll expect you to do as I ask, and if you don't, I'm afraid I'll have to put you in the chair again. You don't know the half about the chair, Joey. You were right about that. I do know how to use the chair. And I will. You can't imagine what can happen in it. And to tell you the truth, you've made it very, very angry, Joey. I think I can control it, but you've made it very angry. Some things are worse than suicide."

Outside, the storm raged lustily as if fed by the insanity of a single house in Franklin Village, while God roared and stabbed the earth with silver daggers again and again.

35

She went inward somewhere around ten-thirty when the storm was just starting to build, and it wasn't until she reached the plant that she started to focus again. She scarcely noticed that the expressway was flooding, but she lasered in on Sinswicki, whose red face appeared briefly under a gray umbrella as she drove through the gate, and imagined (she must have imagined it) that he had looked on her with something close to the respect she deserved. And if she didn't feel the same thing as she walked through the main assembly room, she was at least sure that no one was grinning at her behind her back. Everywhere they were milling and dipping and grinding and boring and assembling things just like they were supposed to do. Barths was nowhere in evidence, but there was a quality in the air she hadn't sensed since Frank's death. The smell of heated oil, melted plastic, and pungent thinners layered the various stations, filings littered the floor, and dust motes rode the cross-drafts of the ventilators like maverick planets. Sandy Raddler nodded to her for the first time since the Labor Day baseball game, and best of all—she discovered when she checked the punch-in cards—Millman hadn't come to work.

The sheet was on her desk right where it was supposed to be, courtesy of Agnes Predamowicz. One sick call: Daryl Millman.

So he was spooked or discredited—discredited, judging by the clues in the plant—or both. It wasn't going to be the same company anymore. It was going to be better.

Funny, she couldn't enjoy it.

She went inward again at the end of a long day, and maybe that was good, because by then the Lodge was flooded and she got caught in the middle of an expressway parking lot between Grand River and the I-94 interchange. The sky was still wringing out clouds in bucketfuls, and the underpasses were oceans dotted with stalled cars. Suddenly it had become a masculine world, with work crews swarming in yellow slickers and men on car hoods. Emergency vehicles winked like fireflies where they could pass through. She couldn't get off on a service drive until after the Davidson at about seven-thirty, and it took another three hours to wend her way through jam after jam along the flooded surface streets and detours of Detroit, Redford, Livonia, Southfield, and finally Franklin Village.

But it was timeless time. She was thinking, brooding, deciding. Edging along in her little cocoon, the world swishing by and the rain drumming, Carolyn Whitehall began her final metamorphosis.

The first thing she decided was that the psychiatrist needed a psychiatrist. All that intellectual weave about deposing Chip. It fit very neatly. The trouble was it was all bullshit. She knew that much. Joey had *always* been afraid of the chair, and he probably never accepted what it stood for. He certainly didn't think of himself as usurping his half-brother. Lucien had been right about the counseling. It could easily become a convoluted, hyper thing, raising more crises than it put to rest, eating away more confidence than it restored. Appointment mills. So they would wing it without Doc Coker.

The second thing was Lucien himself. He was not the man she loved; he was a lover—had been. They hadn't slept together since she had discovered the duplicate chair. When she thought about it, he was still just one big mystery. What did she know about him? Could she share his art? Could they sit on a couch and watch television, his head in her lap? He wouldn't even let her wash his clothes. He was her brother-in-law and their relationship had consisted of his giving to her—advice, support, sexual warmth, a surrogate father for Joey. For a time she had been consumed by that. She had needed him, accepted him, but now she was stronger and capable of a more even relationship. He may have made her stronger, but the irony was that she could see how shallow they were now. When it ended completely—and she had no doubt it would—she would accept it and be relieved.

The third thing didn't come to her until after she had arrived home, hungry and exhausted at ten-thirty, and heard from Luce that Joey was asleep and ate some toast and went to bed and then lay awake for hours and hours. The third thing wouldn't let her sleep.

36

I'*m going to give you time . . . think deeply.*

Joey thought deeply. The rain was a dirge, and his mind rolled through dreary night streets like a funereal caisson, bearing unspeakable thoughts to a place of abandonment. But *he* wasn't going to abandon them. He was the vessel.

You don't know the half about the chair, Joey . . . you can't imagine what can happen in it.

He wouldn't have to imagine. This was the night. A black flag was ascending slowly above the house and the walls were filling with goggle-eyed, giggly things. The certainty of something doom-laden and horrific swam in his bloodstream like alien fish. He lay pathetically on his mattress, feeling totally invaded.

I think I can control it, but . . .

Uncle Luce couldn't control it. Joey had felt the power. He had heard the wail of a million cats or banshees or whatever they were and knew the utter desolation there. It was beyond deadness. A force so sinister that its aura would crumble granite, shatter diamonds. The only thing it wouldn't atomize was the teak of its origins, whose enchantment arose from black seeds buried far deeper than the earth. Joey only knew it had no master. It was a weed. Something that had come up wild and rapacious and been transfigured into an object of human design. The form was malleable, but the soul was perverse and indomitable.

Some things are worse than suicide.

But Joey didn't want to die. With all the surging greenness of a small boy he wanted to live. The instinct for survival was still there, and he feared that moment he knew was coming when the chair would make him want to die. A tremendous wave of self-pity kept crashing on his beach, weighting the objects of the room with an exaggerated sentimentality: the Encyclopedia Brown book he hadn't finished, the soft leather baseball glove he had snagged grounders with, his tape recorder that needed new batteries, the microscope and the Monarch wing as pretty as a sunset mounted on a slide—

Uncle Luce had given him the microscope.

No matter. The worn textures and aging aromas of his child's private environment were ghosting away from him, assuming a hallowed preciousness that could only be longed after. He saw himself as the little boy he was, together with the alchemy of a little boy's touch, transmuting adult debris into make-believe treasures, now lost, lost, lost. The night's postings shared this recession. He could not acquire the outward peace that settled over his room. The clock struck in a distant galaxy, and when his mother arrived late and moved tantalizingly near in her brief preparations for bed, he could not penetrate the membrane of fear and uncertainty that yoked him. Even the rain became remote, chattering litigiously with the slate tiles and the metal downspouts. And some time into the deepest part of the night after the storm had stopped whispering, the chair began.

It was only a breath of sound at first, like the soughing of air under the eaves. He heard it but did not. Not until it called his name in a little huff, louder than the rest. Instantly he was attuned, the remoteness that had encased him opening suddenly like the flexing of a cardiac valve. And it was exactly that inside him. A torrent of adrenaline iced his stomach while his heart jumped to counter with hot blood.

The chair was calling him.

I think I can control it, but . . .

That was a lie. His uncle couldn't; and he wouldn't if he could. The chair was in control. And it would have what it wanted, however long that took. Because it owned time. *(I'm going to give you time. . . .)*

Calling louder now. Louder than he had ever heard it. And he thought he heard a thump, the faintest thump imaginable *(You can't imagine what it's like . . .)*, but absolutely chilling in its suggestion of the chair's animation down in the den.

Joey rolled out of bed, ran to the door. He snapped on the light switch. Nothing happened. You could believe it was the storm. The lightning had gone on hour after hour—God's silver daggers—and once he had heard a transformer explode in the distance. Sometimes the power went out even after a storm was over, when a splintered branch or something collapsed on a power line. You could believe it was the storm. Joey didn't.

But he tried the tape recorder anyway, just to make sure about the power. He could pick it out in the gloom and the AC adapter was plugged in, so he hit the big lever on the left side that he knew said PLAY. There was a tape in it, he remembered, something off the radio. But it didn't want to play. He took the four batteries out next and fumbled through his bottom drawer for the Star Wars flashlight. Maybe two of the batteries would still work, maybe he could scrounge up a combination. He tried them all. Tried them twice, because he thought he mixed them up in the gloom the first time. He wasn't sure how many combinations there were, so he went through some of them a third time inadvertently when he worked it out to twelve pairings— each battery with each of the other three.

Dead. All of them.

He sat on the floor and listened and shivered, because the calling was still going on. Loudly. His name. Was that why the rest of the house couldn't hear it?

253

On his knees now, he grabbed everything he could that would jam under the door. The rocket, the toy saxophone mouthpiece, both tennis shoes, clothes. And then he was back on the bed, huddling. Because the chair had all the time there was, and the thumps and rustles had left the den.

It was like the raindrops, all murmuring at once. You couldn't separate the voices. Lots of voices. Voices to go with the plasmic faces he had seen seething in the wood. A million howls, and only occasionally his name, as if by accidental concert they came together. They must be out of the den now.

Mommy, why can't you hear?

Did it matter? Mommy was not on his side when it came to the chair. Mommy had something wrong with her, had betrayed him even though she still loved him. She would not believe him if he told her what Uncle Luce had tried to do to him. She would be angry, just like she was at Chi-Chi's that day. No one would believe him. He was sick. Psychiatrists got out of bed to see him, he was so sick. When you got sick enough, you did something crazy.

And this was his hour. His hour on the cross.

Mommy, Mommy, why hast thou forsaken me?

They must be on the stairs now, all those ancient children. Coming for him. A regular babble of horror and pain he could smell right through the door. At the very least, he wanted to believe that—that they were still outside the door. Not sitting up in a bathtub behind him. Not in the room, in the closet, in a drawer, under the bed. Uncle Luce did things like that. Uncle Luce must be their father.

And now they were coming down the hall, and suddenly— brilliantly—the room exploded into light, a white-white light that bathed everything in purest detail like fine damask. It would have been welcome but for the ghastly groan that retched up collectively from the throats of the children just outside the door and went on and on and on—

The first one hit it a few seconds later. It shook the frame. And then the handle turned, and the panels seemed to bend a little as the fragile fortifications of a child's desperation compressed beneath the jamb and the door slid slowly inward. . . .

37

Joey, hon?"

Even after he saw that it was his mother, his face remained twisted out of shape by the agony of the ordeal, like the yawning ectoplasms of the chair. But his mother only glimpsed this, distracted as she was by the drag of the door and the awful groaning sound coming from the tape recorder. It had come back on with the power, as had the light in the bedroom. The tape, which had not been rewound, was straining against the mechanism. By the time she cleared the wedges from beneath the door and shut the machine off, Joey's face was pale but normal.

"What on earth were you doing, playing war?" she asked merrily.

He was still too stricken to speak.

255

"Joey? Are you all right?"

"The light went out," he said, in a voice frighteningly vacant.

The steel blue sharpened in her eyes as she ambled to the bed and put her hand on his brow. A little damp but no fever.

"Didn't you hear it? Didn't you hear it, Mommy?"

"I heard the tape recorder."

"It was the chair."

Vexation crossed her face, but she dropped down on the bed and looked at him for a long time. When she spoke again it was with a deep breath and a sense of renewal. "Joey, I made some decisions last night. From now on I'm going to be fearless. If I'm fearless, maybe you'll become fearless too. We're going to analyze everything ourselves, and step by step we'll do what has to be done. We're going to depend on common sense and common sense alone. And the best idea of all had me so excited I couldn't sleep half the night. Know what it is?" She tossed her head and the merriment came back into her eyes. "We're going to tear the chair apart and put it back together."

Tear the chair apart?

"We're going to reupholster the damn thing, Joey! God knows it needs it. It won't hurt what it was intended to be. It'll still be the same chair, only it won't be. You'll see, because you'll help me do it. New stuffing, new cover, new stitching, new tacks—whatever. All courtesy of Minnesota Fabrics. It'll just be a skeleton when we're done tearing it down."

"I don't want to," he whispered in a rush.

She nodded, as if she had foreseen this too.

"You don't want to touch it. I thought maybe you'd enjoy that part, but I can understand that. So I'll do it. You can watch. I'll shred it. I'll—"

"I don't wanta watch."

Inhalation. "Okay. You can stand outside the room. You can hide in the closet or go wait on the corner. But when I'm done I'll show you the pieces, and there won't be an inch of it intact. Just so much fuzz. No pictures, no teeth, no nothing. You'll love it."

They both looked to the door then. Because Lucien was standing there.

"Did I miss a fire drill?" he asked mellifluously.

"It's all right, Luce," Carolyn said. There was something toxic in the exchange of looks between them, something of finality, and this time Joey caught it.

Lucien faked a yawn. And then he was gone.

"Okay, fella," Carolyn said to Joey in another moment. She gave him a squeeze. "We'll do it. I'll pick up the material on the way to work, okay? Okay?"

He shrugged. When you got sick enough, you did something crazy.

38

His mother left early. He heard her shower and pour something from the refrigerator, and then the garage door rumbled up.

It wasn't going to work. He knew that. The chair was going to get them both, and there was nothing he could do about it. If he ran away, Uncle Luce would find him. If he went to other people, Uncle Luce would come and tell them how crazy he was. And if he told anyone about the chair, Uncle Luce wouldn't *have* to tell them how crazy he was.

A minute or so after the car hissed out of the drive, he heard his uncle stirring. It was forty-one minutes past seven when the final insanity began.

They were just a babble at first. He heard them as tiny shouts from the den, but they grew into an aberrant drone like tuning forks in a wind. When they reached a howl, he slipped off the bed and began jamming things under the door again. It was too familiar to strike fresh terror off the flint of his soul. It was old terror. Old and sickening and exhausting. The sparks bit his scalp but his nerves were jelly, washing out of his skin with a rush of blood that seemed to carry the last bit of warmth and vitality down his trunk and into the floor as though a drain had opened. He was barely conscious. Still, he jammed what he could under the door and even wedged the tilted desk chair against the handle. He crawled behind the bed then, into the corner, to wait for the children to come.

The first time he actually heard his name it came out of his own brain, darting like a needle against the inside of his skull. This was not a whisper or a huff but "Joey!" Quite clearly. Then the membrane closed thick and gluey again, encasing a separate tuning fork in the middle of his mind that was beginning to resonate with the ones downstairs.

"Joe-ey!"

An acoustical freak, a Jonah sound of impiety breaking free for a moment before being swallowed by a wail. And then being thrown up again—"*Joey!*"—a scant millisecond before the door boomed open, shattering the desk chair wedged under the handle and gouging the floor with bits of broken plastic.

But the children hadn't come. The children's father had come. And he towered in the doorway as tall and invincible as teak.

"Time's up!" Lucien roared. Three steps, pulling the bed out from the wall. "Are you ready to do it?"

Joey, as palsied as an ancient child, shook his ancient head as if it had skated loose on its moorings.

"You will, though. Most certainly you will, nephew. Because we've got all day to sit in the chair. So you *will* do what I say. Or sit there until you go into shock. And that won't take long. You have no idea what it has waiting for you today!"

Red, raw energy gleamed from his uncle's glance as he took him rag-doll style by the upper arm, and it was only Joey's right

259

foot that touched the stairs at all. He didn't have a very long life to pass before his eyes on his way to extinction, so Joey was through that part of the ordeal before they even reached the bottom step. And by then he was hearing the *pop-pop-pop* sound that Carolyn had heard, had mistaken for the paternal cry of Frank's sleepless soul, only Joey knew of course where it was coming from. All the chair's children were crying together, suddenly breaking through, a unison born of something other than separate agonies: of malice, in fact. The malice seethed like the lathered jaws of some trodden reptile, a great green hungering thing lain long in its own filth and smelling the bones and the blood of what it had been and what renewed it coming nearer, nearer, within snapping distance.

Joey knew nothing consciously of the children of Khi-tan Zor, nothing of the original chair cover still there beneath the old one, red and green and crested with the bloodied shoals of half-savaged infants, but suddenly he knew this: *The malice was not directed toward him!*

Not him!

The cool wind that vibrated the tuning forks rushed into his soul, bringing relief and drying the blood of nightmares. *Pop-pop-pop*. All in unison. The voice of the chair was feelings, and Joey thought in feelings. It broke through in microbursts, driven by a single plea, led by the youngest, the newest.

Chip.

Speaking clearly at last. Calling to Joey in penance. Warning him. Because the chair protected the firstborn, and Chip had trespassed on that. Just like Jacob Alexander, who had dreamed of patricide, and little Bobby Bastard, who had murdered his older brother. Because the chair was where Joey had subconsciously wanted Chip to be. Not in the Lake Erie marshes. Not roaming the world in disembodied form. Flesh and soul in the chair. Whether he had put him there or only kept him there, Joey was the legitimate master. And he understood in some simplified way what the chair wanted him to understand, that he had a genetic will, that he was the present manifestation of the dead and the unborn. The chair protected and purified all its firstborn. What Joey did came out of a sleeping part of himself. A shibboleth of blood.

But now the psychic and the physical had met at a common bridge that only one would get across.

"Well, nephew?"

They were in the den, Uncle Luce inviting him into the chair.

"I won't sit in it," he said petulantly. "Not unless you do first."

Lucien flexed an eyebrow, smirked broadly, then gestured with his palms upraised as he came down slowly on the chair. It was an indelible image that would age into a posture of supplication. Because that was when Joey sprang into his lap, knees first, grabbing the chair arms with all his might.

For the few necessary moments it took, his frail frame seemed welded to the chair's as if the sinews and tendons of his arms had become shafts of teak. The tensing extended to his eyes, which were tightly shut. But he heard the slick sounds beneath Uncle Luce's cries and felt the writhing of the mass that was being consumed and smelled the fetid air that came up through the open maw like a chill web. When all the writhing stopped and the pile was sinking, he jumped off and opened his eyes.

The chair had never let anyone watch before. But it let Joey. Because someone would have to bring down his uncle's things and put them in the seat so that his mother would think Uncle Luce had just suddenly decided to leave. And when that was done, the true living patriarch of the dynasty would have to assume his throne with "a sense of real legitimacy and vindication."

"Joey?"

"I'm in the den, Mom."

"I can't believe this, you're sitting in the chair."

"Yup."

"This is wonderful!"

"Yup."

"I just can't believe this."

"You can believe it, all right. And you know what else?"

"What?"

"I don't think we need to recover it after all."

261

A child believes in St. Nick, tooth fairies, and magic. And in living chairs, if they come his way. The omniscient adult that Joey would become would question the border of fact and fantasy as naturally as the questioning of all articles of faith that live only in blind and trusting memories. Very little scar tissue would remain on his fully vested soul. For one hour he had become a collective force, but the culpability for his actions dissipated in the dream of deliverance—he had had nightmares enough for a lifetime—and when he would think back a month, a year, a decade, to the terror and triumph of the day, it would seem not so much a personal ordeal as the saga of ancient and future children.

> *The Present, the Present is all thou hast*
> *For thy sure possessing;*
> *Like the patriarch's angel hold it fast*
> *Till it gives its blessing.*

—John Greenleaf Whittier
"My Soul and I" (1847)